FREE LOVE BEACH

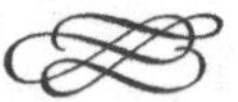

SARASOTA GREEN

*For the women
who came before me*

CHAPTER ONE

February, 2015

The bar opened at 8 a.m. Skylar parked her car in front, across from a bay of moored sailboats, and rolled down her window while she waited. The Florida sun warmed her shoulders through a light breeze. Seagulls squeaked and hollered, splashing in the shallow water of the beach. Skylar studied the colors of the water and the horizon. When she returned home, she would try and paint this.

There was a line outside the door under a blue and red sign that said, The Buoy. A man stood smoking, with a white cockatiel on his shoulder. A woman with electric blue eyes clutched an art portfolio at her side, and a man with a gray-streaked ponytail sat on the bench facing the water, under an American flag.

An older blonde woman swung open the door and said, "Bloody Mary Sunday, everybody!" The people filed in slowly.

As Skylar rolled up the window, she pictured her mother prancing down this sidewalk, as she'd talked about in her letters. It was still so hard to imagine; so different from who she knew her mother to be.

She fished some sunscreen from her purse and rubbed it on her pale arms before she checked her hair in the rearview mirror. Maybe she'd get some sun this week. Her hair almost looked redder here; the purple tones of her highlights were coming out. She took a deep breath and got out of the car.

The bar was dark in the back, but sunlight from the front wall of windows illuminated the floor enough to see her way around. The bartender was already working on drinks for the regulars.

Skylar sat down on a stool, hoping she wasn't taking anybody's usual seat. The dark, smoky air contrasted with the bright rectangle of light glowing in from the open front doors. Black and white photographs hung on the walls. She adjusted her eyes.

"Hey," said the bartender. "I'm Dolly, what can I get for you?" Liquor bottles lined a mirror stretched behind her.

Skylar smiled. "Hi, I'll have a Bloody Mary."

Why not, she thought.

"Where are you from?" Dolly picked up a glass and filled it with ice.

"Ohio." Skylar fidgeted with her phone.

"Lots of people from Ohio here."

"Really?" Skylar asked.

"Yeah. Kenny over there is from Ohio." She pointed at the man with the ponytail, who had a clear drink in front of him, a lemon wedge perched on the side.

"Go Buckeyes." He smiled. Though Skylar wasn't used to talking to adults this early in the morning, she thought it best to make conversation.

"Where about in Ohio?"

"Cleveland, up near Lake Erie. How about you?"

"Middle Falls. Just north of Cincinnati. What brought you to Florida?" Skylar asked.

Kenny scratched his head. "Well, I came down to visit an uncle in '64. And I never left."

Skylar could see why people never left this place. The scenery. Ocean and sky, birds and boats. Her mom had left, she'd just learned in the letters, although Skylar hadn't put the whole story together yet. She wanted to ask the guy about the cockatiel: *How does he just stay there? What's his name? Where did you get him?* But everyone else was acting so normal.

Dolly set the drink down in front of Skylar. "Do you want me to start you a tab? Or are you just having the one?"

"I'll pay." Skylar handed Dolly her card and picked up an olive. She couldn't remember the last time she'd had a mixed drink. Her lips puckered.

"So, what brought you to Florida?" Dolly lit a cigarette. "You have family here?"

Skylar thought about how much she should say, then decided it didn't really matter. She liked Dolly right away, and it had been so long, nobody would probably remember her mother.

"My mom used to live here. She just passed away."

"I'm sorry to hear that," Dolly said. "Seems to be going around lately."

Skylar tightened her lips. "Yeah, thanks. It was the hardest thing I've lived through." Her mom had been sick for a while, but still, it was devastating in a way she couldn't have anticipated. In the blur of her grief, someone had said it gets easier with time, and someone had said it doesn't. "I guess life has to go on."

Dolly reached over and touched Skylar's hand. "Yes, it does. And that's exactly how you do it. You go on, one day at a time."

"When did your mom live here?" Kenny asked. The cockatiel

on the other man's shoulder readjusted itself, flapping its wings for a second. Skylar tried not to stare.

"Fifty years ago," she said. "She always told us she loved the beach, but we didn't know she lived here."

"What was her name?" he asked.

"Kate Ward," she said. "Or, back then it was Kate Wyse. Kathryn."

Recognition washed over his face. He stirred his drink, then bent the straw sideways with one finger so it cradled the outside of the glass as he lifted it. He drank half of it in one gulp and when he set it back down on the bar, the ice cubes clinked.

There was no music playing, which stretched out the awkward silence. The woman with the art portfolio had pulled out a sketch. Skylar couldn't see the picture because of the darkness, but she watched her hands push and pull mechanically across the grain of the white, the delicate sound of pencil on paper.

"Katie Wyse," he said. "I remember Kate."

"You do?" Skylar was surprised.

"Yeah. She used to work here. Way back when it was a biker-bar. Sixty-four was it? Sixty-five? I don't know." He smiled. "I did a lot of drugs back in the Sixties."

All three of the patrons, and Dolly laughed. Skylar laughed too, but then fidgeted. "Everybody did," he said. "In the Sixties, I mean. But maybe not your mom."

Skylar smiled. "Well, she had this whole life here that she never talked about. So, it's possible."

"You remember Katie, right Dolly?" Kenny wiped his hand on his shorts.

"Katie? Who used to sing with the band, Katie?"

"Beautiful girl," the guy with the cockatiel said. "Always smiling." He looked at Skylar in the eye briefly, then looked away.

Katie?

"My mom sang with a band?" Skylar asked.

"Yeah, I remember her," Dolly said in a revelatory voice. "Katie, with the brown hair. Drank vodka gimlets and loved to dance." Skylar couldn't picture her mom drinking and dancing. Just couldn't do it, even though she wanted to. Her mom would dance at weddings sometimes, but drink? Never.

"She left right after I started working here. I saw her a couple of times after that. Heard she got married and started going to church."

"She did love to dance," said Kenny. "I wish I would have been smart enough to take her on a date."

Apparently, this was a smaller town than Skylar thought. Maybe they would know Marco.

"I'm actually looking for somebody she used to know," Skylar said. "Do any of you know Marco Del Rio?"

Dolly's eyes lit up and she smashed out her cigarette. "Oh, *I* remember Marco."

The artist looked up for the first time and her pencil stopped. "Marco Del Rio," she said, "master of the blues guitar." She stared off into the air, tilted her head, and then went back to sketching.

"Marco used to play here," Kenny said. "Matter of fact, when your mom lived here."

He finished his drink and set it against the back of the bar. Dolly retrieved it and made him another.

"Wasn't it his band that Katie sang with? The Whales?"

"The Dolphins," said Dolly. "You're getting old, Kenny." Skylar couldn't believe they all knew both of them.

This was it, why Skylar came. It was a long shot, but her mother had raised her to be a woman of hope.

"Is he still around? Marco?"

The artist looked up again.

Dolly said, "Well, I don't know, honey. I haven't heard anything about him in a long, long time. Kenny, what happened to Marco?"

He stirred his drink. "I heard he moved to New York after the war."

The man with the cockatiel said, "No, he didn't. He moved to Memphis."

"I heard he went back to Texas, where he was born," the artist said. She put her pencil down and lit a cigarette.

"I didn't know him that well," Dolly said. "But our chef did. Hold on." She walked to the back of the bar, opened a door, and yelled.

"Hey Chef, what happened to Marco Del Rio?"

"Who's asking?" a voice said in a New York accent.

"Katie Wyse's daughter. What's your name, honey?"

"Skylar."

The chef peeked his head around the corner and squinted.

"Hey there. Just wanted to get a look at you." He wiped his forehead with a towel. "You look just like her." He hesitated and sighed, "Marco, huh? I don't know what happened to him, but your mom was really fond of him. They were good, good friends." He tugged at his apron. "I love your mom. How is she?"

"Are you Chef, like, Captain?"

"That's me! Frank, but they used to call me Captain."

"I read about you," she said, then felt embarrassed. He was like a big teddy bear, just as her mom described him. "In some letters, from my mom. I didn't think you'd still be around. I mean, Mom's gone. She passed away last winter."

"I'm real sorry to hear that." He wiped his forehead with the towel again. "She never did like the cold much, did she?"

What was he doing still cooking?

Frank leaned forward. "This place hasn't killed me yet, and you gotta do something, you know?"

He cleared his throat and said, "Last I knew Marco moved to Nashville or California or something. We lost touch about twenty years ago."

Skylar's heart sank. She clutched at the letters in her bag and tried to hide her disappointment.

"Well, thanks, anyway. Nice to meet you."

"Nice to meet you too, my dear. I would shake your hand, but I've been chopping fish all morning." His eyes sparkled with genuine friendliness. "Take good care of yourself."

He saluted her, then disappeared back into the kitchen. She finished the Bloody Mary quietly, and asked Dolly if she could pay.

"Sure thing, sweetie. I'm sorry we didn't find what you were looking for."

"That's okay. Maybe I'll take a trip to New York or Texas."

The man with the cockatiel laughed. "What are you looking for that old rat Marco for, anyway?"

Skylar was surprised and not sure how to answer.

"I need to ask him something." If he's even still alive.

As Skylar walked out, the artist discreetly slipped a piece of paper into her hand, then nodded toward the door and turned back around to her sketch.

When her shoes met the sidewalk, the sun hit Skylar's face, and she unfolded the paper to find an address scrawled inside.

CHAPTER TWO

November, 2014

*W*hen they found the letters, it was a sunny day for an Ohio winter. Even though the air felt biting, the sun poured down amidst puffy white clouds. If you only looked at the sky, you might think you were somewhere warm.

Skylar and Curtis sorted through their mom's stuff, Skylar more so than her brother. Though their mom had left detailed instructions on what to do with almost everything, Curtis had never been what they call detail-oriented. He took a lot of breaks between boxes of trinkets and racks of clothes.

Their mom had tried to get rid of things, but she'd been unable to part with many of her possessions, practical or lovely, from her upbringing. Her collection of hat pins was an example. And the junk drawer full of rubber bands and nails. "If a nail fell out of the rafters," she said about her childhood, "we unbent it and used it again, even if it was rusty." Already they'd discarded a chest-sized drawer full of buttons, and two file cabinets of *Country Living* magazines.

"What was Mom going to do with these?" Curtis asked.

"I don't know," Skylar said. "They made her happy."

Though the siblings thought it was too soon, they had to get the house and its collectibles ready for an auction. Neither of them felt emotionally equipped for the job, but since their dad had passed years before, they were instructed by the will to sell the estate within three months. It was November.

Skylar didn't think January was the ideal time for an auction, but in the last few years, she'd decided to do whatever her mother asked of her. The holidays were going to be particularly hard, so they were doing their best, one day at a time.

Curtis was taking a phone call during one of his breaks when Skylar uncovered the blue trunk. She remembered it from their childhood, but she hadn't seen it in years. A red and white-striped Mexican blanket always covered its top.

She moved the rows of shoes, the scratchy blanket, and tried to open it. She'd always wondered what her mother kept in it, but she'd never asked. Maybe old hats and dresses. Maybe the rest of her ceramic cat collection. She had no idea, but it was locked. She pushed the button and pulled on the latch, the metal cool on her fingers. Nothing.

She ran upstairs to Curtis, who was still on the phone.

She mouthed the word: "Key?"

"What?" he whispered.

"I need a key." He reached in his pocket and fished out his car keys.

"No," Skylar said.

"Hold on," he said to the phone, then moved it aside. He had satin-black hair, and their mother's facial shape.

"I found Mom's old trunk in the closet. But it's locked."

"Pry it open. Here's my knife." He'd never had any patience.

"I don't want to break it." Skylar punched him on the arm. "Think about it. Where would she hide the key?"

"Jewelry box." He turned away and put the phone back to his ear.

That's it. Why hadn't she thought of that? She ran back downstairs to her mother's room and found the jewelry box on the dresser. The oak was inlaid with pearl, and her name had been carved in cursive, *Kate.* The box was shiny and delicate, like her mother.

Before she died, her mother had doled out the expensive jewelry to her family. The sapphire wedding ring and an amethyst to Skylar. Her emerald earrings to her granddaughter, and the pearls to her nieces. But inside was every piece of jewelry that Skylar and Curtis had ever bought her.

From the dragonfly necklace she bought at the fourth-grade Secret Santa Shop, to the sterling silver locket from junior high school. Even the tacky blue-green fish earrings, made from wood, that Skylar had brought back from a spring break vacation with her girlfriends. It never occurred to her that her mother had kept all of these, too. She lay down on the bed and let the emotions overtake her.

When she felt composed again and her nose stopped burning, she got up and went back to the jewelry box. This time she touched each piece, held them, and thought about the day she picked them out. Her mother was always so excited when she opened a gift. Skylar wished she would have wrapped more presents for her. She wished she could see that genuine look of gratitude and surprise glowing from her mother's face. Just one more time.

"What's in it?" Curtis's large presence burst in the door.

"What?" Skylar snapped out of the memory.

He put his phone in his pocket. "What's in the trunk?"

"Oh. I didn't open it yet. Did you know Mom was keeping all of this?"

He looked over her shoulder. "Of course, she kept—wow." His eyes got misty. "That's the Minnie Mouse necklace I bought her at Disney World. I talked her into giving me twenty dollars, spent fifteen on ice cream and pop, and got this Minnie Mouse necklace for five." Skylar gave him a minute for his own nostalgia.

"Okay, the trunk," she said gently. Underneath their mother's keepsakes was a skeleton key. Curtis started to grab it out of her hand, but Skylar stopped him.

"I found it." She made a fist.

"I told you where to look." He tried to pull her fingers open.

They ran downstairs, knelt in front of the trunk, and opened the lid. Skylar felt like she was stepping into a time machine.

A musty smell wafted out. There on top was her mom's wedding dress, neatly folded in plastic lining. Her mom said she loved the way it hung off her shoulders on both sides, and the simplicity of the A-frame skirt. Extravagant, and simple at the same time. Their father always joked that he loved the dress because he could see straight through it.

Underneath was a stack of *Rolling Stone* magazines.

Curtis said, "Why would she be keeping these?" He lifted out the stack.

"Be careful." Their mom always said he was like a bull in a china shop.

Curtis studied the covers: Bob Dylan, The Beatles, Bruce Springsteen. "I thought Dad liked *Rolling Stone*."

"I guess Mom read it, too," Skylar said.

She handled the smooth fabric of her college graduation gown. As she lifted it, one of Curtis' demo tapes from his first band fell out.

"Wow," Curtis said. "Curtis and The Dropouts live on!" Underneath the gown were two file folders labeled *Skylar and Curtis: grade cards.* "No way. Look at this!" He opened his and pulled one out. "Third grade," he read, "a delight in class." He smiled. "Sixth grade: Could put forth more effort."

They both laughed. It felt good to laugh.

Skylar wanted to sit back and go through her file folder, but at the very bottom of the trunk she found something else. Two stacks of envelopes, sealed. Addressed.

She pulled them out, careful not to crack the yellowing paper.

"These are all stamped," she said. "*Return to sender?*"

"Who are they addressed to?" Curtis asked. He wiped his nose with a handkerchief.

"All the same person. Marco Del Rio?"

"Who's that?"

"I don't know."

"It's not Dad."

"Well, yeah. Maybe Mom had a pen pal."

"Pen pals usually get the letters and then write back."

"Maybe her pen pal moved."

"Maybe she had an affair," Curtis said.

"Dude, why do you always go there? You're so cynical."

"I'm just saying, I don't think people are meant to be monogamous."

"You say that all the time. Mom and Dad loved each other. Until the end."

"They were bored to death, when they weren't arguing. Do you think they ever, you know—"

"Dude!"

"I'm just saying. Maybe we have siblings we don't know about."

"Old couples argue," Skylar said. "That's just how they communicate. What should we do?"

Curtis never had much regard for anybody's privacy. "We should open them."

"We can't open them." Skylar eyed Curtis. They had scattered the contents of the trunk all over the carpet. Skylar sat down. She already felt like they were invading their mother's privacy.

"Why not? Mom's gone."

"If she's watching over us, don't you think she'd be upset if we read her private correspondences? Plus, isn't it a federal offense?"

"You're so lame. I don't think the feds will come after you if your mom is dead and you open her old mail."

"But they're not addressed to us. What if this guy is still alive? Then, we're opening *his* private correspondences." Skylar dug her toes into the carpet.

"What's with you? It's probably a bill mom sent for some work or something. This guy probably owed her."

He took a stack of letters out of Skylar's hand and flipped through them. "*Seaview, Florida; Seaview, Florida; Miami, Florida; Key West, Florida. Return to sender.* Apparently, she couldn't find him, but she didn't give up on the money."

"But what if they're not bills?" Skylar said. "What if you're right and these are—"

Her mother and father had been married over forty years, happy years, Skylar knew.

"*Now* who sounds cynical?" Curtis said. "We've got to open them." He started ripping at the paper.

"Wait. At least go upstairs and get the letter opener." He rolled his eyes, not before trampling up the stairs and yelling down.

"Where is it?"

"It's by the telephone, in the cup."

"Got it," he said, and ran back down. Skylar couldn't remember the last time she'd seen him so excited. She had no idea what they were about to find.

Curtis handed her the letter opener.

"Come on," Curtis said. "Open up."

"These are all dated 1969. And then one from the Nineties? So, this was after you were born. And after Dad?"

"The Summer of Love," Curtis said. "Maybe Mom went wild."

"The Summer of Love was 1967," Skylar retorted. "She was home taking care of you. I'm just not sure we should read them. You know how Mom used to say, '*Not everybody needs to know,*'" Curtis chimed in, "*everything about you.*'"

He took the first letter out of her hands. "You're such a baby. I'll do it."

"Okay, but I have to be ready." Skylar sighed.

"Your problem is that you always have to be comfortable. You can't go through life being comfortable all the time. It's not rational."

"Dude," Skylar said. "What if—"

Curtis opened the first letter and started reading." Dear Marco," it read. "I remember . . ."

CHAPTER THREE

Fifty Years Earlier, 1964

The day Kate left, her mother sat at their shiny red kitchen table over a cup of coffee, crying. A blue trunk sat between the stove and the back door.

"Please don't go," Rose said. Kate stood on the black and white checkered tile of the kitchen floor, relishing the smell of Maxwell House. She hadn't seen her mother cry since President Kennedy's assassination; Rose had cried for three days.

"Mother, I love you. I want you to be happy. But I want to be happy, too." Kate's dad had already gone to work. He had kissed her on the forehead and said, "Follow your heart, my little free spirit."

With one hand clutched around the coffee cup and one hand flat on the table, Rose said, "The world is not as pleasant and good as you think it is. Don't go around trusting everybody like you do."

Kate's brother walked into the kitchen, straight to the percolator, and poured himself a cup. "What if you can't make it on your own?" he asked. "What if you run out of money?"

She punched him on the shoulder. "Have some faith, Jim. I'll call you if I need you." She hugged her mother. "I'm going to figure it out, okay? I'll write, and when I have the money, I'll call."

"Why don't you just find a nice boy around here and stay close to us?" Rose sighed. "You could get a secretary job and have a family."

Kate hesitated. Her mom knew how heartbroken she'd been when Chad left for the Marines and stopped writing. All of her family knew, but for some reason, they never spoke of it.

"I don't like any boys around here," Kate said. "I don't want to be a secretary. And I'm not ready for another family yet." She regretted the last part as soon as she said it. Her mom lowered her head.

"Are we not good enough for you?" She adjusted a saucer under her coffee cup, which clattered in the swallowed silence. In a quieter voice she said, "I know we don't have a lot of money, but we have enough. Have I not told you how important you are to me?"

"Mother, of course you have." Kate put a hand on her mom's shoulder. You and Dad and Jim are wonderful. I just want to, I don't know, see the world. And maybe write about what I see. It's not forever."

Kate hadn't prepared herself for the heaviness of this moment. She hadn't told anyone that she'd waited on a couple of hitchhikers at the diner who were traveling from New York to Florida, or that she'd been having dreams about the ocean.

"Mom," Kate said. "It's the Sixties. Women don't have to stay home anymore."

Jim jingled the keys in his hand. "All right, Kate. Train's a-leavin'." He grunted as he lifted Kate's trunk with both hands. "What the hell is in this thing, anyway?" Rose had given it to Kate this past spring, on her nineteenth birthday.

Kate laughed. "Clothes. And my books and journals."

She helped him with one side of the trunk. "I love you, Mother," she said, and pushed Jim toward the door.

"Not everybody needs to know everything about you, Kate," Rose called after her. The screen door caught in a gust of wind and slammed behind them. The siblings hoisted the trunk into the back seat, and Kate climbed into the passenger side.

"Why does she always say that?" Kate said, half to herself.

"You know mom's a private person. Maybe she's afraid you're going to write something about her."

Kate sighed. "I mostly write about my feelings and stuff, you know. And books that I read. It's not like anybody reads my journals, anyway."

As he started the car and pulled out of the driveway, Jim changed his tone to the voice he only used with Kate. The big-brother voice. "Are you sure about this?" She glanced in the side mirror and checked her hair.

"No, but I'm not sure about anything, anymore."

"Why Florida? What are you looking for?" Jim downshifted for a stop sign. "It's so hot there."

"You've been there. Didn't you like it?" They had taken a family vacation there years ago. Fished with their dad and swam with their mom.

"Yeah, but I don't want to live there," he said. "I don't think we're meant to always be on vacation. Plus, I hate the way the sand feels on my feet. Gives me the creeps."

"I had a dream that I lived there. At the beach." Kate hadn't told them, which was probably why her mom couldn't accept her leaving. She didn't tell him that her dream contained a map with a shape, which she looked up in the encyclopedia at the library, the shape like a county. The county where she was headed.

He did a double-take at her face. As he turned into the

parking lot of the bus station he said, "Well, it's probably not going to be all cocktails and sunsets."

Jim set the trunk in a line of luggage next to the side of the bus, leaned up against his car, and lit a cigarette. He hugged her tightly, and then tapped her on the small of her back when she turned away. "Call me when you need me," he said.

Kate found a seat and stared out the window. A few other passengers were scattered about. As the doors hissed closed, she waved at Jim one more time, then watched her brother fade into the distance, making a point to keep to herself.

The farther south they traveled, the more vivid the scenery. Green Kentucky hills, Tennessee mountains, and eventually, copper Georgia dirt. She studied her own reflection in the window: pale skin, gray eyes, drab, brown hair. Kate's attention moved inward. What *was* she looking for?

Nobody she knew had done this before. Nobody in her family, anyway. Her mom had only finished the eighth grade before she became a maid and then met Stan. When they married, she quit working and spent her life raising Kate and Jim. She hadn't ever gotten a driver's license.

Kate wanted to go to college. She yearned to go to school and study English, but there were fees and things for books, and she also had to work. She was saving up, but couldn't afford it yet. She didn't dare ask her parents. She didn't want to be a burden.

Most of the other girls in her graduating class had gotten engaged. Some were going to business college. A few were going to become teachers, and a few were going to be nurses. Nobody had done this. Nobody had just left town to see what they could find.

Of course, some of them left town during high school for a time, to "visit an aunt." But everybody knew what that meant. The idea terrified Kate. If pregnant, her mom would have forced her to marry Chad. Which wasn't a problem after Kate refused to go on a date with anyone else after he left for the Marines.

She had gone full-time at the diner, telling herself she was saving for college, and that she would go later. But there was something about the female hitchhiker she'd met. Not only did her dress look so elegant and comfortable, her blonde hair in lazy curls almost to her waist, there was something in her eyes that seemed wild and free.

In addition to leaving a tip, they had left a copy of Jack Kerouac's *On the Road* under their coffee cups. Kate had gone straight home and read it from cover to cover.

That was the night she had the dream. The one so real she could feel the sand between her toes and the rays of sun beaming on her shoulders. *Why not me,* she had thought when she woke up. *Why can't I travel and start my own life?*

She had told her dad first. Stan's own father had been strict and ruled over him with an iron fist, so he had always encouraged Kate to learn and grow and to be herself. In his eyes, Kate could do no wrong. Against Rose's wishes, Kate's dad had phoned one of his fishing buddies who'd retired in the Sunshine State, who agreed to rent an apartment to her.

"He's not so keen on renting to a single woman," her dad had said, "nobody is. So I told him your fiancé got shipped overseas, and you'd probably move home when he got back. Or maybe he'd move in with you."

"Dad!"

"Kate, sometimes a little white lie that's not even really a lie can go a long way."

"You know that's not true, though, Dad. Chad and I are over."

"So stay out of trouble, okay?" His eyes had twinkled when he winked.

"I'll give him cash every month," Kate promised.

"I know you will."

Just when she thought Georgia would never end, the bus passed a sign with an orange on it that said, "Welcome to Florida." Palm trees streamed past her window against a turquoise sky.

She didn't know what she was looking for, but she hoped she would know when she found it.

CHAPTER FOUR

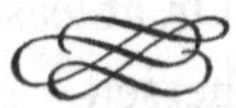

The town was a quiet community on the Gulf Coast called Seaview. The apartment was beautiful. Yellow and blue with a tree painted on the front door. A bungalow, Butch called it.

There was a lime tree in the front yard and tropical flowers out back. The living room was an old front porch someone had refinished with carpet and windows. It even came furnished with everything she'd need: a couch, a full-sized bed, dishes, and pots and pans.

Butch met her out front with his wife. He was a stocky guy in a fishing shirt and khaki shorts. Diana stayed quiet behind sunglasses that matched her pink sundress. Kate handed Butch the first month's rent, and he gave her the rules. No company after 10 p.m. No loud music. Don't bother the neighbors.

She settled in, then scoured the newspaper but couldn't find anything of interest. Secretary, teacher, babysitter. Finally, she walked downtown toward the water, where she found a restaurant right across the street from the beach. A small chalkboard propped up outside read, "Welcome to The Wave: under new ownership." The smell of the ocean reminded her of fishing with her dad and made her smile. She took a deep breath.

The inside walls were sea green. The maroon barstools looked out of place, but she didn't care. She needed a job. Her mother had given her twenty dollars for an emergency only, in case she needed a bus ticket home. Kate promised herself she would never have to use it. Or, at least, she hoped.

She didn't think of herself as religious anymore, but standing inside The Wave, she said a little prayer.

"Johnny Angel" played out of a juke box in the corner. It was early still, 10 a.m., and all the chairs were empty. A tall woman came out from the kitchen and said, "We don't start drinks until ten-thirty. Food at eleven."

"Oh, that's fine. I'm looking for the owner?"

"He's not here right now. Is there something I can help you with?" She had a long, thick blonde ponytail, and she spoke with a certain accent of toughness. Her skin was several shades tanner than Kate's.

"Yes." Kate lifted her résumé out of her briefcase. "I'm looking for a job." The woman looked at her side-eyed.

Kate handed her the paper. The woman wiped her hands on a towel and slid a pair of reading glasses over her eyes.

"Well, this ain't a truck stop and we don't serve breakfast."

Kate had little experience, but she had some. "Right," she turned on her charm. "What kind of food do you serve?"

"Seafood, chicken and burgers. Beach food. Where you from?"

"Ohio." Kate adjusted her blouse that had fallen off her shoulder. "The Midwest."

"What brought you to Seaview?"

"A new beginning, I guess? I love the ocean." She decided to change her attitude to seem more confident. "I can handle ten tables at a time, and that's with refilling coffee mugs every five minutes."

The woman put the glasses back on her head. "Well, the boss is out shopping. He won't be back in until this afternoon." She glanced at the paper again. "Come back around two."

"Sure," Kate said. "Thank you."

"I'm Linda." The woman's face softened and she reached out her hand like a man.

Kate gave her best handshake. "Nice to meet you, Linda."

"Yep. I'll tell him you're coming."

"Thanks," Kate said, and walked out the door.

Instead of going home, Kate wandered out to the beach. It was a muggy August day. White and gray birds trotted away from her in circles as she approached the shoreline. She thought of her mom.

The water spread out before her, blue with a hint of green. A few sailboats bobbed sleepily. Kate wondered if people lived on them, if they were abandoned, or if the sailors just weren't awake yet. The only sound she could hear was the occasional seagull squeaking.

She wanted to sit in the sand, but she didn't want to get her skirt dirty and appear disheveled if she did, in fact, get a chance to meet the boss of The Wave. She could visit the other places on the street and pass out more résumés, but she had a feeling about this one. Plus, she liked the view.

From the water, The Wave's outside deck was made of dark wood. She pictured herself serving seafood and sandwiches, all the while being able to look out at those sailboats on the horizon. Her daydream ended when she heard heavy breathing behind her.

"Hey!" She turned quickly to see a man approaching. He stopped, bent over, and caught his breath about five feet away. He reached into the sand and said, "A sand dollar," and stood up panting. "Is it yours?"

A ring of sweat crowned his white tee shirt.

"Hi." She clutched her briefcase. "No. It's not mine."

He took a step away from her. "Sorry to sneak up on you like that." He brushed the sand dollar against his pants and the sand sprinkled back onto the beach.

She glanced down at her most professional outfit, a skirt and a blouse; she must look silly out here by the water's edge.

"You know, most people out here wear bathing suits and cover-ups." He tugged at his shirt. "Or at least take their shoes off."

Her black flats were covered with sand.

"Right. I'm new in town." As soon as she said it, she clenched her lips. Her mom's voice in her head advised, *not everybody needs to know everything about you. Don't go around trusting everybody like you do.*

"I thought so. I'm Noah," he said. She still wasn't sure what to think of him. "Out for my morning run." He smiled, and when he did, his smile lines creased and seemed to encompass his sun-tanned face in a way that reminded her of the moon. "Where are you from?" he asked.

"Up north, Ohio. How about you?"

"Born-and-raised Floridian. Crystal River, where the manatees live." He was still catching his breath. "It's about an hour north of here. You ever been?"

"No," she said.

"Well, I should take you up there, sometime. Everybody should swim with manatees once in their life." He looked out over the water and pointed to a pier in the distance. "We used to have some out here, but we haven't seen any in a while. I think the boats ran them off."

"Oh," she said. "That's too bad."

"Well, I don't want to bother you. It looks like you're in the middle of something."

"Yeah," Kate said, looking down at her outfit. "I'm looking for a job."

"On a boat?" he asked and smiled again.

"No," she held up her briefcase. "At The Wave."

"Oh, yeah. Heard they have new owners. Sorry I can't help you out. I haven't met them yet."

"That's okay," she said.

"Where are you staying?"

"I rented an apartment a few blocks away." She wouldn't tell him where she lived, exactly.

"I live in town, too. So maybe I'll see you around." A piece of dark hair fell into his face, and he flipped it up casually, back on top of his head. He held out the sand dollar. "You want this?"

"Oh, I couldn't." She'd never seen one fully intact before. It was perfectly round. "You found it."

"I have a ton of them. Here," he said, "it's yours. Welcome to Seaview." She took it out of his hand and studied the flower pattern on the top.

Before she could say thank you, he was running away at a full pace.

"Have a good day!" he called out.

TRUE LOVE SAGA

CHAPTER FIVE

The new boss hired her on the spot. She could wear whatever she wanted, and she would start the next day.

Though a part of her thought she should go out and meet some people or something, she wanted to make sure she could pay her rent before she did anything else. She felt lighter on her walk home, and she stopped into a tiny convenience store on the main drag where she bought herself some food and cleaning supplies.

As the evening unfolded in her new home, she cooked herself a nice meal of pasta and chicken breast and had a glass of white zinfandel. She felt strange, and then realized all at once she felt like an adult: she had her own place, could make her own rules, and she would have time to read. But then, loneliness washed over her.

Kate put her feet up on the coffee table and thought of her dad. She wondered how her parents were, and if Jim missed her. She would write them tomorrow, tell them the good news about her job, and ask her brother when he would like to come and visit.

Just as her eyelids got heavy and her mind dreamy, something snapped her back to attention. A scratching sound. She peeked out of the curtain and looked out into the darkness. The streetlight cast shadows to the end of the sand path, but there was nothing there. She heard it again.

Wishing she hadn't watched *Psycho* with her brother when she was younger, the worst things flashed through her mind.

Maybe Noah from the beach had followed her without her knowing and was trying to break in. Maybe someone had followed her home. Maybe it was a ghost or a spirit who used to live here. Maybe—she shook her mind out of the spiral and told herself to do something.

Kate wished the bungalow didn't have so many windows. She felt exposed. Tip-toeing back through the bedroom, she pulled a broom out from the closet and snuck back to the door. Whatever or whomever it was, maybe she could fend them off.

Approaching the yellow door, she heard the noise again. The scratching came from the lower part, as if a small person were trying to pry it open. Kate took a deep breath, unlocked the doorknob, and opened it. Before she could get the broom handle set, a loud cry rang out, and a cat darted inside past her feet and under the coffee table. *What in the world?*

The cat crouched close to the floor and readied to pounce. Kate peeked back out into the front yard. Two glowing eyes pointed at her. When she saw the outline of a raccoon, she slammed the door in reflex.

Like a Siamese with a line drawn straight down its nose, the cat's face was one side black and one side white. Big and fluffy.

"Well, hi," Kate said. "Please, just come on in." She hadn't spoken to anyone for hours and was glad to hear her own voice. The cat stood up, stretched, and came right up to her. It had blue eyes and a black spot on the tip of its nose, which it used to nudge Kate's hand.

"What are you doing here? You must belong to somebody." It turned around and rubbed again at Kate's hand and purred.

"Aw," she said, "you're very sweet." Kate didn't see a collar, but it still had claws. "You can stay tonight, but tomorrow we're going to have to find your owners." The cat meowed. Kate lifted its tail and decided it was a female.

She laid some paper by the door in case the cat might have to do her business and thought she might as well go to bed. She went back into the bathroom to brush her teeth and wash her face. The claw-foot tub looked white and inviting. As she put her pajamas on, the cat jumped onto the bed and curled up into a ball.

"Okay, Queen Kitty. Would you like to sleep on the bed with me?" Tomorrow she could knock on doors and see if any of the neighbors had lost their cat. Then she'd get ready for the second shift at work. She was excited about her new job and found herself thinking about Noah. There was something different about him from guys back home. Maybe it was just Florida.

As she tucked herself into the covers, the cat stood up, curled, and tucked against her. She was almost asleep again when a slight ticking sound caught her attention. A cross between a ticking and a crawling. What was that?

The ceiling fan above her had its rotating sound but this was different. What was that noise? She flipped back on the light and noticed a softball-sized cluster of bugs crawling in and out of the globe. Little ant-looking things, with wings. A few of them had fallen and landed on her comforter. She scrambled out of bed and panicked.

Gross. What should she do? If she had any problems with bugs, she was supposed to call Butch. She looked at the clock: 12:30 a.m. The cat stood up and waited for Kate to get back under the covers, but she could not. Would not. There were too many of the ant things for her to kill them all. She pulled a blanket out of her closet, turned the light off, and went out to the couch. The cat followed her.

Her brother's voice came to her now, his questions. *What if you can't make it on your own? What if you run out of money?*

If she went home, everyone would know she'd failed at taking care of herself and making her own way.

Kate settled her head on the couch. Her skin crawled thinking about the bugs. The cat let out a quick meow and then hopped onto her lap and crawled across her legs to find its spot. She petted its fur, glad she had a companion, if only for a night.

THE MORNING SUNLIGHT crept in through sheer window covers and Kate made a note that she would need some better curtains. She opened them and looked outside. Everything was so green. The flowers and the trees were their own jungle. The air smelled fresh and pure. Despite the loneliness and the bugs, she loved it. After brewing some coffee and pouring milk for the cat, she called the landlord.

"Did you put some in a bag, so we can see what kind they are?" He had a big and booming voice over the phone.

"Um, no, sir. I didn't. I can't get close to them without, well, screaming."

Butch huffed through the phone. "I'll send the maintenance man around noon."

"Thank you," she said. The cat lapped up the milk.

Before he hung up the phone she heard him mumble, "This is why you don't rent to women. Can't even handle a couple of bugs."

She dressed, avoiding the ceiling fan, and then opened the front door so the warm air could circulate through the house. Queen Kitty crept outside and then sat poised on the front step like a statue.

At exactly noon, a man approached. She stood up from the

kitchen and went to the door. Then she recognized him. He flipped a lock of hair out of his eye. Noah.

"Hi," she said. She was surprised at how excited she was to see him.

He seemed excited, too. Smiling. "I'm here about some bugs."

"You're the maintenance man?"

"That's me." He held up a pair of plastic gloves. "I've come to save the day."

"Thank goodness. Please, come in." The cat darted into the bedroom and under the bed.

"You have a cat?" Noah had on a white tank top today. His muscles drew clear, sculpted lines in his arms. She caught herself staring.

"I let her in last night. On the run from a raccoon. She must belong to somebody."

"Do you mind if I take a look?"

"No, please." She gestured toward the bedroom. He got down on his hands and knees and peered under the bed.

"She looks like Holmes's cat."

"Great," Kate said. "Can we take her to him?"

"Unfortunately not." Noah stood back up. "Holmes died about a month ago. Heard his family let the cat out on accident and it never came back. I can't be sure, but I think it's the same one. The markings on her face."

"She's beautiful," Kate said. "Okay, well, I'll let her back out whenever she wants. That raccoon is probably still out there, though."

"So how about these bugs?"

"They're right up there." Kate pointed.

He slipped his thong sandals off and stepped onto the bed to get a closer look. "Flying ants, all right. Some people mistake them for termites, but they're really old ants. They must have a colony around here somewhere. Excuse me for a minute." He stepped down and walked outside, then returned with a basket of some unidentified granule substance. "Did you get the job?"

Kate fidgeted. "Yeah, I start today."

Noah lifted each of the white landscaping rocks that sat on either side of the mulched path to the mailbox.

"Hired on the spot. That's good."

"Yeah," she said, feeling proud. "We'll see how it goes."

"Found it." He held a rock up. "The colony is right here. Wanna see?"

The skin on Kate's neck crawled again. "No, thanks." She shook her arms to make the feeling go away.

"Ants are actually pretty amazing creatures. You know they build structures akin to pyramids?" Kate didn't want to think about that. "What time do you go in?"

"I'm supposed to be there at four."

He sprinkled the granules up against the house. Lizards jumped and flopped away. The cat came out from under the bed and sat behind Kate's legs.

"She seems to like you," Noah said. "You might have a new cat."

"I guess I need to walk up to the store to get some cat food."

"Is it okay if I come and visit you? At The Wave?" Noah poked at a rock with his foot.

"Of course."

Did she answer him too fast? She gently reminded herself that she didn't have to play by anybody else's rules.

"All right. I'll see you later." He turned and walked down the street, then disappeared behind a palm tree.

"Thank you!" she called after him.

CHAPTER SIX

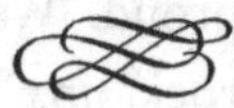

"*Y*ou got the job," Linda said, reaching out her hand again. "Congratulations and welcome to The Wave."

"Thanks," Kate said.

"I'll be training you today, so keep up. My money depends on it." Kate smiled and put her hands in her apron. Linda continued, "It's mostly locals around here, regulars. We get a few tourists in and out, but most people don't come to Seaview unless they know somebody who lives here." She pulled out a notebook and a pen. "I'll introduce you. Let's go."

Kate followed Linda out onto the deck. Seven tables sat along the railing, and one table close to the opposing wall. Two of them had customers and a few of them had empty red cups and pitchers strewn about.

"How are you doing, Sue?" Linda asked.

"If I were any better, there'd be two of me," the woman said.

"Sue, Kate. Kate, Sue." Linda pointed back and forth with one finger and bent over to reset a pair of salt and pepper shakers.

"You're new." Sue had short blonde hair and a round face.

"Yes, I am," Kate said.

"Welcome to The Wave."

"Thanks." It surprised Kate that Sue sat all by herself and at ease. Rose would never go out to eat by herself.

Kate looked out over the water and felt her mind relax.

Sue lit a cigarette. "Paradise, isn't it?"

"Beautiful."

"Sue drinks iced tea or PBR, depending on the day," Linda said.

"All depends on the day," Sue said.

"Keep her drinks full and her ashtray empty, and she's happy."

"Okay." Kate fiddled with her pen.

"Let's bus this table. We've gotta get ready for the night shift."

They collected dirty cups and silverware, put them in a bus tub next to the wall, and wiped down each table. More customers came and went, and Kate followed Linda around.

The Wave's menu was easy to learn, and she found herself training quickly. At the end of the night, Kate sat with Linda as she counted her money.

"You did a good job. I think you're ready to go alone." Linda went behind the bar and poured herself a drink. "You want something?"

"Sure," Kate said.

"I drink gimlets. What do you like?"

"That sounds good," Kate said.

A motorcycle pulled up outside and bumbled out.

"We must have company," Linda said, and in walked Noah.

"Hey." He waved with one hand from his waist.

A twinge of excitement pinched Kate in the stomach. "Hi," she said. "Noah, this is Linda."

"How's it going?" he said.

"I've seen you around."

"I would have come in earlier, but I didn't want to bother your training. How was your first night?"

Kate smiled. "Good. Thanks." He had on jeans and a white tee shirt with the sleeves rolled up.

"Can I get you something?" Linda asked.

"What do you have in a bottle?" Linda stopped writing in her notebook and stood up to move around the bar.

"I have Pabst Blue Ribbon on sale," she said.

"Sold." Noah put a dollar on the bar and sat down next to Kate.

"I'm almost done," she said. "How's your day?"

"I set up a couple of mousetraps and helped put in a window screen. One of our tenants locked himself out and broke his own window last night."

"Really?" Kate took a drink. It was sweet lime and sour.

"Just another exciting day as a maintenance man." He swigged his beer and put it back on the bar.

"Is that your motorcycle?" Kate asked.

"Yep, that's my bike. I've had her for about two years now. She's treating me well." He put his hands in his pockets and shrugged. "How's the cat?"

"Oh, she's fine. I got a litter box and some food today, so I guess I'll let her stay around."

Noah smiled. "Good."

Linda said, "So, Noah, we're getting ready to close up. Do you want anything else before I close down the register?"

"No ma'am. I'm on the bike."

"Kate, we get paid on Tuesdays, so you'll make your first check next week. Tomorrow you'll be by yourself, so you should be able to make some tips."

Kate said a quick prayer of gratitude in her mind.

"Wanna see the bike?"

"Sure. Thanks, Linda. I'll see you tomorrow." She followed Noah out into the warm night. Linda closed the door behind them. They sat their drinks on the front table and Noah pulled out a pack of Marlboros.

"Smoke?" he asked.

She'd only smoked a few times, when her friend Heather talked her into stealing her dad's. He pulled out two cigarettes, and reached over and lit hers first. She coughed at the first drag.

Noah smiled. "I only smoke when I drink. You too?"

"Yes," Kate said. "It's been a while."

"So," he said, "I was thinking about riding out to the beach. Wanna go?"

It was a clear night. She could see all of the stars.

"Isn't this the beach?" Kate asked.

He glanced out over the water. "This is the bay. The beach is a little bit different, you know, the Gulf. The bay opens up to it. There are a couple of cool little watering holes over there, with live music. Do you like music?"

She absolutely loved music. Her father had played the banjo when she was young, and she'd taken piano lessons for a few years. "What kind of music?"

"All kinds. It depends on who's playing. It's Wednesday? I think Marco Del Rio and The Dolphins play tonight at The Parrot."

She'd been on motorcycles a few times with her uncles. She pointed to the bike. "Are you safe?" She was half joking, but wondered how he would answer.

A couple staggered by, holding each other by the waists, cups in their free hands.

"Hi," the man said.

"Hello," Noah answered. "Never had an accident. I won't have more than one beer an hour."

As he took a drag off his cigarette, she noticed his arms again. He was certainly strong.

"Okay, sure."

Noah gave her his helmet, put her apron in the saddle bags,

and she hitched up her skirt and climbed onto the back of the bike. She gripped the handles next to the seat.

"Have you done this before?" he asked.

"A few times, when I was little."

"The trick is to lean with me. If I lean to the right, you lean to the right and that's how we turn. If we're going straight, stay steady."

"I think I can handle that," she said.

He fired up the engine, backed out slowly, and pulled the throttle.

Warm air enveloped her skin as they rode. They turned inland and crisscrossed through some city streets until they reached a draw bridge. Yellow lights flashed and the street in front of them began to rise. It moved slowly, two sides separating until the pavement faced them like a wall pointing straight up into the middle of the sky. If it weren't for gravity, maybe they could ride up into the clouds.

"Out there," Noah yelled over the engine, "is the bay, which flows in and out of the Gulf." The dark horizon was scattered with red and green lights from parked sailboats. "Over there," Noah pointed to the right, "is the Intracoastal. It's a collection of little man-made canals, built for shipping vessels. People started buying up the land and moving there." Houses of different shapes and sizes lined a concrete wall on both sides, some of them with boats dangling up out of the water on lifts.

The bridge lowered, and Noah pulled the throttle again. Kate moved her arms to hold him around the waist. With his body against hers, she felt a little wild. Right before they came to a dead end, they pulled off into a parking lot. The street sign read "Bay Avenue." People mingled around a few tables planted in white sand. Red letters on the building said, "The Parrot." Music poured out of the open doors.

She lifted her leg from the bike and took the helmet off while Noah slid into the parking space. The vodka had warmed up her chest and made her feel a little like dancing. Generally, she was too shy to ever dance in front of anyone.

"Here we are," Noah said, taking the helmet from her and propping it up on the back of the seat. A few other bikes were already lined up. He grabbed her hand. "Ready? I'll introduce you to my friends." Inside, the music was loud, and people were lively. They went straight to the bartender where Noah yelled over the music.

"Shawn, this is Kate." Shawn had four bottles flipped upside-down in two hands, pouring a drink.

"What's happening, Kate? Welcome. What can I get for you?"

Noah ordered himself a beer before asking, "Do you want another drink?"

Sure, why not. She nodded.

"And a . . ."

"Gimlet," she said.

A stage in the corner of the room held a four-piece band. The front man played a bluesy-folk riff, one of the guys played a banjo, there was a stand-up bass guitar, and a drum. A couple of them had sunglasses on.

"What do you think?" Noah said. He handed her the drink and paid Shawn.

"Far out," Kate said. She'd never used that phrase before, but this seemed like the right kind of place for it.

The lead singer spoke over the microphone with a hint of an accent she couldn't place. "We would like to welcome everybody to The Parrot tonight. We are The Dolphins." A couple of people cheered. "We like to play a little music that *you* love, a little music that *we* love, and we hope that you *all* fall in love tonight." He flashed his eyes at Kate.

Of all the people in the bar, he was staring right at her. Her face burned, and she felt herself smile. She thought she should look away, she didn't want to stare, but he had a look on his face, a glimmer in his eyes, some kind of expression she couldn't quite read, but wanted to. He closed his eyes as the band started in on a song.

Noah flattened his lips. "That's Marco Del Rio."

Jet black hair hung straight and shiny around his face, and his bronze skin reminded her of a picture in a magazine. He had an aquiline nose, long and slanted. And dimples.

When he caught her eyes again, Marco smiled sweetly. She couldn't help but smile back again. He looked like a boy and a man at the same time.

He tipped his chin at Noah, and Noah made the same gesture back in greeting.

"Come on," Noah said. "Let's go outside."

She followed him out back to a white picnic table. A '57 Chevy drove by with the top down and a group of people who looked about her age whistled and yelled, "What's up, Moon Dog?"

Noah lit a cigarette and offered one to Kate. She could get used to this, drinking and smoking. Her mom would hate it, but her mom wasn't here.

"So how do you know Marco?" she asked.

"Gorgeous, isn't he?" Kate wasn't sure what to say. "All the girls in the county are in love with him. He's been playing around here for a few years now. He's from Texas, I think."

"He seems nice," she said.

"Yeah," Noah said. "He's *nice*."

Kate looked up at the stars. Maybe she wanted to find a nice guy. *No*, she snapped out of it. She wanted to be able to take care of herself.

"What about you?" Kate asked. She felt the vodka loosening her up. "Do you have a girlfriend?"

Noah smiled. "I don't." He ashed his cigarette into the street and seemed pensive. "You're a young, pretty girl. How come you don't have a guy with you?"

"I don't know, all of my friends were looking for husbands

and I guess I didn't want one yet." She thought about her high school sweetheart, but she didn't want to explain it here, now. "I wanted to live a little, I guess." She shrugged.

The '57 Chevy bounced around the corner, parked, and a group of people piled out, chatting and laughing. A guy draped his arms around both girls, who wore their skirts above their knees. Kate had to keep from staring at their legs. She had on a long skirt, as always.

"Moon Dog, who's the librarian?" The guy removed one of his arms to shake Noah's hand. He had narrow eyes and combed-back hair.

"Hey, man. Ease up. This is my friend Kate. She's new in town."

The guy pulled a flask out of his jeans pocket. "Excuse me." He made an extravagant bow gesture to Kate and said, "I'm Jack Miracle. Pleased to meet you, miss." He reminded Kate of James Dean.

The librarian comment embarrassed Kate, but she forgave him quickly. "You don't have to call me 'miss,' *sir*."

"Ohhh," the driver said, slamming the door, and smoothing his hands over his blonde hair. "She called you, sir!" Kate smiled.

"Quiet, Donny T-Bird," Jack said.

One of the girls reached out her hand and said, "I'm Steph, and this is Peggy."

"Hi," Kate said. "Nice to meet you."

"Welcome to town," said Peggy, lighting a cigarette. "Where are you from?"

"Up North," said Kate. "Ohio."

"Far out," Peggy said. "Steph's from Ohio."

"Where exactly?" Kate asked.

Steph had short blonde hair, cut off in a bob around her chin. "A small town north of Cincinnati."

"Me too! Middle Falls." What a small world, Kate thought.

"Let me guess," Steph said. "Your dad works in a factory,

your mom stays home, and you wanted to get the hell out of there."

It had been a wonderful place to grow up, but she knew the world was bigger for her. "How did you know?" She took a drag from her cigarette. The smoke tangled up in her throat.

"That's why I'm here, too. We go to Florida Gulf College. How about you?"

"I just got a job in Seaview, at The Wave." She glanced at Noah, and he nodded.

"Oh yeah, we've been there," Steph said. "Right down the street from The Buoy. Have you been?"

"Not yet. I just arrived yesterday."

"Right on," Steph said. "We should all go sometime. They have poetry readings on Saturday nights, and we know the owners."

"That sounds like fun."

"Come on," Donny said. "Let's go in and get a drink." He turned to Noah. "Marco's band playing tonight?"

"Affirmative." Noah put his cigarette out in the ashtray on the table.

"Well," Jack said, "what are we waiting for?"

The girls followed the guys in. Jack stopped and turned around and grabbed Kate's hand. "*Come on*, Library."

Noah nodded with a resolved look and followed them. Jack led the pack through the back door of The Parrot and straight to the bar. He yelled and bobbed his head to the music, then released Kate's hand and started up with Shawn.

"They're the local college kids," Noah said. "The guys might give you a hard time, but they're cool."

"They call you Moon Dog?" Kate asked. She was trying to talk loud without yelling.

"Jack's into nicknames. It's a song on the B-side of the Beach Boys album. I usually listen to the B-sides first."

"Donny T-Bird?" Kate asked.

"Donny Turner. His dad's a big county prosecutor. Buys him a new car every year. Last year it was a T-Bird. They've got this huge garage with cars just lined up."

"What about the girls?" Kate asked. "Do they have nicknames?"

Noah laughed. "Jack tried to name Steph 'Blondie,' but she swore she'd beat him up, and I think she meant it. Peggy Sue—"

"Of course," Kate said. "Like the song."

The college girls danced freely. Kate wanted to dance, but she was feeling shy again. Out of all the people in the place, twenty or thirty, her eyes landed on Marco, who was staring at her again. The music stopped.

The band members all lifted their drinks and Marco said over the microphone, "We are going to slow it down for a minute. Bring your sweetheart up to the front if you like." He started the song. It was Elvis. They could play Elvis!

The college guys grabbed their girls and led them out onto the dance floor in front of the stage. Kate wondered if Noah would ask her, but he rested his elbow on the bar and stared at the band. Kate noticed Marco again, smiling at her, as he sang about not being able to help falling in love. His voice was deep and resonant.

"Another drink?" Noah asked.

"Sure." Kate held up her empty glass.

A few other couples took to the dance floor. While Kate waited for Noah, an older guy approached her. She smelled the whiskey on his breath before she saw how red his eyes were. A stench of body odor stung her nose. He grabbed her by the arm and put his face too close to hers. "Let's dance," he slurred.

Before she knew what to say, Noah grabbed the guy's hand and put himself between them.

"She's with me, old man." The guy looked bewildered. Noah stared at him. "Back it up a little bit, please."

"Excuse me," the guy mumbled. He staggered away and onto a barstool.

"Sorry," Noah said. "He's a regular. Lives on a sailboat, I think." The man saluted in Noah's direction. "He's harmless, but I wouldn't dance with him."

"Thanks," Kate said. "He smells pretty bad."

The Elvis song ended, and the band went straight into Chubby Checker's "Twist." Right away the college kids started twisting. Kate knew this one. Peggy waved at Kate and said, "Come on!"

She wasn't sure she wanted to dance in front of all these people she didn't know, but Steph ran over to her, grabbed her by the hands, and pulled her onto the dance floor. Steph's hair flung back and forth when she broke out into the step.

Kate eased into it faster than she thought she would. Everybody but Noah and the old man got onto the dance floor. Even Shawn the bartender twisted while he tidied up the bar. She glanced up at Marco. When she realized she was staring, she laughed, and Noah raised his beer in cheers. Jack twisted in her direction, and then the song was over before she wanted it to be.

"We will take a little break," Marco said, "and be back in fifteen to play some original tunes. I hope you stay around." The guys set down their instruments and Marco walked straight to Kate.

"Hi," he said. "I'm Marco."

"I heard."

He reached for her hand, raised it, and kissed the back of it gently. Her heart fluttered. She took a sip of her drink and licked the lime from her lips.

"What is your name?" His eyes were humble and gentle, deep like the ocean, and green. He was looking at her like she was the only woman in the bar. She was amused.

"Kate," she said.

"Can I call you Katie?" he asked.

"Sure." He tucked a loose lock of hair behind his ear and gritted his teeth. His dimples showed, like he was looking for words. She stared back at him. The way he was looking at her . . . she felt powerful and beautiful at the same time.

Noah came up behind her.

"Marco, great set."

He broke the stare. "Thanks, man. I thought you might like that Elvis song." He tapped Noah on the shoulder with the back of his hand as if they were sharing a secret.

The drummer approached.

"Come on, man. We're gonna light one up."

Marco turned to Kate. "Would you like to join us?"

Noah spoke up. "Nah, man. We're gonna get out of here. I'm on the bike."

Marco raised his eyebrows and tilted his head. "When will I see you again?" He was smiling at her like he knew her.

She tilted her own head and raised her eyebrows. Had she met him before?

Noah grabbed her by the hand and said, "Good to see you, Marco," over his shoulder and led her out of The Parrot, her feet stumbling to keep up.

As Noah started up the motorcycle, the college kids came out of the bar.

"Hey Library," Jack said. "Hope to see you soon! Stay cool!" The girls waved. Noah revved the engine.

"The Buoy on Saturday!" Steph yelled. "Meet you there!"

"See you," Kate hollered, and climbed onto the bike.

CHAPTER SEVEN

The ocean seemed endless in the dark. Lines of beach and tide reflected the moonlight, opaque curves kissing the white sand. She clutched her hands together in front of Noah's stomach and looked up at the stars. She felt kind of fuzzy, excited still, from dancing. She hadn't been this close to a guy in a while. They crossed over the drawbridge, back over the intracoastal, and toward her new home.

Right as they slowed into town and rode by The Wave, Noah said, "If I were you, I'd stay away from Marco Del Rio."

There *was* something about him. Something gentle and kind—and familiar. Jack and Donny, she would understand if Noah wanted her to stay away from them. They seemed kind of rowdy.

"Why?" she finally asked.

"First off, the chances of him taking you on a proper date," Noah said, "are slim."

He stopped the bike in Kate's new driveway, an alley of a sand path. She swung her leg over the seat of the bike and got her bearings.

Noah added, "I don't even know if Marco's his real name."

Maybe Noah did like her, and he was just shy, too.

"Thank you for the ride," she said. "I had a lot of fun." She handed him the helmet.

He turned off the engine and walked her to the door. She turned the key and, feeling daring, said, "What about you? Why don't you take me on a proper date?"

Noah made a face.

Oh gosh. "I'm sorry. I guess I'm having so much fun."

"No, I mean, yeah," he said. "We could hang around again."

He quickly kissed her on the cheek, and put his helmet on. She felt silly as she unlocked her door. He waited for her to get in safely, and then he sped off on his bike without looking back.

Hang around again? As she opened the door, the cat startled her. She wasn't used to having an animal in the house.

The next day Kate had a slight headache and a vague sense of regret. What was she thinking? She was so embarrassed for having asked Noah to ask *her* out. Maybe he didn't like her. Maybe he thought she was ugly or boring, or . . . something. As she tried to shake the negative thoughts out of her head, the cat jumped up and meowed.

"Well, hi, Queen Kitty. How are you today?"

The cat nudged Kate's hand, demanding a rub. Today she would make some money at the least. She went into the kitchen, poured some coffee and a bowl of cereal, and fed the cat. Memories from the night before flowed in and out. She liked Steph. She had danced. And Marco Del Rio. When she remembered his eyes, her heart warmed. Who knew living by the beach would be so exciting?

A knock at the door snapped her from her thoughts. She re-tied her robe and debated on answering.

"Who is it?"

"It's Noah."

"Just a minute." She ran back to the bathroom and checked her hair. Mascara was smeared under her eyes and her hair was tied in a matted, tangled ponytail. Oh my. Should she open the door? She splashed some water on her face, threw on a tee shirt and her black skirt, and then tried to pretend like she'd been awake for hours. The clock read noon.

"Hi," she said as she opened the door. "How are you today?"

"Good," Noah said. "Can I come in?"

"Sure." Queen Kitty rubbed against Noah's legs. He reached down to pet her.

"How are you feeling?" he asked.

"I slept a little later than usual, but I feel fine."

"I was almost late for work." He ran his hands through his hair. "I'm on my lunch break, so I can't stay long."

"Would you like some coffee?"

"Sure."

She poured cups for them and they went outside and sat on the front step. Their shoulders touched. Queen Kitty followed them out. Noah lit a cigarette.

"So, I had a really good time last night."

"I did, too," said Kate, maybe too quickly. "And I like your friends. They're nice."

"Yeah, they're all right," he said. "So, but, um . . . " this was the first time Kate saw him nervous. "Can I tell you something? Maybe you won't tell anybody?"

"Yes." Kate said. She took a sip of her coffee. The mailman walked by, and her mailbox clinked as he put something in it.

"I really like you."

"I really like you, too."

"But, I—" he stammered, set his coffee down, and put one hand in his pocket, taking a drag from the cigarette with the other. "Jesus, this is hard. I didn't want to ask you out last night because, well, I . . . I . . . " he turned his voice into a whisper, "I don't really like you, like *that*."

What? Oh my gosh. Her heart sank.

"I mean, no, it's not you. I'm not really attracted to . . . girls.

At all. And so, if I were then, I would have wanted to ask you out . . . but—"

"Oh my gosh, I'm so sorry," Kate said. "I guess I was having so much fun that I—"

"No," Noah said, "yeah, I mean. It's just that I'm only attracted to, well, you know. It's weird." She put her hand on his knee, trying to comfort him. "I've never told anyone. I mean, my parents caught me with a . . . my friend, in high school, and my dad . . . they kicked me out of the house. I've been on my own ever since."

Kate had heard rumors in high school about two boys liking each other. One day they both came to school banged up and bruised with black eyes. Some guys on the football team bragged about it later, but nobody ever got punished.

He continued. "I mean, I think my parents knew there was something different about me from the time I was young. *I* knew there was something different about me. The boys in the neighborhood were playing cops and robbers, but I wanted to play with the girls, and I liked clothes and stuff."

"Well." She struggled for the right words. "I'll keep it to myself."

He put out his cigarette and exhaled. Queen Kitty darted after a lizard, then jolted back as if surprised by the sound of rustling leaves.

"I wish I liked girls, like that. I really like you. I wish I knew I could like you like that. I had a girlfriend once; it didn't work out." Noah's eyes were focused on the sand. "But it feels good to tell someone." He let out another breath. "I know I just met you, but you have this something about you I trust. And," his eyes turned to her, "I don't have very many friends."

Kate smoothed down her skirt. She wanted to reassure him. "I won't tell anybody." This must be so hard for him. After some time she asked, "What about the college kids? Do they know?"

"I don't think so. I like them, but they're not much for keeping secrets."

"Well, so far you're my first good friend here, and my most favorite tour guide. Will you do me a favor then? Will you go shopping with me? As friends, of course."

Kate wanted to buy herself a pair of blue jeans.

Noah laughed. "Sure."

They shared a long, sibling-like embrace before Noah went back to work, and Kate got ready for her first night by herself at The Wave. She pulled her hair back into a bun, ironed her black skirt, and decided on a blue blouse with a collar.

As she put on her mascara, she told herself how silly she'd been for wanting Noah to ask her out, anyway. She came here to get away from the expectation of marriage and kids, so why would she even let herself get romantically involved with anyone? Looking in the mirror, she promised herself that she would focus on saving money and think about a career, rather than spend her time and energy on a guy.

On her walk to work, she noticed how colorful the houses were painted compared to the bricks and beiges of her hometown. Light pinks, sea greens, bright yellows, every color of the rainbow. Seaview was naturally a cheery place. Neighbors planting flowers or sitting on their porches all waved to her, and nobody looked at her like she didn't belong. She did belong here.

She felt at home. She had her whole life in front of her, and plenty of time in the future to think about love and romance. That's what she told herself, anyway, until she got to work and in walked Marco Del Rio.

CHAPTER EIGHT

Kate faced the bright blue bay and was taking an order when she saw him. He carried a guitar case in one hand and an amplifier in the other. The sun shone on his black hair like a liquid, shining light. His eyes stopped her again, engaged her, like he was speaking without speaking.

"Katie," he said in a gravelly voice. "What a pleasure." She gripped the pen and her order ticket. Heat flushed over her cheeks, and her stomach jumped like popcorn.

"Hello."

He stared briefly, as if he knew something she didn't, then walked past her into the corner of the restaurant and set his equipment down.

Kate tried to focus on the guests in front of her.

"So, that will be a burger well-done, fried shrimp, and a basket of fries?"

"Medium-well on the burger," the guy said. "And grilled shrimp. Are you new or something?"

"Sorry." Kate scribbled the changes in her notebook. "Yes, this is my second day. I'm usually really good at—never mind."

She didn't typically feel flustered on the job. What was Marco doing here?

She put the ticket book in her apron pocket and approached him. "Can I get you something to drink?"

"I'll have a bourbon on the rocks. That's my usual."

"Are you going to have dinner?" Kate asked.

"Maybe later, after my first set."

His first set.

"You play here?"

She fumbled with the server book in her apron. His face. There was something so familiar about him.

"Thursday nights. This is my first one. It is a smaller place than I usually play, but I know the owner."

"It's my first night, too. Well, I trained last night, but today I'm on my own with tables."

Kate was trying to figure out who he reminded her of. She studied his eyes. There was something enchanting in them.

"Well, then. We will throw our first party together." He smiled the dimple smile.

The mirror pep-talk she had with herself earlier returned.

You're not looking for a guy, Kate. You don't have enough money or time for love and romance.

"I better get back to work."

The sound of her shoes echoed against the wooden deck as she retrieved some menus from the cart and handed them to new customers.

When she walked into the kitchen, Linda grabbed her shirt sleeve.

"Kate, who's *that?* Do you know him?"

"That's Marco Del Rio." Kate handed her ticket to the cook. "I kind of know him," she said. "I met him last night, with Noah."

"He's a fox. I'm about to go out there and lay him down on top of table eight."

"Linda!" Kate laughed.

Chip, the skinny cook said, "Keep your man-devouring stories to yourself, please. Trying to work here."

"He does have nice dimples," Kate said.

"Nice dimples," Linda said, "I'm more interested in his package. How old do you think he is?" She peeked her head around the doorway and stared outside.

Package? "I don't know." Kate shook her head and laughed. "You should ask him."

Kate carried refills in paper cups out to her table and greeted a new one. Marco sat on a stool tuning his guitar. He seemed so calm and comfortable today, while her insides were on fire.

Noah pulled up on his motorcycle, took off his helmet, and hung his hands over the rail.

"How's it going?" Noah smiled at Marco. "Marco Del Rio, playing at The Wave in Seaview. How'd they get you over here?"

Marco smiled. "I go wherever they pay me." He was talking through the microphone now. "Check, check."

"Just got off work," Noah said to Kate. "Going to go stare at the water for a little while."

She snapped back into waitress mode. "You want something to drink?"

"I don't get paid until tomorrow."

"I'll get you a beer," Kate said. "I owe you one from last night."

Noah hopped over the railing effortlessly, with only one arm to steady him. Kate went to the bar to retrieve him a Pabst.

Linda came out, and Kate watched her fascination with Marco. He started playing a song, but she had to tune it out to concentrate on her customers' orders.

She finally got into a groove, got used to being self-conscious and uncomfortable. She felt like Marco's eyes followed her every step she took. It was flattering and also bewildering.

She waited on more and more tables, relieved to be making some money. Noah finished his beer and waved to Kate before he crossed the street toward the water and sailboats.

"That Noah is cute." Linda walked by with a tray of drinks in her hand. "I think he likes you."

Kate smiled. "He *is* cute."

She emptied ashtrays, took orders, and walked back and forth from the kitchen, to the bar, to the outside deck.

Before she knew it, she felt like she was throwing a good party, she and Marco together. And Linda.

When he took a break, Marco approached. She tensed.

"Smoke with me?" There was something underneath his question.

She smiled, thinking maybe she should resist.

"I don't like to smoke in front of my customers."

"We can go out back," he said.

Why was she feeling this way?

"Okay," Kate said, "let me check."

Linda said she would watch the tables, so Kate followed Marco out the back door into the parking lot.

The sun and clouds were warm colors now, and a small streak of the bay glowed silvery-blue from where they stood under a palm tree. She thought of postcards.

"So," Marco said. He handed her a cigarette. "Where are you from?"

"Ohio." As she placed it between her lips, he clinked open his Zippo lighter and moved in close to her. The burning in her stomach intensified, and he paused there. A sweet, musty scent lingered.

"Never been there," Marco said, coolly lighting his own smoke. There was something so nonchalant about how he moved. He stepped back on one heel and she studied the way his tennis shoes were tied in perfect white loops.

"You're not missing much," Kate managed. "Farmland, factories." She exhaled all the way out, almost hissing while her mind darted. "But there are some really good people in Ohio. It was a great place to grow up. How about you? Noah says you're from Texas. What brought you here?"

"Born and raised, Texan," he said. "I caught some flak for being the bronze boy with the guitar. My mother's family wanted me to be a doctor or a lawyer." He exhaled. "It is just, well, I love music." Marco's accent gave his words an underlying musical quality. His tongue bounced off the top of his mouth when he made an 'L' sound, and she stared at his lips. "It is the only thing I could ever see myself doing."

Kate thought about what it would be like to kiss him.

"But, I am talking a lot. How about you, Katie?" He touched her waist, then put his hand into his pocket. "What is your last name?"

She felt shy and bold at the same time. Something about him put her at ease and made her feel like her soul might jump out of her skin. "Wyse. Kathryn Wyse," she said. She wanted him to touch her again. "But only my mom calls me Kathryn, when I'm in trouble."

"I bet that is not very often," he said.

"What about you? Is Marco your real name?"

He laughed again. Tilted his head and said, "Marco Alejandro Riviera Del Rio." The way he said it sounded like poetry. "My mom calls me Alex. Everybody around here calls me Marco."

"You speak Spanish and English?" It was a silly question, but her nerves raged. She'd taken Latin in high school and could read it, but was nowhere near fluent.

He smirked, like he was interested in what she was thinking. "We spoke Spanish at home and English at school."

He was easy to talk to. "You look familiar," she said. "But I don't know where I would know you from."

He smiled the knowing smile. "I was thinking something similar," he said.

Linda swung open the back door.

"Newbie," she said, "dinner rush time. Table seven wants their check and table four just sat down." She disappeared as fast as she had come out.

Kate placed her cigarette into the nearby bucket and smiled at Marco.

"Back to work," she said. "Nice talking with you."

"Me también," he said.

More customers had congregated outside. She shook her brain back into work mode, gave table seven their check and swung around to greet the new folks. Around table four, several girls had congregated. She recognized Steph and Peggy.

"Hey," Kate said. "How's it going?"

"Kate, hi," Steph said. "These are our friends from school."

"Hi. What can I get you to drink?"

All of them wore lipstick. She must look so homely in comparison. One of them ordered a soda and the others ordered whiskey sours.

Marco walked behind her, and she felt cool and warm, then embarrassed by her outfit.

"Marco," Peggy said. "Want to come home with me tonight?"

The girls all laughed. Marco smiled and took his spot back up on the stage.

"We are having a party here at The Wave," he said.

"Do you girls want to order anything to eat?" Kate asked.

"No thanks," Peggy said. "We're on a liquid diet."

The rest of the girls giggled.

Peggy yelled, "Play 'Surfin' USA!'" She adjusted her shirt and asked Kate, "Can I borrow a piece of paper and a pen?"

Marco tuned up his guitar.

Kate ripped a page out of her notepad.

A few guys congregated at an opposing table, and Kate

approached them next. She recognized a couple of them from The Parrot. From Marco's band.

"My name's Kate. Welcome to The Wave."

"Katie," one of them said. "I'm Timbale." She repeated it in her head so she might remember, *Tim-ball-ay*. "I play drums with Marco." He was copper-complexioned, short and broad with a round face and squinty eyes.

"Nice to meet you, Timbale. What are you having?" They ordered drinks and food, and while Kate wrote down their orders, she couldn't help but juggle Noah's warning around in her mind, against the idea that she hoped she'd get to be alone with Marco again.

She liked the feeling of his eyes on her.

"By request, The Beach Boys," he said. "I am going to need some back up, so please sing along." The whole place erupted into song. The guys in Marco's band all sang different parts, Timbale drummed on the table, and the girls got up and danced the shimmy, the swim, and the Watusi.

Even Kate and Linda bobbed their heads while they delivered drinks and brought food to their dancing customers. It did feel like throwing a party.

Marco tuned up again, started some percussion on the front of his guitar with his thumbs, and somehow captured a song that sounded like he had a full band on stage with him. There weren't any lyrics in this one, but Steph turned toward the moon and howled a few times.

The sky turned dark blue, purple, then gray, and Noah came back and stood next to the table of girls. Kate served them more drinks, and they got louder and gigglier at Noah's presence. He turned down Kate's offer for another beer and took his place back on the other side of the railing with his elbows propped up and listened to the music. Marco's voice cascaded over the whole town.

Eventually, it was closing time. Kate passed around checks,

collected payments, made change, and then went into the bar area to count her tips. A few of the customers lingered, chatting and laughing. The group of girls and the group of guys, mixing and flirting, straggled in.

Marco came through with the entourage of his band, and two of Steph's friends. When he walked by Kate, he lifted his eyebrows at her as if to say *hello*. Then he headed out the back door.

Steph stopped.

"Saturday, at The Buoy, right? I'm going to read some of my poetry. I'd love it if you could be there."

"Of course," Kate said. "I have to work, but maybe after. What time do you read?"

"It starts at seven-thirty, but I might not go on until ten," she said. "I try to sign up for the later slot. After people have had some drinks."

"I should be able to make it."

When Marco came back in, Linda, who had been sitting quietly on the other side of the bar counting her tips, looked at him over her glasses. "Great show, Marco." She stood up and hurried over to him. "I'm Linda, by the way. Manager here."

"Gracias," he said, adjusting his tee shirt. "Nice to meet you." A drop of sweat fell down his cheek.

Kate caught herself wanting to reach out and dry it, but she stayed still on the barstool and instead began stacking quarters into a pile.

Peggy burst in from the deck, laughing. She walked up to Marco, slipped the piece of paper under the collar of his tee shirt and said, "Call me later." She kissed him on the cheek and left a ring of pink lipstick.

Kate's body pumped with jealousy. Marco pulled the note from his shirt and glanced at it, wiping his cheek at the same time.

"Peggy, come on!" Steph grabbed her hand and dragged her out. The front door closed behind them.

What was happening to Kate? Why did she care?

Marco rolled his eyes, gritted his teeth so his dimples showed, and crumpled up the piece of paper with an apologetic smile.

"What are *you* doing later, Miss Katie?"

Linda raised her eyebrows but kept her head pointed at the piles of money she was sorting.

Kate blushed. "I'm probably going to go home. I need to feed my cat."

Reaching for her drink, she knocked over the stack of quarters. They crashed and clanged and rolled across the wood in all directions. Some fell to the floor. Everybody stopped talking and stared.

Oh my gosh.

"Bravo!" someone yelled. Her faced heated.

Linda smirked. "You all right, Midwest?"

"Fine," Kate rubbed her palms on her apron.

In what seemed like a grand gesture, Marco bent down and picked up the quarters one by one. As he placed them gently back on the stack, he put his elbow on the bar next to her. He was standing very close.

She tugged at her blouse. Noah's voice again. *I'd stay away from him if I were you, Kate.*

She gathered up the stray quarters on the bar and added them back to the stack, trying to assess his danger. Marco picked up a quarter, added it to the stack, and brushed her knuckles with his.

She took another sip of the drink, a bigger one this time.

"When can I see you again?" he whispered.

Everybody still stared.

"I have to work the next few nights." She didn't know if she wanted to resist him, because she wanted him to touch her again. She was too nervous to look him in the eyes this close, in front of everyone. She wanted to kiss him.

"Me también," he said, breaking away. "Maybe I will see you around."

She wanted him to turn and look at her over his shoulder, but he didn't. He tossed the crumpled phone number into the trash can, then disappeared through the green door into the parking lot, with Timbale and the boys close behind. A car engine revved up, and slowly crunched away through the gravel and sand.

"Whoa," Linda said. "He likes you." She lit a cigarette and gathered up her money into one pile.

"You think so?"

"Honey, did you see that body language? I thought he was going to climb up there and straddle you in front of all of us."

Kate laughed. "You're so forward."

"I'm from Jersey. We tell it like it is. Why didn't you get his number?"

"I guess I'm a little old fashioned."

"That must be the Midwest coming out. Don't worry, the beach will shake that right out of you." Linda tapped her cigarette at the side of the ashtray. "You know, though. That guy is the foxiest guy I've seen around here in a long time." She smiled a motherly smile. "He would make me nervous, too."

The front door opened, and a man walked through. Kate expected Linda would tell him they were closed, but instead she got up and gave him a hug.

"Kate, this is my husband, Bobby." He had a long beard. She said hello.

"Kate's the newbie I was telling you about. She's doing great. I'll count down the register if you want to go and finish up wiping down the deck. Just bring the cart in and set it next to the kitchen."

Kate put her organized money into her apron and went outside.

In the silence now, it seemed like the whole town had fallen asleep. As she wiped down the tables and stacked the condiments onto the cart, she felt a certain yearning she hadn't felt in a long time. She didn't want to feel it, though. She was afraid to feel it again. The Big Dipper hovered over the Little Dipper as if it were protecting its young, and she remembered the last time she felt like this.

SHE AND CHAD sat on the porch, looking up at the same two constellations from his parents' house in the country. She rested her head in the cozy handle of his arm. Stars sparkled in between the lily pads of the pond. They talked about the future. About getting married, having kids. He would work for and eventually take over his dad's lumber business, and she would stay home.

The night after Chad gave Kate a ring, his dad, a World War II veteran, told him he was expected to go into the Marines. He had two months to get ready, and soon he was off to basic training.

Kate begged him not to go. She cried and pleaded and promised that she could keep her job at the diner, and help take care of them both while he figured things out, but his family was too influential. He followed his father's wishes, and soon, he was gone.

After he left, Kate's whole world dulled. She felt aimless. She didn't watch the news, because it just made her sad, but she knew from newspaper headlines that there was some kind of conflict in Vietnam.

They wrote letters at first, Chad always saying that he couldn't wait to come home and see her, but the letters got fewer and farther between.

In the last letter she received, he wrote about how he'd met a girl at his last station, and how she was giving him hope. How big the world was, and how he didn't miss Kate as much. He might not come home right away, even if he were discharged.

It said she should try to forget about him.

She took the ring off, put it back in the box, and stashed it in the top drawer of her dresser under a handkerchief. Visions of herself in the future shattered, and months later, when she put her heart back together, she made sure she closed it off completely.

Her heart couldn't be trusted, she'd told herself. She'd learn how to use her mind to make her own way in the world.

"MIDWEST!" Linda's voice broke the memory. "I closed down the register, are you done out here?"

Kate placed the last of the salt and pepper shakers on the cart and rushed it into the dining room. "Sorry, I kind of got lost in the sky out there."

"The beach will do that to you," Linda said. "Let me show you how to lock these doors and we'll get out of here."

CHAPTER NINE

$\mathcal{M}$arco's voice had found its way into Kate's mind and lodged there. She wasn't completely aware of it, but she was happier than she'd been in a long time. It was going so well at The Wave, she was going to be able to make her rent payments. She could take care of herself.

She sang "Surfin' USA" to the Queen Kitty, and the cat meowed. "I know. You're just hungry."

Noah showed up right on time and they rode the motorcycle to J.C. Penney. Kate bought her first pair of jeans, two shorter skirts, and a pair of black sandals which Noah talked her into.

"You can't wear those Pollyanna shoes at the beach," he said. "It's not natural."

She didn't know if she would wear the short skirts, but she was feeling adventurous. Like she was reinventing herself. She tried on a red sundress and Noah nodded furiously.

"You can get rid of that silly business blouse."

On their way out, they walked by the makeup counter.

"Let's get you a makeover," Noah said.

"I don't think I want to. I've have already spent more money than I should have."

"But look. You can do it for free. They'll put some makeup on you, and then you decide if you want to buy it or not."

He flagged down a woman behind the counter. She wore a large beehive of hair—piled on top of her head in a cone shape, and hair-sprayed together—blue eyeshadow, and hot pink lipstick.

"Noah, really, it's not necessary."

"What time do you have to be at work?"

"Four."

"We've got two hours. Let's do it."

Kate reluctantly sat in the chair. The woman introduced herself as Brenda from Nebraska while she shook a bag of makeup brushes.

"What brought you to Florida?" Kate asked. It seemed like the appropriate get-to-know you question here.

"Crazy husband," Brenda said. "I ran away from him in '61 and I didn't look back." She pulled a round brush from the bag. "Are you two married?" Brenda eyed Noah, who was looking at the different varieties of blush.

"No, ma'am." Kate said.

"Good for you." She leaned in closer and whispered, "Men are overrated." She cleared her throat and leaned back. "Who braided your hair?"

"I did." Kate's mom had taught her how to braid when she was small.

"It looks great," Brenda said. "Hold still."

Brenda did everything from apply eyeliner, to paint frosted lipstick on Kate's lips with a brush. After about a half an hour, she put a round mirror in front of Kate's face and said, "What do you think?"

Kate didn't recognize herself. Her gray eyes popped with blue, and her complexion glowed.

"Yeah!" Noah came from behind, so she could see his reflection in the mirror, too. "You look like Kate, enhanced!"

"I do?"

"You do. Brenda," Noah said, "you are a true artist."

"Oh, it was easy." Brenda put the mirror on the glass counter. "She was already glowing."

"Thank you for your time," Kate said. If I decide to buy something, I'll come back."

"You're very welcome," Brenda said. "You know where to find me." She leaned in close again. "And I'm serious about the men thing. Stay single as long as you can."

Kate smiled. "I'll keep that in mind."

As Noah fired up the bike he said, "Do you want to stop at the record store on the way home?"

Kate put her feet on the pegs.

The sky was full of fluffy white clouds. The sun beat down on her shoulders and arms. It was so hot, the air hugged them like an electric blanket. Her mom would hate this heat. Kate smiled at the drivers as they stopped next to cars at stoplights, and Noah nodded at other motorcycle riders. She loved being on the back of the bike. She was so glad she'd met Noah.

Incense swirled around the record store and pleasantly into Kate's nose. Posters and autographed records lined the walls all the way to the ceiling. A guy with long hair and sunglasses sat behind the counter with his feet up. Smoke wafted from his cigarette. He greeted them when they walked in. "What's happening, friends? Make yourselves at home."

Kate browsed the rows of albums, and when she stumbled onto the locals' section, she found a green LP, *Marco Del Rio and The Dolphins*. She pulled it out.

"Noah, look!"

"They're kind of legends around here," he said, matter-of-factly. "Marco spent some time in New York City with some fancy recording people. I guess it didn't work out because he ended up here."

"What else do you know about him?" Kate asked.

"Not much. He's kind of a recluse."

"Does he have a special girl?" As soon as it came out of her mouth, she regretted saying it.

"You could say that. And one in every bar."

But she was curious. "I mean a *steady* girl."

Noah scratched his head with a concerned look in his eyes.

"The last one I saw around for any length of time, who was old enough to be a steady girl, was Gina."

"Gina," Kate said, under her breath.

Noah lifted an album out of the file, studied it, and then put it back down. "Look, Kate. I like Marco. I really do. I think he's the most talented guitar player I've ever seen. But he's got a past, and his career is his priority. A girl like you, he'll break your heart. I don't want to see that happen to you."

"A girl like me?" She tried not to sound defensive, but she was offended.

Noah put his hands in his pockets.

"I mean," he stuttered. "I'm sorry. A girl like you who is sweet, who is . . . lovely." This made her feel a little better, but did he think she was too innocent? Too prude?

"He's got a reputation on the beach, is all. I've seen the broken-hearted girls, the ones who show up at his shows thinking they're the only ones, and it turns out there are three or four of them. It's not pretty." He stuttered again. "I don't— know what he tells them, or how he even handles it. I mean, I get it. If Marco liked guys, then he sure would get tired of seeing me, but . . . ."

Kate reminded herself she was a grown-up. That she was taking care of herself. That she could make her own decisions and decide for herself about people.

Still, questions tugged at her.

"What do you like about him? It seems like you guys are friends."

"Yeah," he took his hands out of his pockets and started

thumbing through the records again. "Yeah, we are. I think the guy has a good heart." He pulled out another album, studied it, and put it back. "He's just really popular around here, you know? That comes with attention. Girls falling in love with him." Noah pulled out the *Surfin' Safari* record. The Beach Boys were posed on a truck holding a surfboard. "He likes the B-sides, too. Like, last night he played 'Surfin' USA' because the girls asked for it, but then he played 'Moon Dawg.'"

Noah pointed to the list of songs. There it was. Song number 11: "Moon Dawg."

"Get this one," Noah said. "The best songs are always on the B-side."

Kate paid for the albums and the guy behind the counter handed them a flyer.

"This Sunday," he said, "at the Gulf College on the green. They're having a Love-In." The flyer was drawn with a green and yellow burst of color. "All lovers welcome. Bring your good vibes."

"A Love-In?" Kate asked.

"Yeah, man," the guy said. "We're gonna see how many people we can get to be intentionally loving and kind."

"Okay, thanks," Kate said.

"You guys seem like kind and loving folks," he added. "Bring your friends."

She followed Noah out of the door and into the heat. Since the bike didn't have a radio, Kate found herself singing again. The Beach Boys, "Surfin' USA."

"You know," Noah turned his head, so she could hear him over the wind. "You've been singing that all day."

"I have?" She climbed onto the back of the bike, clutched his waist, and he revved the throttle. "Do you guys surf?" she asked.

He pulled out of the parking lot.

"We have boards, most of us. But the waves on the Gulf aren't always big enough to catch, unless there's a storm coming or going. We ride over to Daytona when we really want to surf." He sped off, and she let the wind cool her face.

Her night at work began smoothly enough. At the last minute, she had decided to wear one of the shorter skirts. She felt a little self-conscious about her legs, but after she got busy, she didn't think about it again. A duo came in and set up in the corner, Jimmy and Jake. They both had long hair and didn't wear shoes. She served them whiskey while they played bluegrass and chain-smoked. She liked them. Her dad would love them playing Johnny Cash and Merle Haggard.

During their break, Jake said, "Kate, are you married?"

"Not yet."

"I can't believe there's not a long line of men right here trying to buy your supper. You wanna go out with me sometime?"

"Aren't you old enough to be my father?"

"Probably so." He puffed on a cigarette and they started playing again.

As the sun went down and Linda and Kate turned tables and made tips, Kate heard her name from the other side of the railing.

Marco hung his elbows over the wooden rail and propped his foot on the bottom rung. Her stomach flipped.

She said, "Hi. Give me a minute." She went into the kitchen to add up a check and pick up another table's food.

As she carefully set the plates in front of her customers, Marco's eyes followed her.

"Is there anything else I can get you all right now?" she asked.

When they said no, she said, "Enjoy your meal." She put her tickets in her pocket and mustered the courage to approach him.

She flirted. "You can come to the other side of the rail, you know. That's what most customers do."

"I cannot stay. I have a show tonight." He looked down and looked back up. Almost shyly. Was Marco Del Rio shy?

Kate was starting to feel more in her element here at The Wave.

"You look muy bella." He pronounced the last word *bay-a* with a long first *a*. She could listen to him talk all night, studying his accent and watching his lips. She remembered the makeup.

"Oh. I went shopping with Noah."

"Hiiii, Marco," Linda called from the other side of the deck.

"Hola Linda." He turned his eyes back to Kate.

"I wanted to bring you these." He held out two delicate, white orchids.

Kate was a little stunned. As she took the flowers from his hand, their fingertips touched.

He licked his top lip and she thought of kissing him. He ran his palms over his hair and said quickly, "I just wanted to say hi. I have to go to work." He studied her face. Then glanced at her legs and glanced back. Maybe the makeover was a good idea; she felt pretty.

"Miss," one of her customers called, "excuse me."

"I have to go, too. Thank you for the flowers."

"You are welcome." He held one open hand up in a goodbye gesture before he released his body from the rail and strolled down the sidewalk.

"Oh my *God*." Linda scurried up to her. "Did he just bring you flowers?"

A customer put one finger in the air and said, "Excuse me."

"Yes," Kate said, still stunned. "What can I do for you, sir?"

"We need some refills," he said impatiently.

"Sure," she said, and carried the cups to the kitchen. Linda followed behind.

"Holy hell, Kate. What are you going to do with those?"

"I don't know. I'm trying to focus on work."

"Well, who could focus on work when foxy Marco brings you flowers? Here, give them to me." Linda twisted both stems and settled the blooms into Kate's braid. "There."

Though Kate was a little disappointed that she couldn't see them herself, she was glad she was wearing them. She played it off to Linda, but she was thinking the same thing,

Did Marco Del Rio just bring you flowers?

At the end of the night, Kate counted her money and was thankful.

Chip the cook came out from the kitchen and wiped a towel across his forehead. He had long, wiry fingers and his fingernails were black.

"It's Friday," he said. "Where are we going tonight?"

"I have to go home and feed my cat."

Linda was counting down the register. "Me too," she said. "I mean my husband." She and Kate laughed.

Kate sipped a vodka gimlet.

Chip said, "Aren't The Dolphins playing at The Parrot tonight?" Her eyes lit up. Despite herself, she couldn't stop thinking about Marco. "Kate, you wanna go out to the beach with me?"

Hmmm. Kate wasn't sure about this. She wanted to go to the beach, but she wasn't sure she wanted to go with Chip.

"I really need to feed my cat. She's probably starving."

"So, we'll go feed her and then we'll go. I'll buy your first drink."

Though Kate didn't know if she trusted Chip, she convinced herself that it was a short ride, and she would be okay. They locked up the restaurant and she got into his car. She pointed the way to her house, ran in and fed Queen Kitty, and then they headed to the beach.

On the bridge to the island, a full moon dripped across the

water, and Kate thought about how the moon gives the water its movement.

When she and Chip walked through the door, Marco's eyes hit her. Kate smiled, despite feeling shy. She reached up and touched the flowers in her hair, to make sure they were still there.

Chip said, "Vodka gimlet?" He went to the bar.

The band was playing a song she didn't recognize.

It was way more crowded than it had been the other night. Shawn tossed bottles up in the air, caught them, and poured drinks with a smile.

Chip handed her a drink as the song stopped. Kate took a long sip through the straw, trying to save the lipstick still lingering from the afternoon.

Marco raised his eyebrows at her.

He then moved his eyes to Chip as if saying, *Who's that?*

She shook her head ever-so-slightly to respond, *He's not with me.*

Were they really having a silent conversation in the middle of all these people?

The old sailor sat on the same barstool as Wednesday and raised his glass when he saw Kate. She wondered what Noah was doing.

Marco spoke into the microphone. "Miss Katie Wyse is here in the bar, everybody." She smiled. "We've got a special song coming out to you. One-two-three-four."

The Beatles song, "I Wanna Hold Your Hand."

Marco kept his eyes on her. Some pretty girls got up and started dancing close to the stage. He nodded to them during the musical breaks, but as he sang the lyrics, he didn't move his gaze from her.

She couldn't seem to shake this feeling, although she wanted to. Noah's warning. A wave of heat came over her. Was it the drink? His lips, his eyes, or his dimples?

She had a vision of his bare chest hovered over hers.

She looked up at him, his eyes still on her, and blushed again. *Could he feel that?* What was she doing thinking of him like this? There were all of these other pretty girls around.

She should just enjoy her drink and the music.

His hands moved around his guitar effortlessly. The other boys smiled and played, but Marco seemed to be wrapped in some kind of magical aura. Chip stood next to her. It all felt like too much for her body; she couldn't control her thoughts or feelings.

Maybe some fresh air would help.

"Excuse me," she said and walked out the back door.

A car crept by. A woman in the back seat of the Chevrolet held up a peace sign and Kate returned it.

She wished she had a cigarette. Above her, the stars twinkled in a clear black sky. It wasn't much cooler out here, but a light breeze brushed her cheeks.

Just then, Chip was next to her. He put his beer down on the nearby table. Kate was about to ask him for a cigarette when he cornered her, grabbed her arms, and pinned her against the wall.

What is happening?

The hair on the back of her neck stood up.

CHAPTER TEN

"I've been watching you."

She felt his grimy, long fingers on her skin, and wanted them off of her.

Her drink fell to the sand in a thud.

"Chip, I don't like you like that," she said.

"Oh, come on. I see the way you look at me. I can tell you want it." He smelled like spoiled milk.

He moved his grip from her arms to her waist, and his wiry fingers curled under her waistband. The wooden siding of the bar scratched her bare arms.

"Stop," she said. "Let go of me. This is not what I came out with you for."

She pushed against his chest, and struggled to pry his hands from her, but his arms were stronger.

She glanced down the sandy dirt road. There was nobody.

Nothing.

Gravel.

Sky.

"This will be easier if you stop fighting me."

He reached down under her skirt, and put his hand on her inner thigh. "I like your new outfit."

He pressed his face against hers. *No,* she thought. *No.*

She stomped on his foot as hard as she could, and his arms loosened their grip. She swung her arm, trying to catch him in the chin, but she missed and only hit his chest.

He grabbed her by the leg and reached again under her skirt.

"*Come on,* give me some of that." His fingers on her inner thighs and, *no, no, no.*

She was up against the wall; her head knocked against the brick.

"Get off me!"

The door swung open.

Then Chip was ripped from her body and on the ground.

Marco had him pinned by two fistfuls of his shirt.

Kate tried to pull her skirt down to cover her knees.

They tussled in the sand.

Both men rose with their hands up. Chip tried to tackle Marco, but he caught him and drilled his face into the ground. Marco stood up. Hands out, knees bent.

Kate was frozen.

Chip wiped dripping blood from his chin.

"Why don't you go back to Mexico, Del Rio . . . nobody wants you here messing with our girls."

Marco stood firm and steady. "I am from *Texas.* And *you* are messing with *my* girl."

Noah busted through the door, followed by Shawn, the band, and a crowd of people.

"What's going on?" Noah yelled. Marco kept his eyes on Chip.

Tears built. She didn't want them to break through. Not here in front of all these people.

"He tried to . . . " she couldn't put words together. "He, he grabbed me . . . " and then the tears broke.

Noah punched Chip in the eye, and knocked him off his feet.

Shawn grabbed Kate's arm.

She shook it away and lurched backwards.

"I'm sorry," Shawn said. "I didn't mean to." She took another step away from him and hugged her elbows to her chest.

"It's okay," Kate said. "I'm okay."

"Do you want me to call the sheriff?" Shawn put a pen behind his ear.

"No," she said. Noah and Marco shook hands, breathing with intensity.

"Are you sure?" Marco said.

Kate nodded and wiped at her streaming eyes.

"Get him out of here," Noah said.

Shawn scowled. "Get in your car and get the hell out of here, Chip. And don't come back, or I'm calling the law. Consider yourself barred for life."

Chip rolled around on the ground. Kate wanted to kick him in the stomach, but she just stood there.

Marco and Noah positioned themselves like a shield in front of Kate, as Chip got up with one hand on his eye, walked to his car, and started it up.

He rolled down his window and said, "You shouldn't have come on to me, you *slut.*"

Noah and Marco both took off after the car, but the engine revved and Chip sped away.

Marco kicked up the gravel and sand, which landed on the back window like the sound of hard rain.

"Bastard!" Noah yelled.

"If I see him again, I swear I will kill him," Marco said.

Kate tried to breathe.

"All right," Shawn said. "Show's over. Everyone back inside." The onlookers slowly dispersed. "The band has one more set, right, Marco?"

"Yeah," he said. "We have got one more. Give me five, though."

"Sure."

The crowd piled back into the door, except for a few nosy people who stayed outside in a cluster, pretending not to listen.

"Are you sure you are okay?" Marco asked. He didn't reach out to touch her.

Noah lit a cigarette and exhaled loudly. "What a creep," he said.

"I knew I shouldn't have worn this short skirt," Kate said.

"No," Marco said, "a creep is a creep, no matter what you wear."

Kate pulled at the bottom of the skirt, anyway. She felt naked and vulnerable and confused. Had she done something that brought that on? Had she looked at him in some way that he mistook? She ran the situation over in her mind, and the hair stood up on her neck again. She was sweating.

She took a deep breath and held it in to refocus. Let it out slowly. She was okay. That could have been way worse.

She leaned against the wall, still. Her hands trembled.

"How did you know?" she finally asked Marco.

He took a long exhale.

"I watch things," he said. He lit a cigarette and handed it to her. She tried to steady herself. To calm. "I could see his eyes." He breathed out a cloud of white. "I never liked that guy."

"You know him?" The cigarette shook in her hand.

"I see him around. Usually chasing after some young girls."

"Disgusting," Noah said. "I'm sorry I wasn't here earlier. Kate, you okay?"

"I think I'm okay." She felt like she'd been on a roller coaster. Like she just needed solid ground.

"I don't know how to say thank you."

"It is not necessary," Marco said.

"Do you want me to take you home?" Noah asked.

Her stomach turned. "He knows where I live."

"Why don't you come in, Katie?" Marco said. "We will play the last set and then you guys can come to my house. We can light a bonfire on the beach if you want." He flicked an ash from the top of his cigarette and brought it to his mouth. "Make a safe space between today and tomorrow."

She didn't know what to do, what to think, or what to feel.

"With whom?" she asked.

"I won't leave your side," Noah said.

Kate mulled this over. She trusted Noah and Marco. "Okay. That sounds okay."

The band took the stage again. Shawn made Kate a drink.

"This one's on the house."

Noah and Marco escorted her to the corner of the bar facing the stage, front and center. As the guys started pinging on their instruments, Marco spoke into the microphone. "If anybody else wants to force themselves on a girl tonight, we are offering free black eyes and a complimentary ride with the sheriff."

"That's right," Noah said. "Cheers." He held his beer bottle up. Kate scanned the room.

"It might not be a bad idea to call the sheriff," Noah said.

"I don't want to have to think about it again. Does he live in town?"

"I'll find out tomorrow and go pay him a visit."

"You don't have to do that, Noah," Kate said.

"I know I don't have to. The thing is, if he'll do that to you, then he'll do that to anybody. Men like that need to be taught."

Marco flashed his eyes at her, crunched his eyebrows in concern, and then closed them as he sang.

CHAPTER ELEVEN

*A*fter their show, it took a while for the band to load up their gear. Noah and Kate climbed on the bike and followed the guys in their cars. Wispy clouds passed over the moon.

A few miles down the road, they took a slight turn off the main road where small houses sat unassuming on the beach. At the end of the sandy road was a white trailer, with an aqua VW bus in the driveway. Noah pulled in and cut off the engine quickly. It was so quiet. Stars spattered the sky.

Steph, Peggy, Donny, and Jack had shown up for last call at The Parrot, and Marco had invited them over as well. They all stood in the driveway smoking and talking, waiting for an invitation inside. After Marco and Timbale unloaded their gear, Marco came to find Kate. He reached out his hand to her and sang another verse of the Beatles.

Kate put her hand in his and followed him to the front door. "Are you okay, Bella?" he asked.

"I think so," she said.

When he opened it, a sweet-faced, black and white dog leapt out and jumped at his chest.

"Hey, Henry. Easy." Henry jumped up again, and then jumped up at Kate. She reached out her free hand. Henry nuzzled her palm and gave her a quick lick to the fingertips.

"He listens half the time. He hears me all of the time, but only listens half. ¿Es verdad, chico?" Henry let out a happy growl.

"What kind of dog is he?" Kate asked.

"He is part husky, and part German Shepherd. Thank goodness for the shepherd, because otherwise he would always run away." Henry wagged his tail and ran out into the driveway to greet the other visitors.

"Come in," Marco said to Kate. "We will meet you out back," he called to the others. The trailer was smaller than it looked from the outside, but it was tidy. Quaint. "It is not much, but it is mine." The trim was painted green and blue, the dishes were clean in the strainer, and three guitars hung in the living room above the couch. A blue and white surfboard was propped up in the corner.

"It's great," she said.

"I wish it were bigger, you know, more room for Henry and me, but, such is the life of a broke musician."

He led her through the kitchen to the living room.

"This is where all the magic happens," he said. "Songwriting, I mean."

"Noah and I picked up your album today," she said. "I can't wait to listen to it."

"Which one?"

"There's more than one?"

"Well, there is one with The Dolphins, and then there is one that I recorded solo."

Kate fidgeted with her hair and realized the orchids were still there. "We got the one with The Dolphins, but I'd love to hear your solo music. The B-sides."

He stared into her eyes before he smiled, as if he were questioning her sincerity, and his voice deepened. "The B-sides. I bet you would."

A defense came up between them. "What does that mean?"

"Nothing, I guess. Lo siento." He sighed. "I am sorry. It is weird having your art out there for people to listen. I mean, it is one thing to play live, because everybody is having an experience. And I can play cover songs, you know, other peoples' music. But it is another to think that someone is sitting around when they are by themselves and analyzing your most intimate secrets."

He slicked his hair back and licked his lips. Kate stared at them.

"Secrets, huh?" She poked him on the waist, where he had touched her the other day. She let her hand linger for just a moment before she put it back at her side.

"Well, I do not know. I mean, for a song to be good, it has to be honest, right? From the heart. But, it is harder than you may think for a guy to spill his guts and then record it for eternity."

"Hey guys!" Timbale hollered from the back door. "Fire's going, and we just lit a joint."

Marco led her through the back door where everybody else had congregated. It was like stepping through a mystical door.

Beyond the firelight and the group of people, all Kate could see was water and sky. Stars and moonlight. The ocean turned over itself in crushes of white on black-blue. The sound of the waves mixed with the wind and drowned out all other noise.

"This is beautiful," Kate said. Marco squeezed her hand. Henry ran from the edge of the water and back, like a rabbit on the flee, and sprinted by just long enough to lick Kate's hand and nuzzle Marco's leg, before he shot back out to the water.

"Someone is excited to get out of the house," Marco said.

Noah was watching them from the bonfire. He smiled and shook his head.

"Hey, you lovebirds, thanks for joining us," said Steph.

Kate blushed. Peggy rolled her eyes.

"You want to hit this?" Timbale's cheeks were puffed like a blowfish. He coughed and handed what looked like a cigarette to Marco.

Marco took the joint from Timbale as if there were an art to it, lifted it to his lips, and inhaled.

"You can pass this if you want," he said. Kate loved the sound of his voice, deep and musical, even though he wasn't singing.

"You might just have to show me how?"

He leaned his head in. With his eyes, he seemed to be asking for permission, if she trusted him. When she said *yes*, though she didn't say it out loud, he leaned in closer, parted her lips with his, and exhaled the smoke into her mouth.

His lips and tongue touching hers. He lingered there. His eyelashes against her skin. Then he pulled back. It tasted like earth, the way corn fields smell mixed with smoke.

"Hold on to it for a moment, then exhale," he whispered.

"It's puff-puff-*pass*," Steph said, and she bounced over to them to retrieve the joint from Marco's hands.

"So, Kate. I heard you almost got groped by Creepy Chip earlier. Come over here and tell me about it."

"Yeah, Library. What happened?" Jack asked.

There were a few chairs and two striped blankets lying around the fire. Steph and Peggy sat in chairs, and Kate led Marco to one of the unoccupied blankets. Noah and Jack stood on either side of a cooler, where Timbale kept pulling out cans of beer and handing them to people.

"I'll have one of those," Kate said. She sat down with her knees folded properly, toward Marco, who had settled with his legs out, his body balanced on his hands, as if he were in a lounge chair.

The fire crackled and spit sparks into the air. Timbale handed her a beer.

"Gracias," she said.

"De nada, Señorita."

Marco showed his dimples at Kate's attempted Spanish.

"I don't know, Steph. It was really weird. I mean, that's never happened to me before."

"Consider yourself lucky," Steph said. She sipped her beer. "I heard Marco and Noah both showed up in the nick of time?"

"Like superheroes," Kate said.

"That's us," Noah said. "Batman and Robin. Straight out of the comic book." Noah snorted as he laughed, and everybody started giggling.

The walls of Kate's mind were falling into relaxation. She put her hand on Marco's knee. His skin was smooth.

"I didn't think I was acting like I liked him."

Steph said, "Guys like that are just waiting in the background for some girl to intimidate. It's disgusting, really. I'm all for free love—"

Jack cut her off. "*Yeah*, you are."

"Hey—" Steph pointed at him, and then leaned in closer.

"Hey what?" He twisted his face into sarcastic innocence.

"Don't soil my reputation, please." She slapped his chest.

"I didn't say anything about your reputations." He annunciated the plural "s." Peggy giggled.

Steph went on, "Free love between two consenting adults. Not between one horny creep and a defenseless girl."

Kate recognized her. From the diner.

"Steph, did you used to have long hair? Down to your waist?"

"Yeah, why?" She sat straight up.

"I remember you. From the diner in Middle Falls. I waited on you last year. You were passing through with a guy."

"That's me!" Jack said.

"Oh my God, Kate, that was you? You look totally different!"

Kate sat up, too. "You said you were going to Florida. I read the Kerouac book you left. That night I had a dream that I lived here, and I woke up and decided that if you could do it, then maybe I could, too."

"That's so crazy, Kate! I can't believe I didn't recognize you!"

"But you said you were coming from New York."

"Yeah," Steph lit a cigarette and exhaled. "My mom had this crazy idea that I should marry this guy from my high school. I only went out with him a few times, but he was kind of a jerk. Anyway, my mom told me that if I didn't say yes when he asked me to marry him, that she would kick me out."

Peggy and Donny and the rest of the crew started talking amongst themselves. Kate was glued to Steph's story, and Jack nodded his head in over-exaggerated attention.

"I went out with his best friend from the football team. We parked one night by the falls and he—let's just say he didn't like the word, 'no.' I ended up with bruises. Got out of the car, but I had to hide in the woods until he gave up looking for me. The next day at school he told everybody that I did it with him. The girls, even my friends, stopped talking to me. People were whispering that I was *fast*." She laid down on her back and fixed her eyes to the clouds. "My mom told me that I was a disappointment. That I had to marry one of them to save the family reputation."

"Long storriiiies," Jack said.

Steph punched him playfully in the leg. "I'd met Jack at the community pool."

He held up his beer. "We bonded over Dickinson."

"I'd applied to Gulf College already. My dad only let me go because it was a Methodist school. So when I ran into Jack and he said he was traveling for the summer, I jumped at the chance."

Jack pointed his finger in the air. "We went to the Village, saw Niagara Falls, and I delivered Miss Stephanie safely here to the beach."

Kate couldn't get over the fact that she'd met them before.

Steph's eyes squinted and she laughed. "We might have also swung by to let the air out of what's-his-name's tires, and I might have written the word 'no' in lipstick all over his windshield."

"It was truly art," Jack said.

They all fell into a comfortable silence.

The water whispered gently, and something changed in her. A gentle nudge that maybe all of this was destined to be. A feeling, like a warm ball of energy moved from her belly button to her chest, then dispersed into the air. She suddenly felt drawn to the water.

She heard her voice saying the words, but they came from somewhere deeper inside than she understood.

"Does anybody want to go and put their toes in the water with me?"

Noah caught eyes with Marco, who spoke first.

"I will walk you down there," Marco said.

Kate briefly looked at Noah, who shrugged and shook his head like he was saying, *don't say I didn't warn you.* Though she wasn't aware of it, it was too late for her. Marco was the moon, and she was drawn to him like the tide.

Henry followed them down to the edge of the ocean, galloping and jumping all the way. Marco picked up a stick and tossed it here and there. Henry was eagerly fetching, splashing, sitting, and wagging his tail for the next chase.

Marco stayed quiet, as if just taking everything in.

Kate had pushed the earlier event out of her mind, concentrating on how many stars she could see. She saw one falling, and then two. The moment felt suddenly more sacred.

"Look," she said to Marco. "Falling stars."

She felt the pull of the ocean on her body and was getting ready to lead Marco into the water, when Noah approached.

"Kate. Can I talk to you for a minute?" Henry laid the stick at

Noah's feet. He picked it up and threw it into the water. Henry splashed away.

She gave Marco a look and he nodded. Noah gently clasped her arm and led her just far enough that Marco might not be able to hear them over the waves. Marco lit a cigarette and looked out toward the sky.

"What are you doing? I'm not sure this is smart."

Kate said, "I'm fine. We're standing on the beach." She didn't know how to explain her amazement.

He put his hand back into his pocket.

"Well, I mean, we're all stoned, and—what happened earlier."

"I'm fine. It's so beautiful out here."

"I know you're fine, Kate. I just don't want to see you get in over your head."

She wanted to reassure him. "You're the best friend I have here. I know Steph and Jack from home. This is where I'm meant to be."

He shook his head. "I'm going to be right up there by the fire. If he tries anything crazy, just yell for me."

Kate gave him a long, warm hug.

Noah put his head down and walked back up over the sand dune. Henry followed him with the stick in his mouth. Kate watched them go, and noticed the rest of the party couldn't see her from where she was standing.

She could only see the tip of the bonfire, the flame licking up toward the sky.

She walked back to Marco.

"Let me guess," he said. "He wanted to warn you."

"He's looking out for me."

He flicked an ash from his cigarette, and the orange of it sailed in an arch before it disappeared. "That is good. Noah is a good guy."

Kate slid her hand into Marco's fingers, against his palm. She took his cigarette, inhaled a drag, then laid it down in the sand, reminding herself to pick it up later. She exhaled, put her body against his, and finally put her mouth on his lips, the way she'd been wanting to all week.

He kissed her back, gently at first, and then passionately. Her whole body burned with yearning. He tasted like sweat and smoke. When the kiss wound down, he put his hands on her waist. "That wish came true much more quickly than I thought."

"Falling stars," she said.

But then his face flattened. "Whatever Noah said, I am—" Kate put one hand on his mouth and shushed him. She replaced her fingers with her lips, kissing him again, softly. She then crossed her arms and removed her shirt.

"Take me swimming?"

His eyes widened into surprise. He took his shirt off with one hand.

"Así lo desea."

She did wish. As they stepped into rolling waves, Kate wrapped her arms around his shoulders and her legs around his waist. The water was cooler than the air.

He carried her with one arm as if she were weightless. When they were chest deep, Kate noticed the water sparkling. Tiny glow-in-the dark specks of light followed their movements like fairy dust.

"What's that?"

His arms held her tightly, her chest against his

"Phosphorescent algae. It happens once a year." A wave crashed over their heads, unexpectedly, and knocked them off balance. They both staggered up, laughing, wiping the matted hair from their faces.

He quickly gathered her up and said, "I am sorry. I was captivated by you and not paying attention."

He moved wet strands of hair from her face. She put her hands in his hair and smoothed it back out of his eyes. He wrapped both of his arms underneath her now.

"It's like magic," she whispered, running her fingers through the tops of the waves. "I feel like I'm surrounded by stars." She leaned back into the water and wondered where the water ended and the sky began. A soft wave pulled her hair.

"You are magic, Bella," he whispered back. At the sound of those *'L's*, she sat up and kissed him again. He held her tighter, his body fitting perfectly with hers, the longing between them trying to quench itself.

He stopped one more time to say, "You are beautiful, Katie," before he waded farther out so they were completely encompassed by water and stars.

The waves rolled in and crashed beyond them on the sand. The moonlight glowed on their bare shoulders. It felt like they were swimming in the Milky Way itself, as they rocked and danced with the pull of the ocean.

CHAPTER TWELVE

November, 2014

"Wait, no. I can't." Curtis waved his hands at Skylar, who was surrounded by a pile of letters, reading their mother's words out loud.

Skylar smiled. "There are no details. Just swimming." Curtis had long since silenced his phone and Skylar had made another pot of coffee. She was glad she'd taken off work for a few days.

"But, Mom . . . drinking and smoking? And now, skinny-dipping with a Mexican dude?"

"Wow," Skylar said. "I know you didn't go to college, but I didn't think you were racist."

"I'm not racist."

"Can you hear yourself?" Skylar took a sip from her mug. "You're not more worried about this Chip character who almost raped mom?"

"Are you hearing *yourself*, Skye, this guy's got mom smoking pot."

Skylar laughed. "It was the Sixties. Everybody smoked in the Sixties."

"But Mom?" Curtis's face turned from his normal adult seriousness to a twelve-year-old kid's disappointment, as if he'd gotten clothes for Christmas instead of toys.

Skylar continued, "Back then they didn't have to worry about people putting weird stuff in it. Like hard drugs. And it wasn't so strong."

"Where'd you learn that, Skye?"

Skylar chuckled. "I read, Curtis."

"What else did she do that we don't know about?"

"I don't know, but if you let me keep reading, then we can find out."

CHAPTER THIRTEEN

August, 1964

Seagulls pecked around the campfire. It had burned to embers, and small tufts of smoke wafted out into the August wind. Kate was lying on a hammock. The morning sun warmed the blanket covering her.

Noah was laid out in a chair next to the fire, with a beer can in the sand next to him. Jack slept in a chair beside Noah, and their bare feet were touching. As she wiped the sleep out of her eyes, Kate heard a crumple sound under the blanket. She pulled out a note.

Katie Bella, it read. *I had to leave you this morning to go to an interview. Here is my phone number. I hope you call. 555-1148. I enjoyed our night swim, Marco.*

Kate's body shivered at the memory of their night.

Noah grunted and growled, then opened his eyes. Before he drew his foot away from Jack's, he studied the way their toes were touching. Then he saw Kate was awake and sat straight up.

"Good morning," he said.

"Hey," she said.

"How was your night?"

"It was nice." She was trying to keep her balance sitting up in the hammock.

"Did Marco try anything funny on you?"

Kate smiled. "He was a perfect gentleman." She was glowing from the inside out.

"You guys were out there for a long time," Noah said. "I guess we fell asleep." The cooler still sat next to the fire. Kate wondered if Henry was inside.

"I'm hungry," Noah said. Jack rustled awake. "Hey Sleepy, you guys want to go get some breakfast?"

"Yes," Jack said, opening the cooler before his eyes opened completely. He peeled the tab from a beer can and took a sip. "It's still cold. Where'd everybody go?"

"Marco went to an interview," Kate said, and then she felt sheepish. "I don't know about everybody else."

"Is my car still here?" Jack asked Noah, taking a long drink.

"Do you have the keys?"

Jack felt around in his pocket. "Yep! Hot dog!"

Kate and Noah laughed.

"Hey Library," Jack said. "You ever been to Cindy's Diner?"

"No," she said.

"They serve beer with breakfast."

Kate smiled.

"Well let's go," said Noah.

"Don't you have to work?" Kate asked.

"It's Saturday," Noah said. "I'm off."

Cindy's Diner, a place with shiny red tables and a black and white checkered floor, reminded Kate of her mom's kitchen. She wondered how her mom was doing and told herself to write to her when she got home today.

Steph and Peggy were already there, eating breakfast. "We

tried to wake you guys up," Steph said. "But you all were out-like-shout."

Noah and Jack pulled a table up next to theirs and they all took seats.

"Where's Marco?" Steph asked. Kate didn't know if she wanted to tell everybody about their night.

"He went to an interview," Kate said.

She ordered a soda, the guys ordered beers. Peggy and Steph drank Bloody Mary's.

"You should try a bloody, Kate. Takes the edge off," Steph said.

"I have to work later."

"Oh, right. But you're still going to come to the reading?"

"Absolutely," Kate said.

"So," Peggy said, "what did you and Marco do last night?"

"We went swimming," Kate said matter-of-factly. "Oh, and in the water was the phosphorescent algae," Kate remembered with awe. "It felt like we were swimming in the sky."

"Damn," Jack said. "It figures Marco would get you out in the water with the algae running. Man, I don't know how he does it. Lucky bastard."

"What do you mean?" Kate asked.

"Nothing personal, Library. But let me guess. He told you he wasn't seeing anybody, and he seduced you."

Kate didn't want to lie, but she didn't want to tell them the truth, either. The waitress delivered their drinks. Kate thanked her.

"We just, swam. And talked." This was mostly true. They did swim, and they did talk. But she hadn't thought to ask if he was seeing anybody else. He certainly hadn't acted like it. Techni-cally, *she* seduced *him*. She felt her lips curling up into a smile, but paused, cleared her throat, and decided to leave the rest of it out.

"I suppose, Library," Jack said, "that our superhero Noah here has already warned you about Marco a hundred times."

Kate didn't say anything. She realized she was stirring her soda. As if it needed stirring. She stopped.

"Marco's got some serious skills," Jack said. "I mean, I can shag a woman if we're in the right atmosphere, but Marco can shag any woman, any time. He's just so slick like that." Donny nodded. "Score one for you if you resisted him," Jack held up the beer in a cheers gesture. Noah blocked his face with his menu. Kate wondered if they could see her squirming. "I mean, he's got more notches on his bedpost than I have hairs on my legs." Jack stuck his leg out from under the table.

"Gross," Peggy said, punching his arm. "We're eating."

Kate felt sick to her stomach.

"Excuse me," she said. "Which way's the bathroom?"

Steph stood up and said, "I'll show you."

"Noah, would you order me an omelet?"

"Sure," he said.

In the bathroom mirror, Kate was embarrassed about more than the mascara smeared under her eyes. She splashed cold water on her face, wiped at the black shadows with a piece of toilet paper, and wished she had a toothbrush. What had she gotten herself into? She didn't want to regret the night before, but she was starting to.

Steph spoke to Kate's reflection. "Hey." She turned on the water to wash her hands. "I can see the way you feel about Marco."

Kate didn't know what to say. Steph continued. "I just wanted to tell you that I understand. I've known him for a couple of years now. He's got a good heart."

At this, Kate's insides settled down a little. "But, they're right about him. There's a different girl every week." Kate was trying to swallow this. "But hey, I'd do it for a week if I could." She laughed. "He doesn't like blondes, though. Only brunettes." She shrugged her shoulders.

If Kate were blonde, would he have resisted her? This all felt like too much. She didn't know what to think.

"Thanks," Kate said.

"No problem." Steph tossed her hair in the mirror. "I feel awful, and I look like a freak." She laughed. "Happy Saturday."

"You look fine." Kate tried to tidy up the braid in her hair. The orchids must have fallen out during her swim with Marco. She was sad they were gone; she had wanted to press them into her journal.

"So," Steph rested her hand on the doorknob. "Did you do it with him?"

"Steph!"

"Come on. We're friends now. You can tell me."

Kate just shook her head. "We swam, and we talked."

"That doesn't sound like Marco to me. He didn't even try anything?"

Kate was amused. She really did like Steph.

"He flirted with me a little, you know. And I flirted back."

"Oh my gosh. That's it? You have *got* to loosen up."

Steph opened the door and Kate followed. When they got back to the table, Noah studied Kate's face.

"You all right?"

"Just needed to splash some water on my cheeks."

"So, Library, about Marco," Jack said. The waitress began delivering their breakfasts. Kate smiled and thanked her again. All eyes were on Kate.

"Listen," she said, asserting herself in front of her new friends for the first time. "I think you all might have an unhealthy obsession with Marco Del Rio."

"Oh!" Jack said, "Hot damn. Maybe we do."

Peggy laughed, "I'd obsess about him all night if he'd let me.

And then once in the morning." The rest of the table erupted in laughter.

"You guys," Kate said, "all I'm saying is that he didn't sit around all night talking about your love lives."

They all got quiet. Then Jack said, "Only because his is much more interesting. What *did* he sit around all night talking about?"

"Life. You know, music." They'd sat on the beach staring at the stars until they'd dried off, shared a cigarette, and hadn't spoken much at all. By the time they got back to the campsite only Noah was awake, and he hadn't asked any questions.

She hoped they couldn't see through her story. As she ate and avoided their questions she decided, if Marco was in fact going to break her heart, she wasn't going to let everybody else watch it happen.

CHAPTER FOURTEEN

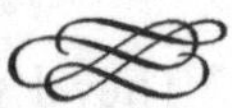

The Queen Kitty lectured Kate with meows. "I'm sorry I left you here alone for so long." She fed her, opened the front door, and sat on the step with a notepad and a pen.

Dear Mother, she wrote. *I hope you are doing well. I found a job and made a few friends. Girls from the local college. You would like them.* Would her mom like Marco? Maybe. Probably, but she might not like him for her. *Please tell Dad and Jim that I love them and miss them. Love, Kate.*

She put the letter in an envelope, added a stamp, and walked it out to the mailbox. She hadn't checked the mail since she'd been here, so there was a stack of coupons and one letter inside, from her brother. *Dear Kate,* it said, *Mom misses you something awful and I worry about you every day. Did you find a job yet? Are you taking care of yourself? Don't do anything stupid. Love, Jim.*

This made Kate smile. *Don't do anything stupid,* he said. Had she done something stupid with Marco last night? The Queen Kitty was done eating and came to sit on the step. Kate petted her smooth fur and replayed the evening's happenings through her mind again. The whole night, after they got to Marco's house, felt like a dream. It was beautiful, more beautiful of an experience than she'd ever had with anyone.

Her mind wandered to Chad.

He had talked her into losing her virginity in the back seat of his Mustang. She almost cringed to think of it. He was like some maniacal animal, tearing at her as if she were only flesh and bones.

Because they were engaged, she didn't feel like she was betraying God or her family. She thought it was to be her wifely duty, and she might learn to get used to it. But she always felt used and empty when he was done.

She didn't know it could feel like it did last night. Like it was meant to be. Like her soul yearned to be so close to his that they might for a minute, become one.

There were things about her that not everybody needed to know. But was it too fast? Maybe. Had she been under the influence? Yes. Marco seemed to have a spell on her. She definitely shouldn't tell anybody else. She didn't want them to think she was *that* kind of a girl.

Was she *that* kind of a girl?

Queen Kitty jumped on a lizard and chased it into the yard.

Like Steph said, what was wrong with free love? Kate wasn't promised to anyone else, nor did she see marriage on the horizon of anything she wanted to do soon. So what if she wanted to make love to Marco Del Rio? So what? But did he have a girlfriend? Oh, she hoped he didn't have a girlfriend. That would make her feel bad. Why didn't she ask? She was too caught up in the magic of it all. His eyes, his lips, the moonlight, his skin glistening under the stars.

A wave of shame began to crawl over her before she pushed it away. No, she thought to herself, I will not feel guilty for such a beautiful night. She reached into her pocket and pulled out the note Marco had written. *I hope you call*, it said. Maybe she should call. No, she thought, I don't want to seem too desperate.

I'll wait for him to call me. But he didn't have her number. Maybe she should call? She picked up the phone and dialed the first three numbers.

She wanted to tell him that she usually wasn't like that. It wasn't an everyday thing for her to find herself bare-skinned and swimming with a guy she'd just met. Maybe she should tell him how she felt about him, that she hadn't ever felt like this about anybody else.

Kate put down the phone. She would just wait. Maybe he would stop by and see her at work tonight. She took a shower and got ready for work. She hoped she wouldn't have to see Chip.

At The Wave, a new chef greeted her in the kitchen.

"I'm Frank." He was big and friendly. Kate studied his eyes, hoping he wasn't creepy, even though she'd worn her blue jeans today.

"Nice to meet you. I'm Kate." She wanted to ask him how he got here, but before she could find the right way to say it, he said, "I'm a friend of the boss's. The other restaurant I worked at just folded so I'm here until further notice."

Linda came into the kitchen. "I see you've met the new Captain." She squeezed his arm and said, "He's the one in charge here now. The boss told us this morning. Do what he says, or else." Linda raised a fist.

Frank chuckled. "I'm not all that bad. But yeah, I'll be handling the night-time kitchen, and the inventory, and the boss wants me to do some managing of personnel."

Kate wondered if this made Linda feel threatened. "Managing of personnel?"

"Mostly making sure that we keep guys like Chip out of here." Frank leaned over the cutting board table on both of his palms.

"We heard," Linda said. "I'm sorry."

"How did you hear about that?"

"It's a small town, missy," Frank said. "Be careful what you do and who you tell." His eyes shined and she wondered if they knew about Marco. But how could they know?

"Kate, are you on?" Linda said. "We've got new guests at table one."

Kate greeted the table, looked out at the bay and thought, no matter what happened, this job was a blessing. She took their order and went back into the kitchen.

"Ladies," Frank said, "We're going to run some seafood specials tonight. I've got some fresh grouper from the guys out on the docks. We're going to grill it in a garlic butter and serve it with a potato and a salad."

"How much?" Linda asked.

"Three-ninety-nine," Frank said.

"Aye, aye, Captain," said Linda and saluted. The nickname seemed to suit him.

As the restaurant got busy, Kate glanced at the corner where the music usually played. There was no live band tonight, so Linda had turned on the radio. As if teasing her, the DJ played "Surfin' USA" and "I Wanna Hold Your Hand." Kate kept glancing down the street. Hoping Marco might appear. All night she watched and waited, but he didn't come. The sun set again, and Sue-the-regular pointed at two dolphins in the distance.

"You know, dolphins mate for life."

Kate didn't know if she believed her. She smiled, anyway, emptied an ashtray, and said, "That's nice."

After closing, as Kate was finishing up, Linda and Frank came out on the deck to smoke. Linda offered a cigarette and Kate decided she could use the break.

"So," Linda said, putting her hands in her apron. "How did it go with Marco last night?"

How did it go with Marco last night? How did they know?

Frank stirred an orange and pink drink. The ice cubes clinked around her hesitation. He bent the straw, looking at Kate with his amused eyes. She felt found out.

"Marco Del Rio?" Frank asked.

Linda took off. "Yeah, Captain. Marco Del Rio brought her flowers here yesterday. And then she went to the beach to see him with Chip, and we know how that turned out. Marco and Noah blacked his eye and sent him packing, and then they all went to a bonfire at Marco's."

Kate was exasperated. "How do you know all of this?"

"Honey," Linda said, "in Seaview people know you've taken a wee before you even flush the toilet."

"Oh my gosh," Kate laughed. "You guys are crazy."

Frank looked at Kate again, way too knowingly, way too excited. "Marco Del Rio," he said, but this time with his forehead wrinkled in question, mixed with a tone of warning.

"Please," Kate said. "Not you, too."

"What do you mean, me too?" He flicked an ash from his cigarette, raised his eyebrows, and used the voice that her brother used. "I take it his reputation proceeds him." When Kate didn't say anything, he said, "And you've been warned?"

"Yes. Everybody has warned me." She took a puff from her own cigarette. The menthol cooled her tongue. "He brought me flowers, okay? It was sweet."

"Aye, very sweet indeed." He shifted from one foot to the next. "And if we could count up all of the women who are sweet on Marco Del Rio, then we'd have quite a bouquet. Plus, one tiny flower."

"I told her," said Linda, "I'd like to do him in the dining room. But I'm married. I can't. She's not."

Kate said, "You guys."

"There's nothing wrong with having fun with all of the wrong ones before you find the right one," Linda said. "But I think he likes her. You should have seen the way he moved around her the other night. She was sitting at the bar, and he came all up into her space. Like this." Linda got really close to Kate and looked at her dreamily.

"Linda, stop." Kate couldn't help but laugh.

"Oh," Captain said. "If he likes you, then you're really in trouble." He chuckled again.

"So," Kate had enough of this. "My friends are reading poetry down the street at The Buoy. Would you two like to join me?"

"Can't," Frank said, putting his cigarette out in the ashtray.

Linda said, "I promised Bobby I'd be home right after work. I ordered him some chicken tenders."

"Those are for you?" Frank said, "Of all the good seafood dishes I make, you order chicken tenders?"

"They're for Bobby," she said, "not me."

"All right you guys," Frank said. "Are we ready to close up?"

"Shots first?" Linda asked.

"Sure." Frank poured three shots of vodka and sweet lemon juice, and Kate, Linda, and Frank held them up.

"Here's to a new adventure for me," he said. "And hopefully a good adventure for you both."

"Cheers," Linda and Kate said in unison.

An adventure, Kate thought. That's how I should treat this thing with Marco, whatever it is. Like an adventure.

It was a strange feeling to walk down the street by herself. Kate kept looking over her shoulder, afraid that Chip might be following. She walked faster.

The Buoy was dark and smoky. Mostly older folks sat on bar stools staring at their beers, and chatting softly, but in the back corner of the bar by the cigarette machine, was a small stage with a microphone and Kate's new friends. Jack was on stage, rapping about something Kate couldn't quite hear. Steph found her quickly and greeted her.

"Hey," Steph said. "Glad you came." They hugged.

"Sure," Kate said. "This is cool."

All along the walls were black and white portraits of people Kate only faintly recognized.

"Cool, right?" Steph said. "There's Ginsberg, and Hemingway."

"The writers," Kate said.

"Yep. Rumor is Ginsberg stops in here to have a beer when he's in town." Steph turned to Jack. He had a glass of bourbon in one hand and sunglasses on. "Poor Jack," she pointed. "He just wants to be heard and nobody's listening."

"Let me get a drink and I'll sit with you." Kate waved at Peggy who sat at a round table near the stage.

Kate ordered her usual and Noah came in.

"Hey," she said. "Can I get you a beer?"

"Sure." An old man scooted his stool over on the carpet so that they could squeeze in.

"Hey, No-aaah," the bartender said. She had long blonde hair and wore thick, black eyeliner.

"Hi," he said.

"Is she flirting with you?" Kate asked.

Noah just smiled and sipped his beer. "I just came from the beach" he said. "The Parrot."

"Really?" Kate wanted to ask about Marco.

"The Dolphins were playing."

"Cool," Kate said. She left two quarters on the bar.

Noah seemed apprehensive. "Gina was there."

"Who?" Kate asked.

"I just thought I should tell you. Gina, Marco's ex-girlfriend was there, sitting front and center."

Great, Kate thought. She wanted to change the subject. "And how about Creepy Chip?"

"About that. I stopped by his house today."

"You didn't have to do that."

"I wanted to," he said.

"What did you say?"

"I told him that if he ever came within twenty feet of you again, that my biker buddies and I would break his hands, knuckle by knuckle, finger by finger. And the rest of his body parts, one by one." Noah stayed nonchalant as he spoke. "I don't think he'll bother you again."

"Thanks." Kate said.

"No problem. I don't really have many biker friends, but I think he got the point, anyway. What's Jack up there talking about?"

"Speaking of Jack," Kate said. "I saw your feet touching this morning." Kate didn't want to pry, but she wondered if he might want to talk about it. "Was that on purpose?"

Noah stared into his beer. "Jack is complicated. Let's go listen."

They sat down at the table with Peggy, Steph and Donny. Kate tried to focus on Jack's performance, but she couldn't. Noah had brought up Gina the ex. Uggh. What was happening to her? She had never considered herself to be a girl who obsessed about a guy.

"And the flame will burn regardless," Jack said, "of you, or I or the midnight sky." He waved his arms and almost spilled his drink. "We will continue turquoise dreams, since nothing eternal is as it seems. I'm Jack Miracle, thanks for listening."

The table of young people clapped, and the older folks at the bar ignored him. Jack came down from the stage.

"What's up, Library, what did you think?"

"Far out," she said.

"Steph, you're up next." Jack downed his drink and danced over to the bar.

Steph took the stage. For the first time since she met her, Kate thought she seemed fragile, almost shy. When Steph finished, she took a little bow.

"Steph," Kate said, "that was lovely. Did you write that?"

"Yep. A few nights ago."

"That was really great. You're brave."

Jack returned with a bourbon and six shots of something brown.

"Bottoms up for my poetry friends," he said.

The whiskey burned and fizzled in her stomach when it met with the vodka. Jack had a cigarette behind his ear that he took down and offered to her.

She thanked him as he lit one for himself.

Peggy, who hadn't said anything other than hello, said, "So, Kate, did Marco bring you flowers today?"

"No," Kate said.

"Did he call you?"

"He doesn't have my number," Kate defended.

"Where is he now?"

Noah butted in. "He's at the beach, working." He swigged his beer. "You sound like the FBI."

"I'm just curious." Peggy spoke with an aloof look and an innocent tone, but Kate sensed something different.

"Who's reading next?" Kate asked.

"We're done," Jack said. "You just caught the tail end."

Steph said, "We read all that we brought. Or else I did, anyway."

"Me too," said Jack.

A woman approached.

"Great job tonight. Thanks for coming out."

"Library," Jack said, "this is Thelma. She and her husband own the place. They're the reason we can get up and express ourselves." Jack did a fancy bow.

"Nice to meet you. I'm Kate. I really like your place."

"He calls you Library, does that mean you read?"

"I love to read."

"What's your favorite book?" asked Thelma.

"Oh, wow." Hardly anybody ever asked her that. "It would

have to be *Their Eyes Were Watching God.* My grandmother left it to me in her will. First edition."

"Hurston," Thelma said. "Zora Neale Hurston."

"You know that one?"

"I like a good love story. Especially one where the female protagonist does what she wants."

"Free love," Kate said, and looked at Steph. "I've never thought about Janie like that before."

"She was ahead of her time," Thelma said. "Do you write?"

"Not much," Kate said. "Letters, and in my journal."

"If you ever scribble any poetry then we'd love to have you read here."

"Thanks," Kate said. Maybe she would start to try to write poetry. She had hardly written anything at all since she'd been here.

"Well, I better get back to the office. I'm behind on my paperwork. Nice to meet you."

"You too," Kate said, finishing her drink.

"Let's go out to the pier and smoke a doobie," Jack said.

Peggy and Donny nodded.

Kate was tired. Her mind was full from the week. "I'm going to get going. Feed my cat. I could use some rest."

"I bet you could," said Peggy. Kate ignored her.

"I'll take you home," Noah said.

"Aw come on, guys. It's beautiful out," Steph said.

"I better not."

"I need some rest, too," Noah said, looking at Peggy. He slapped Jack on the back.

"Love-In tomorrow, on the green," Jack said.

Noah looked at Kate. "We'll be there."

CHAPTER FIFTEEN

When Kate got home, she opened the window and crashed into her bed. It had begun to rain. The week's memories swirled through as she closed her eyes. In her dreams, she saw her mother's crying face at the kitchen table. She saw her bus ride. She heard music. And for a split second, she saw Marco Del Rio sitting on a stool with his guitar, singing to her.

In the morning she took a long bath, thinking of the way Marco touched her body. Longing for his eyes in hers. Longing for his lips. Though she thought she had been in love with Chad, she'd never been so mesmerized by a man before. She put on the new red sundress and decided to let her hair down and stay curly.

Noah picked her up on the bike and they rode over a bridge, across the bay from where they worked in Seaview. They didn't pass too many cars, and the island seemed rather deserted until they got to the college. Kate wanted to tell Noah about her night swim with Marco, but she was afraid he would further discourage her. She didn't want anybody else to taint her feelings more than they already had, so ultimately, she kept quiet.

"You all right?" he asked, as he parked the bike and they dismounted.

"Yes," she said.

"You haven't been singing at all today." He winked at her.

Around the corner of a giant building, a crowd of people gathered. Kate had never seen anything like it. Girls in sundresses danced barefoot in the grass, guys in bell-bottom jeans with their shirts off shook and moved to the music. Different kinds of smoke wafted around from various clusters of people on blankets.

"Welcome to college," Noah said. On one side of the green, a band played. She scanned their faces, searching for Marco, but he wasn't one of the guys in the band. Trying to shake off her disappointment she said, "Do you think Steph is here?"

"Moon Dog!" Jack waved from a nearby blanket. Peggy and Donny sat on a blanket with their limbs entangled, kissing. Steph was wearing a white sundress and had a bandana wrapped around her head. A pile of flip-flops sat in one corner of the blanket.

"Library, shoe deposit," Jack said. "Mandatory." Noah and Kate both took off their shoes and put them in the pile.

"Kate!" Steph said. "I've got something for you." She knelt down above a picnic basket and handed Kate what looked to be a brownie. "Magic brownies."

"Magic?"

"I'll have one of those. Magic," Noah said to Kate, "special ingredients. Might make you laugh a lot."

Kate sat down. The guy from the record store stumbled by and when Kate said hello, he acted like he didn't recognize her and kept walking. She nibbled on the brownie. It tasted a little earthy.

Peggy and Donny continued to act like they couldn't get enough of one another.

"Free Love," Noah said. He sat down next to Kate and put his elbows on his knees. "And speaking of free love, look who's here."

Marco Del Rio emerged out of the crowd like an apparition. Kate rubbed her eyes, wondering if the brownie had kicked in already. He wore black jeans and had a pack of cigarettes tucked into the sleeve of his white tee shirt. He hesitated, and then walked straight toward her. She couldn't see his eyes from behind his sunglasses, but she could tell from his dimples that he was smiling.

"Hey," he said to the group, but faced Kate. Peggy broke her embrace with Donny and smoothed down her skirt.

"Marco!" Steph said, "Dance with me!" She grabbed his arm and twirled herself underneath it. He moved with her for a second, laughing, before he eased his way over to Kate and sat on the very corner of the blanket next to her. He shook hands with Noah and nodded to Donny.

"Hola Bella," he said quietly. "*¿Cómo estás?*"

"Shoes in the shoe pile," said Jack, dancing wildly. He waved a silver flask in the air. Marco slipped his shoes off and Kate found herself staring.

"Brownie?" she offered.

Steph said, still twirling, "That's the last one. If you can get Kate to share it, I would."

He opened his lips a little, and Kate broke off a piece and put it to his mouth. His tongue touched her finger as she pulled it away. Her body tingled.

"Thanks," he said. She kept her eyes on his lips. He put his arm around her. Though she relished this, and wanted to cuddle up against him, everyone's warnings hit her brain all at once. Assessing him again, she knew she didn't have to protect herself from him, but maybe she needed to protect both of them from the others. She stood up and said, "Dance with me?"

Damp grass and cool mud seeped between her toes. Marco took her hand. She shook it away until they got to the middle of the dancing crowd and their friends could no longer see them. She locked eyes with a girl who was staring at Marco.

"You're quite famous around here," Kate said, beginning to move. There were two bites of brownie left. She took one bite and fed the other to him, this time, letting her fingers linger in his mouth, the suction of his tongue. She glanced back at the staring girl, who turned away. Kate's whole body burned. He grabbed her by the waist and pulled her close. She retracted.

"What is it?" he asked. She kept moving her feet.

"Everybody's staring at us."

"I am sorry. It comes with the territory."

"Hey, Marco," the record store attendant approached. "How you doin' man?"

"Good," he said.

"Hey, we sold out of your albums this week at the shop."

"That's great," he said. When Marco didn't say anything else, the record store guy wandered away.

Marco put his hands on her waist again.

"I can't see your eyes," she said.

"I am in disguise." Then, as if considering it, he slid his glasses up onto the top of his head.

"Better," she said. His body moved in synchronicity with hers.

"I cannot stop thinking of you and swimming with you in the stars. Can I kiss you?"

She shook her head. Too many people.

"Ah, she is shy." He took her hand and twirled her around, then pulled her body close to his. His other hand settled on the small of her back. When she smiled and pulled back, he appeared frustrated.

She pleaded with his eyes then. Without words, she gestured to their friends over her shoulders, and all the other strangers watching them. She shrugged. For just one moment, she let him see her, unguarded. Her fear of being found out and talked about.

"Claro que sí. Why did you not say something? Let's get out of here."

Kate resolved to let Marco lead her through the crowd by the hand. Then she thought of Noah. He would be worried about her if she left without saying goodbye. She squeezed Marco's hand and said, "Just a minute." She hurried through the crowd and found the blanket.

Peggy and Donny were back at it and Steph and Jack were dancing. Noah still sat on the same spot.

She cupped her mouth and put it to Noah's ear. "I'm leaving with Marco. Please don't tell anybody, okay?"

He started to shake his head. She said, "Thank you!" And dashed off.

A guy with curly, waist-length hair handed her a daisy. "Pretty flower for a pretty lady."

She smiled and continued running. When she came to the clearing where she'd left him, Marco stood talking to a brunette, curvy in all the places Kate was not curvy. He'd put his sunglasses back over his eyes.

The girl stood close to him, too close for Kate's comfort. She had shiny, straight black hair and her hand placed on his arm. Kate's stomach flipped. The girl kissed him on the lips and danced away into the crowd. Kate held her breath.

"Bella," Marco said.

She might as well say something. She couldn't hide her jealousy forever.

"Who was that?" Her voice came out in a high-pitched tone.

"My sister. I am sorry I did not get to introduce you. She is on some kind of new drug." He laughed. Kate exhaled. "She was trying to tell me something about the neon universe." He peered out over the crowd and shrugged. "I hope she is careful. Where did you get the flower?"

"Oh . . . a guy," she pointed over her shoulder.

Marco held his hand out to hers and said, "I want to be the only guy to give you flowers." He rubbed his thumb against her palm. "I know about a beach where nobody goes. Henry likes it there."

They picked up Henry and rode in the VW bus. Kate let the wind blow through her hair and studied the clouds as they drove over bridges and causeways, past marinas. Maybe she should talk to him about how she felt, but she didn't want to ruin the moment. Henry bounced around the back of the bus, from window to window, and squeezed his muzzle out into the air.

Cars and people became fewer and farther between, until they pulled onto a sandy dirt road and wound around mangrove trees. Finally, the road opened onto a strip of white sand against blue water.

"Welcome to Sand Dollar Beach. Or, Marco and Henry's Beach." There were no cars or other humans to be seen. Henry did his growl-talking and panted at the door.

As Marco turned off the engine, he reached over, put his hand on her bare knee and moved it up her skin just slightly, inside her thigh. "I cannot resist you, Bella. It is unlike me."

He released his hand, but she felt suddenly wild. He shuffled his hair with both hands, so it fell around his face. Before he could open the driver's side door, she crawled into his lap and sprawled her legs over his. He kissed her long and hard.

She glanced up to see Henry, watching from the back aisle, and she giggled. "Can we let him out?"

"Yes, Bella," Marco said, breathing heavily.

Kate slid open the door and Henry darted out into the sand. She pulled the door back to a crack and crawled back up into the driver's seat. He cradled the back of her neck with one hand and pulled her forward to look into his eyes.

CHAPTER SIXTEEN

Kate woke up to a knock on the window. A police officer holding a baton. Her body was still folded into Marco's. She pulled away from him and lowered her dress. Marco had drifted off himself, but now he was wide-eyed. He helped her crawl back to the passenger seat, made sure she was decent, and then pulled up his jeans and buckled his belt. He rolled the window down slowly.

"Mr. Del Rio." The officer leaned forward and raised his eyebrows at Kate. "I believe I have your dog." Henry wagged his tail beside the man and barked like a greeting.

"Oh, great. Thanks, Joe. How are you?" The word *Sheriff* curled over the badge on his chest.

"I'm fine, Marco. What are you doing out here?" The sun was setting over the water.

How long had they been asleep?

"I just brought the lady out to watch the sunset," Marco said coolly. "This is Kate. Kate, Joe." Kate reluctantly waved. "How is Silvia?"

"The wife's fine. You know you can't just let your dog run

around freely, even out here." Sheriff Joe tapped his baton in his palm.

"Yeah, Joe. I am sorry. We only let him out for a minute, and he must have taken off." Kate noticed her panties on the dashboard. She leaned forward, snatched them up, wadded them up into her fist and sat back down.

"You all right, miss?"

"Yes, sir. I'm fine."

"Are you just saying that, or did he tell you to say that?" Her mind was fuzzy. The sheriff moved one hand to the revolver on his side.

"We were just getting some rest before the sun goes down," she said.

"I bet you were. I know all about what Marco does in here."

Marco braced one hand on the door. "Look. I am sorry about Henry. We will put a leash on him, okay? Thank you for finding him. He has a lot of energy."

Joe tapped on the hood now with his baton. "You know the park closes at sunset, so don't go shacking up here all night." He leaned in. "I know a boy like you wouldn't want to be caught with a white woman after dark, illegally parked, right?"

"Right," Marco said, his lips now flat. "Henry, get in the van."

The dog ran around to the door, pried it open with his nose, and hopped in. Kate slid the door closed, holding her dress down with one hand.

"Thanks, Joe. You are the best." Marco rolled up the window.

He closed his eyes and put his forehead against the steering wheel. Kate put her hand on his back and rubbed it back and forth. "You know that guy, too?"

He raised his head. "I swear, it is like nobody around here has an interesting life. Everybody seems to want to see me lose, somehow." Kate wasn't sure what to say. "I am sorry you had to see that."

"He seems like a jerk." She thought about the incident from start to finish. "I hope he didn't see me, like—"

Marco pointed to the windshield. "Tinted windows. You still want to watch the sunset?"

Kate leaned over and kissed him.

"Yes," she said. "Are you hungry?"

"Do you like lobster tail?" He started the van. "I know of a place."

"I haven't had it before," she said.

"A week of firsts for you, then?" They wound out of the park and over a few bridges before coming into a tiny beach town, this one smaller than Seaview. A general store and some boats were lined up against a dock, and one restaurant on stilts hung out over the water.

From the parking lot, she could see a few fishermen sitting on wooden barstools. White birds dipped in and out of the bay. Large pelicans with beaks like big scoops sat on the pylons of the pier. The smell of salt water hovered around them.

Kate had forgotten to grab their shoes from the green, so they were both walking around barefoot. "Cuidado. Be careful of splinters from the boardwalk." One of the pelicans dove off its stoop as they approached and flew away. "Nobody knows us here." Marco led her by the hand. "Your privacy is granted, Bella." He tied Henry up by the leash to one of the wooden poles. "Good boy. I will bring you some steak if you are good." Henry sat down and sneezed.

They walked to a small table facing the water. The sun had turned brilliant fuchsia and orange and reflected on the glass-calm sea like a watercolor painting. "Los dioses are showing off," Marco said. A worker in a tee shirt lit the tiki torches surrounding them in the sand, then the candle on their table.

They sat across from one another. She ordered white zinfandel, and Marco ordered a bourbon while they waited on their dinner and shared a cigarette.

When they were apart, there were a thousand things that Kate wanted to know about Marco. But now, while they were together, it was enough for her to just gaze into his eyes. As if reading her thoughts, he said, "I could get lost in your eyes, Bella."

Kate blushed. "What's it like to speak two languages? Do they get mixed up in your head?"

Marco grinned. "Sometimes." He sipped his bourbon. "I think in Spanish, and also . . . feel. Depending on who I am talking to, I either translate or . . . sometimes the Spanish words come out before I think about them, or the English words do not give the right meaning. Are not as . . . how do you say . . . *authentic*-feeling."

"It's neat to listen to everybody talk here," she said. "The different accents from different places. But I'm surprised being from Texas you don't sound more like . . ."

"John Wayne in a cowboy movie?" He laughed.

She giggled. "Yeah, I mean." Maybe that was rude. "I've never met anybody from Texas before."

"it is okay to ask questions. I am glad to be your first," he said.

She took in their surroundings. Blue and green-painted wood, nautical decorations, a fish tank against one wall.

"See the dollar bills?" He pointed.

One-dollar bills were nailed to the walls one after the other, with names and small messages written on them. "The fishermen hang them up when they have a good catch." He took another sip of his bourbon. "With their names. That way, if they do not have a good catch the next time, they can still get a burger and a beer when they come from fishing."

Kate smiled and sipped her wine. Even though she'd only known him for a short time, she felt a deep affection for him that she couldn't explain. Maybe she should ask him if he was seeing anybody. Maybe she should ask him about his past. Instead, she fell back on what she knew. Small talk.

"Tell me about New York," she said.

"Well," he rubbed his palms on his shorts. "It is crowded. Busy. All of the time. It is nice because there are more people, and less people calling me boy, you know? But it is too busy for comfort. Too many people. Plus, I am not meant to live in the sky."

"Live in the sky?" Kate tasted her sweet wine again.

"All of the apartment buildings have, like, one hundred floors." He laughed. His lips. She leaned across the table and kissed him, shyly. From her mind to her midsection and below, her energy cascaded like a waterfall. "The beach is my style," Marco said. "You are my style, Bella."

"What about Texas?" She put her foot against his smooth calf. He reached down and ran one finger up her leg.

"It is big. *Hot.* In the country there are farms and ranches and land as far as you can see, and in the cities, it is also crowded."

"Is your family there?"

"Sí, my parents. But my sister is here. Sometimes I think she follows me, just to keep an eye out. Though she is the one who needs supervision. She can be wild." He smiled with affection. "How about your family? Are they all in Ohio?"

"I have one brother, Jim, who's older than me, and my parents."

"And they were okay with you leaving your home to come to the beach?"

"Well, not really." Kate smiled. "My mom wanted me to stay, but my dad helped me get an apartment. My mom has some idea of what my life should be like, like I should fit into some kind of box. I tried for a while, but I just . . . don't fit."

"Ah, I understand," Marco said.

They both thanked the waitress when she brought their food. Marco got up to pour water in a bowl for Henry, and then returned. They ate in comfortable silence. The lobster tail was equally buttery and delicate.

The sun slipped under the water and slowly set in pulses of light that turned green, then blue, gray-black. Kate lifted a piece of lobster tail to his lips, and he offered her a piece of steak.

After Marco paid the bill and they gathered up Henry, Marco fed the rest of his steak to the eager dog, which he chomped up quickly, and then swallowed in one big gulp. They walked back to the van and rode home.

When they got close to town Marco said, "Spend the night with me?"

IN HIS LIVING room under the guitars, he laid her down on the velvet fabric. His eyes sparkled with passion and innocence. She ran her fingernails over his stomach muscles, the tight curves on either side of his lower back. She felt like a flower, opening for the rain.

He sat up and caressed her hair out of her face. She hadn't noticed the yellow specks of his eyes, light tiny bursts of sunshine in the green. "Let's go swimming, Bella."

He led her by the hand into the moonlight.

The sand glowed and sparkled against the black night. They waded out until the warm waves touched their shoulders, and Marco embraced her again.

After a while, he lifted her out of the water, her legs still wrapped around his waist, carried her up past the sand dunes and laid her down next to the bonfire. He lit a match for the wood and a cigarette for them to share.

Kate cuddled up on the blanket and stared at the sky.

"We should have drinks." He handed her the cigarette and disappeared into the trailer, then returned with a beer and a glass of whiskey. Henry followed him out, greeted Kate, and then shot out toward the water, splashing in the tide.

"Can I have some?" Kate asked, pointing to the glass.

"What is mine is yours, Bella." He lit a joint, and offered it to her, but she declined. He pulled her close, their bodies' energy entwining in the night, and he blew the sweet smoke into her mouth, then followed into a long kiss.

They didn't talk for a while, they just held each other and looked at the stars, listening to the waves rolling over in the sand.

"Do you want to lay in the hammock with me, Bella?" He grinned from ear to ear like a little kid. "It is very Mexicano."

From the hammock she saw another shooting star. "You are like a porcelain doll," he said as he kissed her again. "Sweeter than vanilla and more intoxicating than wine."

"It's like living in the sky," she whispered.

"Como vivir en el cielo." Marco ran his hands up and down her legs and said, "Come into my bed, Katie."

He picked her up and carried her through the door to his room. A blue lava lamp rolled over in the corner on his night-stand, and Henry laid on a pile of blankets in the other corner.

Over the wooden headboard hung a painting of two white tigers, lying together in the jungle. Beneath the painting was a circular decoration with tan fur, feathers and indigo and gray beads hanging down. When he saw her looking at it he said, "For good dreams."

He pulled down the navy-blue bedspread and tucked her body gently under the covers. He lit a stick of incense, opened the window, and she watched the smoke rise like a kite string.

"Henry. Tiempo privado." Henry dipped his head down and reluctantly left the room. Kate was in such a state of ecstasy, she wasn't sure she could talk, even if she wanted to. "Música?"

"Marco," she whispered.

"Guitarra acústica." He placed the needle on an album and crawled in bed next to her. He pulled her back toward him and caressed her chest and stomach with his strong fingers. "Katie Bella," he whispered back.

As the harmonies mixed through the bedroom, it was like he instinctively knew where to touch her, what she was thinking, how she was feeling. She felt loved and alive and *seen*, and wasn't sure how she'd stepped inside this magical life.

It was as if last week she had been a girl, and this week she had become someone different; as if it were always going to happen this way. As if he were always waiting there for her to walk into The Parrot, as if she were always going to, and there was no other way.

Marco cherished her with his lips and tongue. He watched her eyes and responded to her body. Skin on skin and limbs wrapped together. He was playful and careful, respectful and gentle, then determined and serious. They laughed and then held onto moments so they might last, so they might reach the same heights together. She closed her eyes and gritted her teeth, and let the waves of pleasure roll over and through her.

He maneuvered her body the same way he maneuvered his guitar. Like he'd been playing it for centuries, in every one of their lifetimes. Like it was the only thing he could see himself doing. Like her dreams were always leading her here, to this time and place, to him.

She had promised herself she was not going to trust her heart again, but now it was pumping and sacred and on fire. This, just this, was all that mattered. When their energy was spent, they stayed entwined, breathing together in the light of the lava lamp, the sound of the ocean kissing the earth outside under the stars.

"Can I tell you something?" he asked. He kissed the top of her head, and inhaled, as if he were taking in her scent. "It is not meant to scare you." The record had stopped. She didn't feel scared, she felt . . . peaceful. Like all was right in the world. Maybe she had finally found what she was looking for.

She nuzzled her head into his neck. "I have been having this dream," he said. "For a while now. I don't know, maybe a year?" She took a hold of his strong right hand, and tucked it against her belly. He squeezed her hand. "I am walking with a girl on the beach at night. I am older, and I am trying to see her face, but I cannot. I am happy though, you know? I feel peaceful and like everything is all right."

He kissed her cheek and then turned so he could see her. His eyes vulnerable and amazed, a faint light glowing from them.

"Once a month I have been having this dream, but I have never seen the face of the woman. And then the night before you walked into The Parrot, I saw your face. *You and I*, we are walking on the beach at night. Sometime in the future. We are older, and we are holding hands and you are smiling."

She tried to keep her eyes open, to take all of this in to remember it, so she could write it all down in her journal. How would she ever describe this feeling she had? It didn't scare her, his words gave her a mysterious sense of faith. She fell into a deep and beautiful sleep.

CHAPTER SEVENTEEN

"So this is what you mean by busy?"

A woman stood over Marco's bed with her hands on her hips.

Kate was disoriented; she'd been dreaming on another planet, in paradise, and now she was—where was she?

Morning sunlight glared in from the window. Marco sat straight up and rubbed his eyes. The Love-In, the sunset, and the dinner date flashed through Kate's memory and now . . . who was this?

"Gina," Marco said. "What the hell *are you doing* in here?" Kate tried to shake the cobwebs from her mind.

"I see you have company." The woman crossed her arms. Kate realized she was completely naked under the blanket. She had no idea where her dress was.

"Invited company. You do not live here, anymore, ¿recuerdas? How did you get in?" He picked his shorts up off the floor. "Leave. Please."

Kate wanted this to be a bad dream. She wanted to wake up again, and be cuddled against Marco's body, with the morning ahead of them. Another morning of ecstasy.

"The back door was open," Gina snuffed. She looked at Kate, "Who are *you?*"

Kate sat up and held the comforter against her chest.

"Gina." Marco raised his voice. "Get out. You cannot just walk into my house at any time you want."

"You know he's never been faithful to any woman for any length of time," Gina snarled, her eyes like wet glass. "He'll treat you like a queen for a month and then you'll be old news." She looked back at Marco, "I suppose she's new in town."

Marco slid his shorts up quickly and stood, taking a step toward Gina while he fastened his belt. His voice turned into a low-tone growl. "Gina. Get. The hell. Out. Of my house." She stepped back toward the door as he approached her, then she put her hands on his waist.

"Hey, baby. I just missed you."

Marco gently removed her hands from his waist and walked her backward toward the door.

Where was Kate's dress? Her adrenaline was kicking in. She scanned the room for any sign of red.

"Hey," Gina said. "Let's just try to work it out."

Marco growled again, closed the sliding glass door in her face, and locked it behind him. He returned to Kate.

"I am sorry, Bella." He ran his hands over his hair and rubbed his face. "She is loca—crazy."

The sound of a car spitting gravel under tires gave Kate a quiet relief, but also made room for the anger. Kate's insides were caving in.

"Where's my dress? Please, just take me home."

"Listen," he said. "Por favor." He sat on the bed next to her. "I am sorry. She should not have come in."

"Yeah, well, she seemed to feel pretty at home here."

Kate knew this was out of line, but what else could she say? Oh, no problem? Your ex-girlfriend, or maybe present girlfriend just walked in on us in bed like she owned the place? It's fine?

"¡Chingada!" His tongue bounced off the top of his mouth. She thought of his lips on hers.

Despite her body lighting up she said, "Find my dress, please? I'd like to go home, now."

The incense had burned to a sliver of wood, but the scent lingered. Kate felt sick. Marco retrieved her red sundress and her panties from the floor under his clothes, then closed himself inside the bathroom. She slipped them on quickly, wrapped her hair in a bun, and walked out to the van. She folded her arms and waited.

The heat was stifling. Her stomach ached.

As he spilled out into the driveway from the back door, he struggled to put his tee shirt on and pleaded. "She and I are not together anymore. I promise. She is apparently having a hard time comprehending." He pointed to his temples with both forefingers. Marco glanced around the house and stared to the back.

"Apparently."

"Look. I asked her to leave. I took back her key. She has no business just walking in, and I am sorry that happened with you here. After our noche sagrada." Kate didn't know what that last word meant, but she wasn't going to ask.

"¡Chingada!" He slammed the door, gripped the steering wheel, and hung his head over it, the same way he'd done after the sheriff left. Kate didn't want to talk to him any more today, but what was he looking for? Was Gina still around somewhere or something?

"She took my dog," he said in defeat.

"What?" Kate wasn't sure she heard him right.

"We bought Henry together. I paid for him, she named him. She fucking took my dog again."

"Again?" Maybe this is what everyone had been warning her about. Maybe this is why everybody kept telling her to stay away from him. "I told you," he said, swirling an index finger around his ears, "she is loca."

Kate didn't know how to feel. "Noah told me she was at your show on Saturday. Front and center."

Marco winced. "I cannot control who comes to my shows."

"And apparently you can't control who comes into your house, either." She felt guilty as soon as she said it. He tapped the steering wheel three times with his forehead. "Just take me home, please." Kate didn't want to go home, but she didn't know what else to do.

He put the van in gear, shook his head, and he let out a long, hard sigh. They drove in silence. Kate's whole body shook with anger and jealousy. She tried to manage her feelings. She would not cry over this, over him. She'd wanted some adventure, right? *To live a little*, she'd heard herself tell Noah. And here it was.

They got stuck at the drawbridge which was letting a sailboat pass through. He reached over and touched her knee. Her body tingled against her will. She brushed his hand off.

"Katie Bella," he pleaded, "Por favor."

"Please, what?" She needed some time to think. She didn't know how to put what she was feeling into words. If the college kids found out about this, they'd certainly have a heyday. But she wanted to talk to Noah. Or she wanted to talk to her mom.

She didn't know what she wanted, but she needed to be alone.

He parked in her driveway, and leaned over toward her face, eyes as deep and green as the ocean. She wanted to kiss him; she wanted to crawl into his lap. She wanted to succumb to him again and again, to replay the night before.

Instead, she opened the van door and slammed it behind her.

Her heart slowly closed down. She told herself that she wouldn't let it open again, for anybody else. For a long time.

Kate collapsed onto her blankets. The ceiling fan went

around and round in the silence. What had just happened? She'd just had the most beautiful few nights of her whole life, and suddenly it felt like a nightmare.

Who did she think she was, anyway? Did she really think her connection with Marco competed with the other girls? That she was someone special? Of course not, what was she thinking? She was just a number. A girl in the front of a long line of girls. Another flower in a big bouquet. And now her turn was over. She wondered how many others there were.

Did he make love to Gina the same way he'd navigated her? In the ocean and the hammock and the couch? It was too much to think about. She fell asleep and woke up with just enough time to scramble to get to work. She put on her blue jeans and walked toward the bay.

When she got to The Wave, Captain was flipping burgers on the stove. "Happy Burger Monday."

"It's Monday. That makes sense."

"What's the matter with you?"

"Nothing." She opened the door to the salad cooler to take inventory, or, to try to ignore the conversation. "I'm fine."

"You don't look so fine."

"Thanks for the compliment."

Linda came into the kitchen.

"That's not what I meant. I mean you look—sad?" She was really going to have to try to disguise her feelings a little better.

"Kate, table two is down if you want to take them."

"Great," she said, trying to sound cheery. "I will."

Kate faked a smile for the rest of the night. She went through the motions, taking orders, serving beers, refilling sodas.

During clean-up Linda said, "Midwest, come in here to the bar. We've got something for you." Linda and Captain held up shots, one for her.

"Cheers," she said, half-heartedly.

"What happened to you?" Linda said. "Last week you were the happiest girl I've ever met, and this week you're like, blah, or something."

"I feel kind of blah." Outside a motorcycle pulled up. Noah came in, putting the sunglasses on top of his head. Jack trailed behind him, then Steph.

Jack sat at the end of the bar and put his elbows down. "Hey Library, how'd it go with Marco last night?" Kate looked at Noah with disdain.

"I didn't tell him." Noah raised his hands like she was an officer who was getting ready to arrest him. "He guessed."

"Oh," Captain said under his breath. "Well, this explains something."

This town was too small. "Linda, can we pour my friends a drink before we close up?"

"Sure," she said.

"So," Jack appeared to be feeling no pain. "Library. Marco. Spill it. What happened? Did he conquer you?"

Noah backhanded him in the chest. "Dude. Leave her alone."

She didn't want to talk about it. She didn't want to think about it. But she needed to defend herself here before the truth got around.

"He took me to the beach to watch sunset, and then we went out to dinner."

"Dinner?" Jack said, lighting up a smoke.

"Marco does *not* just take girls out to dinner," Steph said.

"It's true," Captain said. "He barely leaves the house unless he's playing." He leaned in over the bar. "Did he pay?"

What was that supposed to mean? "Yes, he paid. And then he took me home."

Noah said, "I stopped by your house this morning, and nobody answered the door."

She glared at him. He averted his eyes. "I must have still been sleeping."

Linda leaned over and made Kate look her in the eye. "Has he called you?"

"I don't really have time for going steady, or going on lots of dates."

At least if she didn't see Marco again, she wanted to be able to stop having to answer questions about him. But Kate didn't consider it until she lay in her bed that night, after maybe one too many drinks at The Buoy.

She would have to see him again. Because he played at her job, every Thursday at The Wave.

THE NEXT FEW days went by like a dull blur and Kate went through the motions. She needed to relax and reflect, so on Wednesday, she packed herself a turkey sandwich and walked down to the beach, settling on a place where the sand was uncrowded, where she could think and swim. She had only taken one bite of her sandwich when a seagull dove down and snatched it out of her hands. It scratched her fingers with its claws, and chills ran up her spine.

So much for relaxing.

Thursday came around and Kate found herself nervous about what she would wear. She had a little extra money from the week, so she decided to ride the bus to the department store and buy some of that makeup that Brenda had recommended. Part of her felt silly for doing it, but the other part of her wanted Marco to see how beautiful she really was, and what he was missing out on. Even though she was done with him.

Brenda's beehive was perfectly in place, and she remembered Kate. "How are you?" she asked.

"I'm okay?"

"Where's your friend?"

"I'm not sure. Probably working."

"He was cute," Brenda said. "But you haven't gotten yourself wrapped up in a guy, have you? Some of these beach guys can't take a hint."

"No, I haven't." Kate was getting used to not being completely truthful. "Can I buy a few of those products you used on me the other day? I'm thinking about the eyeshadow and the blush."

"Yes, ma'am. Let me do your face again."

Kate sat down in the chair. "First," Brenda said, "they tell you that you're beautiful and you're the only one for them." She dipped a padded brush into eyeshadow. "Close your eyes." Kate tried not to blink. "Then, they get you to marry them, somehow. You've watched too many Marilyn Monroe movies, is the problem. So, you do all the dishes and the laundry, for years. As if that's a job that makes you want to jump their bones." Brenda opened the glass display and picked through small packages. She pulled a circular container close to Kate's eyes, then seemed to be satisfied. "When you wake up to the whole deal, you find out they've been sleeping with their secretary since the day you met." She put a round brush in rouge and turned Kate's face by her chin.

"I told him, I said, you're sleeping with your secretary, that's great. Might as well train her up to wash your dirty underwear and your stinky socks because I'm done with it. And I hope she likes to listen to you snore over the sound of the late show. Purse your lips." Brenda dipped a small brush in pink and stroked it over Kate's mouth. "Should I tell her that you pass gas in bed all night and then have the nerve to ask for sex in the morning?"

Brenda paused and looked her in the eye. "I took the money I'd been stashing in a coffee can in the back of the closet, and I didn't look back. The poor bastard. I bet the house is filthy." Kate smiled. "If any of these beach guys ask you to marry them, you should run the other way. And I think you should go with the lip gloss. It makes your eyes stand out. See?" Brenda held up the mirror.

Kate studied her reflection. She didn't look that bad.

"The products will be five-fifty," Brenda said, as she packed them up in a bag for Kate. "The advice is free."

CHAPTER EIGHTEEN

Kate's heart was already burning on Thursday when Marco walked onto the deck with his guitar. She tried to ignore him, but he approached her, albeit tentatively, hands in his pockets.

He stood on his tiptoes and then lowered, bending his knees like he was unsure of what to do. He took a step toward her.

"Hi, Kate," he said.

Kate? He'd never called her that. "Hello," she said without meeting his eyes. "Can I get you something to drink?"

"Bourbon, please. How are you, Bella?"

"I'm fine." She spoke the way she responded to all her customers. "How are you?"

He was trying to be warm; she could tell. But she didn't dare fall for it. She kept her hands busy as she talked.

"Fine."

"Okay, then, I'll be right back with your drink. Would you like a menu?" She could do this all night. She hoped.

"No, gracias," he said.

She walked away, trying to ignore the way her midsection tweaked with a pang of pleasure.

"Marco's here." Captain stood in the kitchen and did his signature lean against the heat window, like he was taking the load off his feet to listen. "So, how *are* we?" He shifted to one leg.

"We're fine."

"Did he bring you flowers tonight?"

Kate poured a bourbon and a soda.

"Well, that would have been a smart move," Captain said. "Everybody says he's so smooth."

Kate shook her head, tired of the topic. Then there he was, peeking into the kitchen.

Before Kate could say anything, Marco kissed her on the cheek and said, "Mi amor. You have been walking a tráves de mis sueños." She glanced at Captain, and only for an instant into Marco's eyes. Marco raised his eyebrows quickly, and then slipped back out of the kitchen.

Uggh. He was relentless.

"Well, *that* was pretty smooth." Captain turned back to the stove and tended to the beef he had on the grill, which had begun to sizzle. Kate's stomach growled. When was the last time she'd eaten? Linda came in and opened the salad cooler.

"Specials tonight," Captain said over his shoulder. "Five grilled prawns with steak, rice, and broccoli. Six-ninety-nine."

"What's a prawn?" Kate asked.

Linda laughed. "A giant shrimp. I swear we'll make a Florida girl of you, yet." She pulled a salad out of the cooler and then asked, "What did Marco say?"

Captain said, "Can I?" He wiped his forehead with a white towel and shuffled from one foot to the other. Kate rolled her eyes. "He said, *she has been walking through his dreams.* But he said it in *Spanish.*"

"Ahh," Linda shrieked. "So romantic. I'd do him on the salad counter. What did you say, Midwest?"

"I am done with this." She walked out, delivered his drink

without making eye contact, and then continued to wait on the dinner rush.

Kate and Linda moved about, taking turns with orders, tables, and drinks. She refused to look at Marco, even though she felt his eyes on her. Even though his guitar sounded like a spell, and his velvet voice called to her spirit. Even though she kept trying to lock down the drawbridge, to talk her heart out of burning, and opening, to talk her body out of throbbing when a memory crept in.

Why couldn't she do this? Why couldn't she control her heart?

Marco's friends came in, and she brought them beers. "Hola Timbale," she said.

"Hola Katie." Steph came in, and some of her college friends.

"Kate," Steph said. "They're opening up one of our poetry classes to the public. You wanna join?"

"Maybe. How much does it cost?"

"I'm not sure. I can let you know."

Pretty soon they were throwing a party again, Kate, Linda, and Marco and their closest friends.

During a cigarette break, Kate found herself fantasizing that Marco and she would leave together, go the beach, and talk out the happenings from the other day. Maybe she could at least give him that, right? After all, what if he was telling the truth about Gina? What if she was really a crazy girl who refused to let him go?

And what if he really wanted to be serious about Kate? To officially go steady? They hadn't even had that conversation. She thought of his strong body on top of hers. The hammock and the stars. She had to snap herself out of it.

If he asked, maybe she would give him one more chance to explain. And she would evaluate it from there. Like a grown-up, Kate thought, she would talk about her feelings like a rational person and then decide if there was any future with

Marco Del Rio, famous local musician, friend of many women.

When she walked back out onto the deck, a young girl with brown hair and glasses was perched at table eight, the closest table to the stage. The girl swooned, legs crossed and one foot pointed at him.

Kate knew he saw the look on her own face, but she couldn't help it. He saw her pain as if she had said it out loud. His eyes pleaded with her again from the stage, as his hand moved around the neck of the guitar.

But Kate's heart crushed and crumbled.

Who needed love, anyway? She didn't need a guy for anything. Like Brenda said. She should just run the other way.

"Welcome to The Wave," Kate said. "What can I get you?"

"I'll have a vodka and orange juice."

"Menu?" Kate asked.

"No thanks. I just came to see Marco."

"Right," Kate said. "Great."

At closing time, Kate continued to give Marco the cold shoulder as casually as possible. She tidied up the deck while he smoked and laughed with his friends. Every time she found herself looking at him, she peered away before he could catch her eye. The brunette seemed to know his friends. She stood in the middle of the group, laughing, giggling and stealing glances at Marco.

Kate tried to ignore his eyes, his lips, his body. When he approached her, and put his hand on her waist, she felt everyone watching. She stepped back from him and said, "You don't have a tab. Do you need something else?"

"Te necesito," he whispered in her ear, his low voice soft and pleading. "I need you to talk to me." When Kate scoured the crowd, only Timbale was looking.

She made herself turn away and walked back inside to the bar.

"Shots," Linda said. "Kate, here you go." Kate took the hard liquor from Linda. Last year she wouldn't have dreamed of drinking liquor or smoking, but she drank it down so her throat burned, then accepted a cigarette from Linda and lit it up. She could at least ask about Henry. No, she wasn't going to. She didn't want to give him the idea that she cared.

"Let's do another shot," Kate said. "That one was delicious."

"Are we okay?" Captain asked.

"We're fine," Kate said.

He leaned in close to her and said, "Who's the brunette?"

Kate brushed her hair back. "The next flower in the bouquet, I guess."

Captain pulled at the bottom of his chef coat and stopped asking questions. Kate downed the other shot before cheers-ing with them.

"All right," Linda yelled out to the deck. "Party's over. You don't have to go home, but you can't stay here."

The crowd spilled into the bar, talking loudly all at once. Everybody else seemed to be feeling pretty good. Steph said, "Kate, we're going down the street to The Buoy. Peggy and Donny are supposed to be there."

"Yeah," said Jack. "They can't keep their hands off one another lately."

"They're going steady," Steph defended. "Let them be."

Noah was strangely quiet and had been so all night.

Kate didn't feel like being alone. "I'll meet you there."

Captain and Linda watched like an audience, as Marco and his friends headed toward the back door. From the corner of her eye, Kate saw him turn around one more time to look at her. She blew a cloud of smoke over her drink and tried to shake him off.

The juke box played Elvis in The Buoy. Peggy, Donny, Steph, and Jack huddled around the bar at the back end. Kate walked in alone. Steph said, "We thought you might bring Marco." Kate took a deep breath. "I'm sorry," Steph said over the music, "is that a sore subject?"

They did some more shots, and Kate spent most of her night's tips buying round after round. Donny's dad had lent him his sailboat for the weekend, and it was tied up out at the dock.

When the bar closed, everybody stumbled out to the boat. Donny gave them the grand tour.

"This is the helm," he said, pointing at the wheel of the boat. He led them down below. "This is the galley, or kitchen, and this is the main salon, or in land-lubber speak, the lounge. There is the head," he pointed to the bathroom. "Pump once and pump twice to flush, and the cabins are in the stern and the bow. Now, let's have drinks."

Noah mixed everybody gin and tonics. Peggy and Donny sat at the helm, and everybody else dispersed into various places on the deck and the cockpit. "Tunes?" Donny asked. He put the needle on the record player and Kate heard Marco's voice, singing out over the bay.

"This is his original stuff," Steph yelled. "Have you heard it?"

"I have not," said Kate.

"He's good." Steph flicked ashes of her cigarette over the bow of the boat. "We all thought he was going to be the one to put Seaview on the map."

Kate's whole body buzzed with liquor. She couldn't focus on the words but looked out over the water. Marco was going to be hard to forget. Around here, anyway. Lights from the coast popped up on the horizon, blurred, and moved in yellow and white spots. Kate felt a little woozy.

"Noah, I haven't seen you in a few days, what's up?"

He shot a glance at Steph and Jack, who were deep in conversation at the bow. The music was loud enough.

"I kissed Jack," he said.

"Really?" When he didn't answer right away she said, "Can I have one of those?" She gestured toward his cigarette.

He pulled out his pack and shook one out. "You know," he said, "you should probably just buy your own pack."

"What did Jack do?"

"He kissed me back. It was nice." Noah leaned in closer. "But then the next day was kind of weird. It's been weird ever since."

"Have you guys talked about it?"

"I tried to mention it, but he changed the subject."

"At the Love-In?" Kate asked.

"After it got dark. We were all hanging out, getting buzzed. Donny and Peggy and Steph disappeared, and the music was playing. Somebody had brought these technicolor lights. We were all feeling pretty high, you know? Loving. Dancing. So, I laid one on him." Noah gazed out at the water.

"But you said it was nice?"

"I mean, he seemed to like it at the time, but, I don't know now. He pulled away from me quick. You know, he says he likes girls."

"I kissed Marco," Kate blurted out. For some reason she thought Noah was going to be surprised.

"I know," he said.

"You know?"

"He told Donny you were 'sweet as honey.'" Noah put his fingers up in imaginary quotation marks.

"They're friends?" Kate had never seen them even talk. Marco kissed and told? She put that on the list of things she didn't like about him. Though other than his apparent female associations, it was a very short list.

"I guess so. Do you think I should go sit by Jack?"

Though Kate wanted to talk more about Marco she said, "I don't see why not. It's a beautiful night."

Noah got up and settled next to Jack and Steph. Marco's voice echoed all over the water, all over Kate. Her body was numb; her heart closed off. She could just sit and watch the stars with her friends. She had made good friends.

Peggy stood up. "Because you're a fucking asshole!"

"Whoa, Peggy Sue," Noah jumped to his feet. "What's up?"

"We're having this romantic night and then he says his ex-girlfriend's name? Jane? Why do I have to hear her name every night, Donny? You're not fucking over Jane?"

Steph said, "Peggy, chill out, man. We're all just having a good time, relaxing on the boat. You guys can figure this out."

Peggy poured her drink in Donny's lap. "Fuck you!" As she climbed off the side, the boat rocked back and forth against the fenders.

"Should I go with her?" Noah asked.

"She's fine," Donny said. "Her car is right there by the bar."

"But maybe she shouldn't be driving?" Kate said.

Steph chimed in. "Peggy will drive whether you think she should drive or not. I say we let her be. Maybe she'll come back after she cools off."

Jack said, "T-Bird, it's generally a bad idea to mention the ex to the new girlfriend, capisce?"

A quiet took over them. Marco's voice was the only sound, singing something about the sky.

Donny didn't seem too bothered. "You guys wanna get out of here? Or do you wanna stay docked?"

"Where would we go if we went?" Kate asked.

"Cindy's diner. Open all night."

"I think we should stay here," Jack said, "sleep it off and then go eat when the sun rises."

"That's probably smartest," Steph said. "What's your dad got for sleeping on this boat?"

"Cabin in front," Donny said, "cabin in back."

"I'm just going to stay out here and look at the stars," Noah said.

"Me too, mate." Jack said. "Thanks for the hospitality."

Peggy's storming out had rattled Kate a little, but she didn't want to mention it. "This is pretty far out. I'd like to own a boat someday."

Donny flashed a smile at her then.

If she would have registered what it meant, if she would have not been so numb but would have recognized it, then she thought, much later, that she could have prevented what happened next.

Steph said, "I'll crash in the front cabin, if you want to crash in the back one."

"That sounds fine," Kate said.

"I mean. We could probably both crash in one cabin, but I think that would require cuddling."

Kate laughed. "I'm hip to whatever."

The gin finally took her over, and Kate didn't remember stumbling to the front cabin. She remembered seeing Noah and Jack, with their legs bent toward one another, hoping they were having an interesting conversation. She remembered saying goodnight to Steph, and Steph laughing. "Are you blitzed Library? See you in the morning." And the next thing Kate knew, she was waking up with Donny's body on top of hers.

"You're just like honey, like Marco told me."

Kate came to. She was disoriented, but aware.

A pain.

Donny?

She struggled under his weight. He had her wrists pinned up over her head. "What are you doing? Get off of me!"

"What's the matter, *señorita*? Am I not as big as Marco?" He smelled like vomit.

"Get the hell away from me!" she pushed him.

She pushed him again at the chest with all her strength. He stood up, holding the sheet with a fist below his waist. Kate tried to cover her whole self with the blankets. She still had her shirt on, but, pants?

What are you doing? Kate thought. *What is happening?* "Get the hell away from me. You're—you have a girlfriend."

What just happened? Kate pulled her knees up against her chest and backed up against the mirror on the wall. She heard a stomping on the stairs and saw Noah's silhouette.

"What's going on?"

Kate was stunned. Noah grabbed Donny by the throat. "What the fuck, man. What are you doing?" Donny held the blanket at his waist and Noah pushed him against the wall. "What the fuck are you doing to her?"

Steph and Jack appeared. Kate's voice trembled out. She didn't recognize it as her own. "I just woke up. I don't know . . . what he's doing."

Noah slammed him against the wood again and said, "You think you can stick your dick wherever you want, whenever you want?" Noah was bigger than Donny, and stronger. He punched him in the eye, and it instantly swelled.

"Kate, are you all right?" Steph rushed around the guys and put her arm around Kate's shoulder.

"Fucking creep," said Jack. "I knew you were a creep, but really?" Noah slammed him against the wall again. And with a crazed look in his eyes, punched him another time. Donny touched the blood seeping down his face, but he didn't fight back.

"She wanted it," Donny said. "Can't you see how she's just bursting with free love? Marco said she couldn't get enough." Noah punched him in the stomach, and Donny folded forward.

"I was asleep," Kate said. "I just woke up and—"

"You asshole. How dare you?" Steph gathered up Kate's jeans from the floor and pulled her from the bed, past the guys, to the bow of the boat. Kate, stunned and crying, put her pants on leg by leg. "I didn't want that," she said. "I didn't ask for that."

"I know," said Steph. "Fucking men and their sick, fucking

superiority complexes." She wiped Kate's eyes. "Let's get out of here."

Steph half carried Kate as they crawled off the boat. Kate's legs were heavy as lead, and she kept stumbling over her feet. They made it down the dock and found their way to Peggy's car. Peggy was in the back seat, passed out.

"Peggy, get up. We've gotta go."

"What?" Peggy rustled.

"Keys," Steph said. "Where are your keys?"

CHAPTER NINETEEN

Steph exhaled a fog of cigarette smoke out of the car window. "The dorms should be back open by now. What time is it, Peggy?"

"Seven-thirty."

Steph lit another cigarette and handed it to Kate.

"What happened?" Peggy asked, rubbing her eyes.

"Your creepy boyfriend just raped Kate."

That word stung Kate's bones. *Rape?* She hugged her knees and shook and smoked. Her eyes burned; her body hurt. She could still smell his stale body odor on her skin.

"Are you sure?" Peggy asked.

"Pretty sure," Steph said, "that if a guy puts his dick in you while you're sleeping, that it's called rape."

Kate hugged her knees tighter. She tried not to feel anything. She tried not to think.

Peggy seemed to sober up quickly. "Fucking creep is right. I'm done with guys. I'm sorry; I—are we going to call the sheriff?"

"It's up to Kate." Steph turned to her. "Jesus, you're white as a ghost. Do you want us to call the sheriff?"

Kate shook her head, *no*. She kept shaking her head, *no*. She wished she would have been awake, so she could have said *no*.

DAYS CAME AND PASSED, and Kate went through the motions. She went to work, paid her rent, and came home. She barely went out. Noah came by and picked her up every night at The Wave, so she didn't have to walk home alone in the dark.

Sometimes he came in and chatted, and sometimes he didn't. When he invited her out, she would say that she needed to save money. She needed to feed her cat. She needed some rest after a long workday.

Most nights she woke up in the middle of the night feeling like someone was in the room. She'd get up and check the door, look out the window, curl back up and hug herself to sleep, feeling that any minute she could wake up to Donny's face again, hovering over her.

Noah had beaten Donny up badly enough to put him in the hospital. The sheriff came around questioning them, and when they told him the story, he said there was nothing he could do unless Kate filed a report. Kate didn't want to do that. Donny's major was criminal justice, and his dad was the biggest lawyer in the county.

She didn't think the sheriff would believe her, after he'd seen her that day on the beach with Marco. She didn't want to go through the shame of explaining that she had been drunk. That she had been passed out. That she had been drinking to close off her heart.

Kate didn't tell her brother, or her dad, either. She didn't know what they'd do. And what would her mom say? That she had been drinking too much. That nothing good happened after ten o'clock.

Kate believed, deep down, that somehow it had been her fault. She'd set out to drink too much that night, to forget

Marco Del Rio and her heart. It all just got out of hand. She still felt confused about the whole thing, filthy. And somehow, guilty.

There was talk around town. People stared and whispered. She detached from her friends at work, distanced herself from her college friends, and on Thursdays, she served drinks to Marco, the new brunette, and all the other girls who came around.

CHAPTER TWENTY

November, 2014

Skylar stopped reading. In Curtis' face, she saw a sadness she hadn't seen since the funeral.

He scratched his chin. "I'm guessing Mom never told you about this, either."

Skylar shook her head.

"I don't understand. Why didn't she tell someone? The authorities?"

"It's not that easy." Skylar wondered if her mom had told their dad.

"I don't understand. I just—has something like this happened to you?"

Skylar hadn't ever told him.

"Yeah? What the hell, Skylar? Why didn't you tell me?"

She put the letter down.

Her therapist had said that it was healing to talk about it, if the topic ever came up. She never brought it up. "It was college." She cleared her throat. "I was at this frat party." Maybe she hadn't dealt with it all. "I passed out on the couch, and when I woke up, my pants were on the floor and I was bleeding." She felt a stabbing pain below her waist. "But there was nobody around."

Curtis scooted closer to her on the bed. "Why in the hell didn't you tell me?"

"It's confusing," Skylar said. "I didn't know how. It's not just me. It . . . happens . . . "

To more women than not, she'd learned from her therapist. It was the last time she had more than one drink in front of anybody she didn't know.

"If you don't tell anybody, then it's more likely to happen to somebody else."

"I know," Skylar said. She hadn't felt these emotions for years. Shame, guilt, embarrassment, fear: second-guessing her choices after it happened. Sick to her stomach.

"Why the silence? I thought we told each other everything?"

"Well, what would you have done if I had?"

"I'd have flown to campus and—"

"Killed him?"

"Probably."

"Right. And then you would have been in trouble. Why didn't I tell the police?"

His voice softened. "Yeah."

"It was a frat party. It was my word against thirty rich freshman boys, who were already training to be in the 'good old boys' club.' I guess I wasn't brave enough. I just wanted to feel okay again."

"I need some air." Curtis stood up and stretched his legs. He let a tear slide down his cheek, hugged her and said, "I'm so sorry," before he headed up the stairs.

CHAPTER TWENTY-ONE

November, 1964

Winter came to Florida. The nighttime air was cooler than Kate imagined it would be, a wet-cold. One Thursday she stood out back at work, dragging from a cigarette. Letting herself shiver. She had not brought her winter coat to Florida.

Marco had been hiring out his gig at The Wave for a while now to his friends, but tonight he must not have been able to find a cover. Her heart didn't flutter anymore when she saw him, anyway. He was simply another character at the beach in a blur of characters. She navigated his presence now as if a giant sheet of ice surrounded her body.

When the door opened after his set, she jumped momentarily until she saw him. She put her eyes onto the gravel and stayed still. Maybe he was getting something out of the van, but he stopped.

"Katie Bella. How are you?"

"I'm fine, how are you?" She had her arms wrapped around her waist, hugging herself. She tried to relax. She hadn't spoken to him in anything but niceties for weeks. But she had wondered about his dog. "How's Henry?"

"He is good," Marco said, taking a step forward. Kate took a step back. "I got him back. And I changed the locks again."

"That's good."

There was one question she'd been rolling around in her mind lately about the bad night. She had been irresponsible, drank too much, and had put herself in an unsafe situation. This she had learned. This she knew.

But there was this one piece she couldn't rationalize or believe.

Maybe it was the way the beach tonight in the dark reminded her of a first snow in Ohio, and she missed her family. Maybe she missed connecting with someone she loved. Maybe she was ready to talk about it. Something in her warmed, and she asked in a whisper. "You told Donny?"

The confusion and hurt all welled up in her eyes.

"I *am so sorry*." His deep voice cut through the shield she'd built around her, but still she would not let herself feel. "Donny was worried about Peggy. I was trying to reassure him." He took a step toward Kate, and then put his foot back. "I guess I said too much." He studied her face. "I am sorry."

Although his vulnerable expression pained her, and she wanted nothing more than to crumble into his arms and cry, she changed her mind. All these months she'd been able to stay together, to stay composed, and now, here, she was losing control. She couldn't feel all of this. She wasn't ready. It was too much.

"Great set tonight," she stammered. She flicked her cigarette into the bucket and walked inside.

Noah joined her inside the apartment after work, and she poured them both a glass of chardonnay. He was acting funny again, his quiet confidence transformed into something that she couldn't quite place.

"What's up with you, Noah? I can tell you're thinking hard about something." She sipped her wine and took off her work shoes. "How is it going with Jack?" Queen Kitty jumped up on Noah's lap.

"I got a draft letter today. They're calling me into the Army."

Kate couldn't believe it. "What? What are you going to do?"

"I guess I'm going to go and be a soldier. For our country." He made a fist and swung it up like Rosie the Riveter, from the old World War II posters.

"Noah, no. Can't you get out of it somehow?" Her face crinkled.

"If you keep moving your face like that, you'll get wrinkles." He sighed. "I don't think so." He gulped some wine and pulled out a cigarette.

"Can't you go to Canada or something?" Kate hadn't read the newspaper in a while, but the chatter around work was that the conflict in Vietnam was getting worse. She could not imagine her life without Noah, even for a few days.

"I'm not much for cold weather, Kate. Plus, it feels like I would be on the run."

"But there has to be some other option."

"If I were enrolled in school or something, but . . . ." He laid his head on the back of the small couch and stared at the ceiling. "There is a box that I could check on the paperwork," he closed his eyes, "that asks if you are . . . like me. But, my family. My safety. The government. I can't."

Kate tilted her head.

"I leave in three weeks. Basic training, and then, I don't know."

"Why you?" Kate asked.

She knew other guys were getting letters too, but so far none of her friends. Everyone had to sign up on their eighteenth birthday, but Noah was twenty-one.

"I have a feeling that the sheriff and the county prosecutor might have had something to do with it. About Donny."

The hair rose on Kate's arms. "You mean after the night on the boat?" She tried to rub off the chills.

"I was surprised they didn't press charges against me. I mean, I roughed him up pretty bad. But then, I knew they didn't believe me. Donny's story was that I was coming on to him. He said that he punched me in defense. Not that he, you know, you."

Kate couldn't believe it. "Do you mean if I would have gone to the sheriff then maybe this wouldn't have happened? What about Jack? Did they get his story?"

"Jack's, you know, Jack. He doesn't want anything to do with the law. I told them it was all me. That I was only defending you. But, we can't think about what ifs and maybes now. I'm going to go, Kate. I'm not afraid to serve our country. I'll be proud to."

Noah lowered his voice. "I would do that again, in a heartbeat. Donny deserved every punch I gave him." He stubbed out his cigarette, "I might have killed him if Jack wouldn't have been there. I grew up having to fight. I didn't have a choice. Sometimes everything just goes red. I, you know, lose my mind." He straightened up. "You're my best friend."

"Oh my gosh, Noah." She moved to the couch, hung her arms around his neck and hugged him. She didn't say anything for a while, just hugged her friend, wondering for the right words. "You're my best friend, too."

Noah sat back up. "Which is why I wanted to talk to you about Marco."

"Marco?" Kate slid a Marlboro out of her pack and opened one of the windows to the sound of night crickets. A beach breeze came through the screen and dispersed the smoke.

Noah seemed guilty. "After the night at his house, the campfire, I changed my mind about him. And I should have told you,

I invited Marco to the Love-In." He rubbed his palms on his jeans. "He doesn't normally come out much during the day, you know, he likes to keep a low profile." He passed Kate the ashtray from the table. "I know I warned you about him, but, I've been studying people who love each other for years. Watching the way people look at one another and trying to figure out how to get what they've got." Kate set the ashtray on the side table and focused on his words. "I see the way you tune up when he comes into the room. And I see the way he looks at you. Of all the girls that come around, I've never seen him look at anyone like he's dreaming. When he asked about you that night at The Parrot, his eyes lit up and something came over him. He's different when he's with you. People can change," he said. "I think he's changing."

Noah crossed his legs and his foot bounced, his thong sandal hanging from his toes. "So, I told him you would be at the Love-In, and that you would be happy to see him." Queen Kitty stood up, turned herself on his lap, and laid back down. "I'm sorry I didn't tell you. I shouldn't have gotten into your business."

This was news. Kate remembered the beautiful day and night with Marco. Watching the sunset. Dinner on the water. Her body and her heart warmed up. "That was one of the most amazing days of my life," she said, almost in a whisper.

"Have you talked to him yet? After the Gina morning?"

"No, not really."

She had asked him how his dog was.

"Love just doesn't come around all the time, Kate. When your heart opens up, you have to honor it. Listen to it. Even if it's in a different package than you thought it would be in. All of us have a past. Real love can embrace that, and figure it out."

Kate stood, found the wine bottle and topped off both of their glasses while considering his words. "What about Jack?" She took a large gulp of the buttery white. "How's it going with him?"

Noah shrugged. "When we're alone, we laugh and kiss and talk about our dreams. But then whenever people come around, he turns on his bullet-proof personality, and it's like I don't even exist." Queen Kitty nudged his hand for an ear scratch. "It's not safe, I know, but he barely *looks* at me in front of anybody. Even you and Steph. It makes me feel kind of cheap, you know? Like, I don't mean anything to him."

Noah's eyes hazed up and Kate didn't know if it was the wine, the smoke, or the emotion. "I just want to spend more time with him, I guess. I like the way I feel when we're alone together. When nobody else is around."

This touched Kate in a deep place. Somewhere subconscious that she had been ignoring.

CHAPTER TWENTY-TWO

The day Noah shipped out, Kate got a call from her father. It was unusual for him to call her long distance, though she was so glad to hear his voice.

Stan asked her how she was doing, and when she answered briefly, he said, "I have cancer."

"What, Daddy?"

"The doctors tell me there are some treatments available, so I'm just going to follow their lead." He paused, and she tried to process his words. "Don't stop your life for me, Kate. Your mom tells me you're really happy there in Florida. She worries about you. You know how your mom is. But I know you've got a head on your shoulders, so don't come home on my account."

"*Dad.*" She choked back the cry rising in her throat.

"My little free spirit. Follow your heart. I'll be okay. I'll have your mother call you next week when we know more."

She never argued with her father, and so she didn't now.

"I love you," she said.

"I love you, too."

Kate hung up the phone in disbelief.

Jim called the next day.

"Don't tell Mom and Dad I called you. I talked to the doctors. If you want to see Dad alive, come home. Soon."

She folded herself to her knees, sat down on the floor, and cried.

At work that night, Kate felt chilled to her bones. It was Thursday. Marco played and sang on the deck, but even the locals must have been hunkered down to avoid the cold. There were hardly any customers.

Linda left early and so it was only Captain, Kate, and Marco on the clock. A few brave regulars straggled in to have dinner, but nobody stuck around to listen to the music.

A light fog hovered over the water. "Do you want my jacket, Katie?" Marco asked when they were alone on the deck. "I can see you are freezing."

A numbness like Kate had never known had overtaken her. She didn't have the energy to resist him tonight.

"Okay."

He draped his jean jacket over her shoulders and gently pulled her closer to him. Her body responded, as it always had, to his touch. She smelled the musky scent of his cologne from the collar and remembered being wrapped in his sheets and tangled against his body.

"Thank you," she said, and pulled away. She sat down at table eight and lit a cigarette.

"What would you like to hear, Bella?"

"How about some Bob Dylan?"

Marco rolled his eyes and said, "Whatever you wish."

He played, "The Times They Are a Changin'." Kate smoked and thought about her dad. About Noah. How had life gotten so complicated in such a short time? Gray clouds moved over the bay, in front of the moon, and Kate wished she could see the Big Dipper.

A pelican dove through the mist and disappeared again, as quickly as it emerged.

"I wrote a new song." Marco squinted his eyes. "Would you like to hear it?"

"Okay," Kate said.

He started the music right away, as if he didn't want to talk himself out of it, and he led with the guitar. The sound waves tugged at her. Marco looked down at his hands as he played, then he sang.

"She's covered in stars. She's holding my heart." Kate had a vision of their first night, swimming. "Her body is bathed in moonlight, swimming at midnight, I'm wrapped in her arms."

As the harmonies swirled around her, she felt like her soul was being lifted around the edges of her body.

"She's holding my soul," the guitar twinkled. "I've lost all control. Her eyes are like sunset horizons, and I can't stop smiling, she's so beautiful." He raised his head from the guitar to meet her eyes. Kate put one hand on the table to steady herself.

"Now she's in my dreams," he almost whispered, "and she is my queen. But she doesn't see, how she affects me, when we are at sea." Certainly, he wasn't singing a song about her, right? She was just one girl, in a long line of girls. A daisy in Marco's big bouquet of women.

Maybe it was about Gina. Maybe it was about the new brunette, who had been absent for a couple of weeks, to Kate's delight. No way he had written a song for her.

This is what she thought, but what she felt was something different.

"Now we're in the bar, I'm playing guitar," Kate suddenly couldn't keep his gaze. It felt too powerful, too penetrating. It might overtake her. She fumbled in her pack for another cigarette, even though she'd just finished one. "She's hiding her eyes away, there is fog in the bay, but she has my heart."

Kate lost track of where her body ended and where the sky began. As if the world was trying to turn magical again.

And then he rolled into Spanish, "Regresa a mí. I am not

what they say. Forget all the stories they told you, I just want to hold you, you are the girl of my dreams." He peered at her and smiled shyly.

"Sus ojos son como nadar en las estrellas, your eyes are like swimming in stars. Your smile is like sunshine, your mind is like diamonds, I just want to know who you are." He fell deep into an instrumental then, and Kate lost herself, despite herself. Despite the warnings, and the other girls. The drawbridge was opening.

He slowed it down and sang quietly, "If this is a dream," she tried to peer at him, but she felt naked and averted her eyes. "Then I'll stay asleep. I wish you could see, how you affect me, to infinity."

He ended in a sweet, high riff of harmonics that made Kate's toes tingle, a sensation that traveled all the way up through her body and into the foggy night.

She wanted to fall into his arms. She wanted him to hold her safe while she cried, and cried, and cried. She wanted to kiss him, she wanted to touch him, she wanted to fold into his body and let him have his way with her, him and only him. Kate wanted to wake up every morning in a dream; she wanted to feel this magical forever.

But before she could say anything, Steph tromped out to the deck, in a scarf and a hat, with Captain right behind her.

"Hey guys, how's it going?" Steph assessed Kate. "You okay, Library?"

It took her a few seconds to form words.

"I'm just, hot. I mean, cold. I mean, Marco was playing a song, and I got kind of, lost in it." She knew Captain saw her blushing, but he didn't say anything.

He reached over Kate and ashed his cigarette. She wasn't exactly blushing. She was burning.

"Thank you," Marco said to Kate as if he were saying it to an audience of thousands, and then he adjusted the strap against his chest, tucked his guitar under his arm, and lit his own smoke. "It's new." He held Kate's eyes with his. "I'm still working on it."

"Good job, Marco," Steph said, in a tone as if she were talking to her little brother. "So, Timbale's playing at a jazz club on the other side of town, you guys want to go?"

CHAPTER TWENTY-THREE

The four of them piled in the van. Marco drove, and Kate sat in the passenger seat. Captain and Steph bumbled around from the back seats to the mattress in the way-back. Captain asked Marco a million questions, as if he were a movie star.

Kate stayed silent, enjoying everyone's company, wondering if what had just happened, had really happened.

The three shared a joint, and Marco leaned into Kate as always, to kiss her, and exhale into her. She caught a faint brush of his lips and his tongue before he got out of the van and opened the door for her. She was *feeling* again. Like she lived in a neon universe. In love with her life, with adventure, and with Marco.

A thought of her father crawled in.

"What is the matter, Bella?"

"I miss Noah. And—" She wanted to tell her friends about her dad, but for some reason she didn't. "I'm having a really nice time." He squeezed her hand, and they walked toward a one-story building with a small spotlight above a sign that read,

"Junior's Place." A man with dark skin and braided hair greeted them at the door.

"How's it going?"

"Good, Man," Captain said.

"All right. All right."

Steph said, "We came to see Timbale."

"Right on. Dollars for the musicians?"

They paid the admission and walked into the smoky bar. Marco held Kate's hand at her back.

"What do you guys want?" Steph asked. A woman sat at the bar in a sparkly red dress, smoking a long, skinny cigarette.

Steph approached her. "Hi, I'm Steph and this is my friend Kate. Is it okay if we sit here?" She gestured to the open bar seats.

"Sure," the woman said, "I'm Melaney. Welcome to Junior's."

"Thanks." Steph leaned in and squeezed Melaney's hand. Kate smiled.

There were maybe a hundred people here, dancing and laughing. When the bartender came over, he greeted them warmly. Kate adjusted her eyes to focus.

"What's happening?" he said.

"We're here to see Timbale," Captain said, not missing a beat. "He plays drums with Marco."

Marco waved his hand from the hip. As they received their drinks, a guy on the other side of the bar lifted his drink in cheers. They all cheers-ed him, and then cheers-ed each other. The band played some blues and then some jazz; the lead played the trumpet with a mute on it, so his notes sounded like a human cry.

"This is the kind of music I love," Marco said. "Real music comes from the soul." Kate hadn't heard anything like this before. She watched and listened as the band seemed to create their own emotions with the sounds.

The music felt light, and then heavy, and then light again. As if they were having their own journey. The tone of the room changed with them. Someone yelled, "Yeah," when they seemed to be celebrating, and then when the music quieted, and the trumpet man played a solo, someone said, "All right."

Everyone clapped when they finished. Marco whistled. "Timbale says they do not even rehearse. These guys are so good, they just show up and know how to play together."

Timbale set down his drumsticks and came over to greet them. "Hola Katie."

"Hola Timbale." Kate loved their familiar banter.

He winked at Melaney then greeted the others. "How do you like the show so far?"

Jack staggered in. Kate was surprised to see him. "You left me, Steph, what's with you?"

"You were taking too long, Jack. I'm glad you made it. How'd you get here?"

"I caught a ride." He wasn't wearing shoes.

When the band started playing again, the lead singer said, "We're going to need everybody to get on their feet for this one." They started in on an upbeat song. Marco led Kate to the dance floor.

A man with glowing eyes approached them and said, "Do you know The Frug?" He demonstrated a dance like the Twist, but with his upper body shaking and rolling to the music. He gestured to Melaney at the bar, and she put out her cigarette and joined him. Kate and Marco followed their moves and laughed.

Pretty soon, Captain and Steph and the whole bar were dancing. The room moved and pulsed with big, exuberant fun. She and Marco twirled and rolled and shook and gyrated, keeping up with each other's bodies. Melaney stepped in to dance with Marco, the gentleman stepped in to dance with Kate, and they stayed in the moment, checking in every so often with the others' eyes.

It had taken her mind off the sadness.

At the end of the show, they piled into the van and rode back out to the beach to Marco's house, to wind down and finish the night. Timbale had brought Melaney over, and Captain and Steph were enjoying each other's company.

Henry was delighted when Marco opened the door. He greeted them with his wet nose against their hands, and then ran outside. Kate noticed one of the guitars was missing from the walls.

"Where is your guitar?"

"I had to sell it," he said, matter-of-factly.

"What for?" It was probably none of her business.

"To take care of my daughter," he said.

The music in Kate's head screeched to a halt. "You have a daughter?"

Marco ran a hand over his hair and when Kate didn't say anything, he continued. "Yes, I have a daughter."

He has a daughter? Is that something that he should have told her?

"Noah did not tell you," he said. "Of course, he didn't. Noah is a confidante. Her name is Lily. She is three. I try to see her as much as I can, but her mother is complicada."

"Noah knows about her?" *Why didn't he tell her?* Kate paid special attention to the tone of her voice. "Where does she live?" Kate's world was crashing down against her again. Marco has a daughter? And with whom, and was this too much for her?

"In Clearwater." He reached for his wallet and pulled out a polaroid picture of a beautiful bronze-faced child with dimples and black curls. "When I get to see her, I take her fishing, and we look for dolphins."

Though she had wanted to take him out into the ocean and play in his eyes, sit around the campfire and banter with their friends, she wasn't sure she could take this last bit of information.

The neon universe seemed dull all of a sudden, her mind cloudy again.

"I think I need to sleep. I'm really tired."

"Sí, this is bothering you," Marco said. Could he always read her face? "I wanted to tell you, but I did not want my past to scare you away." He touched her cheek. "I was waiting for the right time . . . do you want to talk about it?"

"I'm just very tired." She turned away from him to sit on the bed. When would she be able to actually talk about her emotions?

Kate took a deep breath and tried not to implode with the news of her father, and now this. She was confused.

"You can rest in my bed." Marco took her hand.

As he pulled down the covers he said, "When you are ready to talk, I am ready to listen. But I will give you time."

She stayed silent and closed her eyes.

"I am going to sit with our friends, but I will come back to be with you. Eres mis sueños," he said. "Of my dreams."

She didn't feel much like a dream girl right now. He kissed her on the forehead.

Her eyes jolted open. "Will you lock the door?"

Marco lowered his eyebrows, but he went to his dresser, opened a small wooden box, and pulled out a key. He hesitated, and then pulled out a brown leather bracelet, braided, with an anchor charm hanging from it.

He sat back down on the bed. "I want you to have this." He tied it around her wrist and rubbed his finger up and down her arm. "It is made by my mother, for protection. If you get stuck anywhere, anytime, my heart is the place where you can always anchor." He kissed her softly. "Lock the door from the inside. I will keep the key here." He slid it into the pocket of his jeans. He closed the door behind him. Kate got up and turned the lock.

She wrapped herself in his scent, and remembered their nights in the ocean, under the moon. Her mind wandered to

Lily. Marco's daughter was a symbol of love, for sure, but a symbol of love without Kate. With someone else. He had this whole other family, this love, this life that didn't include her?

The world had overwhelmed her. She closed her eyes.

She dreamt she was throwing stones into the grand, large ocean.

Abruptly, she awoke at the sound of the door and her body tensed.

"Marco?"

"Sí, Katie. It is me." He crawled into bed next to her. She smelled campfire on his skin and kissed his shoulder blade before falling back to sleep. When she woke up, there was a train whistle in the distance. Marco's arms were wrapped around her tightly, his body spooned her from the back.

She rubbed the sleep out of her eyes and thought about her dad. She needed to tell Marco that she had to go away for a while. The song he'd played for her rang in the back of her mind and her heart welled up. She remembered dancing at Junior's. She kissed him on the shoulder again.

He stirred. "What time is it?"

"It's eight-thirty."

"Oh my gosh," he said, rubbing his face. "I am late." He kissed the back of her neck, put on his shorts and a shirt, and came to kiss her once more.

"Are you okay?"

"It is my day to pick up Lily. Make yourself at home here, okay?" He rushed out the door.

Kate found her clothes and wandered out to the bonfire where she found Captain and Steph, Timbale and Melaney bundled up, yet still asleep by the fire. Henry was inside, and the ocean rolled over itself.

Before she left, Kate decided to leave Marco her phone number. On a piece of one of her waitress tickets she wrote,

Dear Marco, you left me too early. I enjoyed your song and our dance, Kate. 555-2468.

She didn't want to wake everybody else up, so she walked down the beach.

The water was cool, but at least she felt something.

She picked up shells and petrified wood, and threw them into the water, hoping she could throw her worries away, saying a prayer with each one. She threw one for her father. She threw one for her mother. She threw one for Noah, and she threw one for herself and Marco. After the others got up and around, Timbale drove them all back to The Wave, and Steph drove Kate home.

Steph sat straight up, with her hands at ten and two, a cigarette in her left hand and the window rolled down. "So what happened with you and Marco?"

"We slept. What happened with you and Captain?"

"Oh my gosh, he's so much fun."

"Steph," Kate said. "My dad is sick. I need to go back home for a while."

"Oh my gosh, Library. I'm so sorry."

In the next few days, Steph helped her pack up her clothes and agreed to keep Queen Kitty for an indeterminate amount of time.

Kate kept the anchor bracelet on, and every time she saw it, she wondered if Marco would call. The first day she thought, *he's probably just busy.* With his daughter, or with whomever else. The second day she thought maybe she should call him, but she didn't.

By the third day, she had let the thoughts creep in of the other girls. *Gina. The Brunette. Lily's mom.* Maybe he was busy with them. What was the use, though? She didn't know how long she would be away. She boarded a bus, and soon found herself back home in Ohio.

CHAPTER TWENTY-FOUR

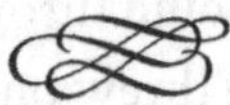

Snow fell from gray skies. The winter chilled her from the inside out. Christmas came and went.

The days at the hospital blurred into weeks, and Kate moved through the world like a ghost, with no physical body, and no thoughts of the future. She didn't leave her dad's side.

The doctors operated, and gave him radiation, but it didn't take long before his body rejected the treatments. Before he fell into a coma, he held Kate's hand and said, "My little free spirit, keep following your heart." With that, they said goodbye.

Kate held her mother's hand as they met with the preacher and made funeral arrangements. She sat with her brother on the porch and snuck whiskey with him from a flask, while he told stories that Kate hadn't heard before. She bought herself a new black dress.

"Dad was really proud of you," Jim said.

At the funeral she wouldn't let herself look at his body in the casket. That wasn't her dad in there; his spirit was gone, and this was just what was left.

His volunteer firefighter buddies showed up in their dress blues. Kate, her brother, and their mother stood greeting a line of never-ending people, when someone came out of the crowd that Kate didn't expect. Chad.

His blue eyes struck Kate from the middle of the line. She hadn't thought about him since her first week at The Wave. His blonde hair was clipped short, his jaw was squarer, and he had filled out into muscles. She didn't know if she was glad to see him. She felt very, very numb. Quiet and resigned.

He came through the line and greeted her mother. For a minute, Kate thought Rose might break down, though she hadn't yet. He shook Jim's hand, and then he hugged Kate in a warm, familiar embrace. Too warm, and too familiar. Kate didn't want to feel anything.

"I'm sorry about Stan," he said. "You look great."

"Thanks. You too. Are you on leave?"

"I've been discharged. I broke my ankle on a mountain in Qui Nhon. They sent me home for civilian work." He gathered her shaky hands with both of his. "I'm home, now, Kate. I can be home with you."

Home with you? She released his hands, rubbed hers on her dress and said, "Thanks for coming."

"Of course. You would do that for me."

Kate hadn't even thought to ask. A pang of guilt touched her in the stomach.

"How are your parents?"

He fidgeted in his pockets. "They're good. Mom's still baking pies for church every Sunday. Dad's still preaching anti-communism. In some ways everything's the same."

Everything wasn't the same. He stared into her eyes. Everything was *very* different. *She* was very different. But this wasn't the place to explain that.

"I need to greet the rest of the line," she said.

"Can I stop by? After this?" He turned to Kate's mom, who had been pretending like she wasn't listening. "Do you need any help around the house?"

"Yes," Rose answered for her. "We'd love to have you stop by." Her voice broke in a stifled cry. "I'm sure Kate could use a friend right now."

Kate's eyes welled up, but she kept her lips closed tight.

The house had a deafening emptiness, despite the train of people that came in and out, bringing food, bringing up memories, asking how Kate and her family were doing. The quiet moments were painful. "We're doing as well as can be expected," Kate's mom repeated.

Heather, Kate's best friend from high school came, a bottle of wine hidden in her winter coat. They bundled up, and the two of them sat out on the front porch passing the bottle back and forth, making small talk. A layer of snow had settled on the ground and Kate yearned to be warmed by the sun.

Cars cluttered the street. People chattered from inside. She pulled out her cigarettes and lit a match.

"Wow," Heather said. "This is unexpected."

"My dad just died."

Small snowflakes fell around the red brick pillars of the porch in the darkness like tiny butterflies. One of the streetlights flickered and buzzed. Heather's auburn hair poked out from under a pink wool hat. Kate was unable to feel anything but cold.

"Well, let me have one of those." Heather said. "It's been a long time." The scent of sulfur lingered after Heather sparked her flame. "How was Florida?" She coughed.

How was Florida? Kate hadn't had time to think much about it with her dad's doctor's appointments, and then him getting so sick, and then his body giving out. After that there were decisions. What kind of casket, what kind of burial, when and what time. Contacting family and friends.

She still wore the bracelet with the anchor, and when she noticed it on her arm, most of the time in the bath, she thought of Marco. She would topple and turn the memories of him, think of Steph and Linda, the moon and the ocean.

"It was fun. I really felt like myself there."

"What did you do?" Heather took a swig out of the bottle and handed it to Kate.

Kate leaned back in the chair. "I went to a Love-In."

"You did! I've been wanting to go to one of those! They had one over in Helen Park. But Harold keeps telling me they're drug-fests. He won't go."

"There are drugs there, but you don't have to take them." Kate tasted a memory of the brownie at the green.

"What was it like?" Heather asked. "Were there lots of real hippies?"

Kate laughed. "What's a hippie?"

"You know, like a Beatnik. Crazy poetry people who refuse to conform. I guess they travel around barefoot and write, and listen to jazz? I think I saw one once when I took the girls to the park."

Were her friends hippies? Maybe Jack. Maybe not. He had been known to go hitchhiking barefoot, but then lots of people were hitchhiking, and lots of people went around barefoot, especially at the beach.

"It was like a lot of people sitting on blankets, and handing out flowers, and dancing. It was like everybody bringing their best vibes together on purpose. And, I can't describe it, but I felt like I was, you know, buzzing with love when I left." Heather nodded in amazement. "And the feeling, like, lasted for a while."

"Buzzing with love," Heather said, "right on." She reached out her hand for the bottle.

The front door swung open, jingling the sleigh bell her mom hadn't packed up from Christmas. Kate startled, and then settled into a comfortable sense of entitlement, not caring what anybody else thought of her, even Chad.

She handed the bottle to Heather.

"Hey Chad," Heather said. "How's it going?"

He wasn't exactly thin before, but now he was bulky. He carried himself differently, straighter, and more intense.

"How are you," he said, squinting his eyes.

"I'm as good as can be expected," Kate said.

"Are you *drinking?*" He stared at the wine bottle. She took a drag off her cigarette and exhaled a large cloud of smoke into the snowy air. "And smoking. Well, that's different."

"Lots of things are different." Kate focused her eyes on the streetlight. It wasn't something she would have said a year ago. She would have silently let him have his own thoughts, without asserting herself.

"Well, I would have brought some beer if I would've known," he said. "Does your mom know?"

She looked over her shoulder to the window, covered by curtains. "I don't think so. There are a lot of people here."

"Your dad was a good man," Chad said. He touched her arm. She pulled away. She didn't want to talk about her dad. It was as if her own heart was missing.

"I think Jim is taking it really hard," Kate said. Her brother's eyes had been red and swollen since before the funeral. She hadn't seen him cry since they were children.

"As to be expected," Chad said. Kate hated all these things that people said when someone died, but she knew there were no other things to say.

He pulled a flask out of his pocket. "You girls want a hit?"

"Sure," Heather said. She took a drink, made a pucker face, and handed it to Kate.

"How's Harold?" Chad asked, as if it were a duty.

"He's fine," Heather said. "I left him home with the girls. The baby just turned one." Kate took a swig of bitter whiskey, and it warmed her up.

Heather had married her high school sweetheart. After graduation they bought a house, and she worked as the secretary for

Harold's contracting company. They had two daughters. Though Kate wanted to be supportive, and to be a good aunt, she had let that slip away when she moved. She had only met the first baby, when she was very small.

Though there was a time when Kate thought that she would be a good mother, she felt like she would have to trade her own life for it, until she made some money by herself. She felt like now, she might never get married and have kids. Maybe she was too selfish.

And somehow that had settled into her bones like the Ohio cold.

"Let's get out of here," Kate said. "You guys want to go somewhere?"

"I just bought a new Mustang," Chad said. "Where do you want to go, Kate?"

"Anywhere but here." She yearned for the ocean. For the adventure, for the music. For her friends.

"Wanna go out to my pond?" Chad said.

She didn't want to replay any memories with him, no matter how familiar they were. If their past came up, she didn't have the energy to deal with it.

"No, somewhere else?"

"The waterfall," Heather said. "River Road." Kate had only been there one time with Chad, and it had been an innocent enough night. At least if it were clear out there, she could see the moon reflecting on the water.

"Okay," Kate resolved.

Heather downed the bottle of wine, but not before offering the last drink to Kate. Kate swigged it and said, "Would you take the bottle?"

"Sure. I have to go, anyway. Harold's probably panicking by now, trying to get the baby to sleep."

"Right. Thanks for coming." Heather held her for a long time, and Kate fought the tears. After sniffles and promises to call, Heather tucked the bottle under her shirt and disappeared through the door, sleigh bells echoing into the void of night.

Silence and distance rose between them until Chad said, "One more?" Kate took another drink of whiskey, and then she let him lead her through the crowd of mourners, and out the front door. She tried to be as cordial as she could, but most of it was just a blur.

CHAPTER TWENTY-FIVE

$\mathcal{T}$he moon was only half-full, and clouds drifted past it in waves. Small puffs of snow fell and melted on the windshield. Chad pulled up to the edge and cut the lights but kept the car running. A deep limestone cliff dropped off twenty feet beyond them.

They sat on the hood of the car and their breath fogged up the air between them. Kate was cold, but she didn't want to get too close. Her down jacket had been hanging in the coat closet where she'd left it, and she was grateful for it now. The hood was still warm underneath them.

The falls cracked as a giant icicle fell into the river below, a faint trickling water sound.

"What was Vietnam like?" Kate asked. Chad tipped up the flask he had refilled on their drive. The falls reminded Kate of the sea.

"My work there was classified. I'm not at liberty to talk about it." He took a second sip before he handed it to her. "I got lucky, though, that I enlisted when I did. The word is they're going to be sending more and more guys, and they're not necessarily going to be able to choose their missions."

Kate still hadn't been following the news. She was afraid for Noah, so she just kept praying for him. That he was safe. That he was at ease. She had expected to get a letter from him in basic training, but she didn't. And now he didn't even know her address.

"My friend Noah is there. Noah Lee. Have you heard of him?" The whiskey burned her throat but warmed her chest.

"Doesn't ring a bell." He pulled out one of his own cigarettes. Kate shivered. "You made new friends, huh?" His tone was accusatory. Kate wasn't in the mood to be accommodating.

"I did."

"How many?" he asked.

She felt this on a different level. "I met good friends. The right ones."

"I hear it gets really hot there in the summer."

"It does. Hot, and the air is heavy." She used her gloved hand to warm her cold nose. "But I might go back."

"What do you mean, you might go back?" Chad scooted closer to her. "I'm home, Kate. I have a good job. We can have a future together. We can settle down and raise a family now." His jacket rustled over the hum of the engine as he reached over and put his arm around her shoulders.

The waterfall crackled. Another piece of ice fell from the falls and disappeared into a shattering echo.

She had put all possibilities with Chad into a tiny golden box in her mind and closed it. Then somehow, the box had disappeared.

"You just, stopped writing to me."

"Things got complicated."

Kate lit another cigarette.

Complicated.

The sound of footsteps crunched in the snow as two figures approached them. A tall scraggly man in a stocking hat and hood emerged. Chad jerked, reached in his pockets, and pulled out a knife.

"Chad," Kate said. A hound dog sniffed around in the snow at the man's feet.

"Who's there?" Chad asked.

"Billy Martin. Just taking my dog for a walk. I'm cool, dude." He put both of his hands out. Empty green gloves holding a leash. "I live up on the hill." The man told his dog to sit. "Are you cool?"

Chad settled his body. "Yeah, man, we're cool. Sorry." He turned to Kate. "I guess I'm always on alert these days." He put the knife back into his pocket.

"No problem, man," the guy said. "Are you a soldier?"

"Yeah." Chad rubbed the top of his head. "Just got home."

"I'm sorry for what they're doing to you over there." The dog sniffed at Kate's feet, and a small pile of snow stuck to its nose.

"I was just serving our country. There's no shame in that."

"Right," the man said. "Usually at this time of night, me and Boomer here say our prayers." The dog's ears perked up. "I've been praying for you all, but do you think what America is doing over there is right?"

Chad glanced at the flask and exhaled a line of white smoke toward the guy. "What do you do for work, Mr. Martin?"

"I work at the steel mill. Two months and I'll have thirty years in. Can't wait to get the hell out of the heat."

"Do you think it's right? What you're doing there?"

Billy didn't say anything. He pulled a cigarette out from his own chest pocket and said, "It makes me a living," and then he trailed off, looking over the falls.

"Yes, sir," Chad said.

"I should probably be getting home," Kate cut in. "Mother will be worried."

"Yeah," Billy said. "You'll freeze to death out here."

"Nice to meet you," Kate said, and they climbed back into the car.

"When's the last time you ate?" Chad asked as he warmed up the car and blew air into his gloves with his mouth.

"I'm not sure. The morning, maybe?"

"Let's stop at the diner," he said.

She didn't want to spend any more time with him, but she was hungry, and thinking of eggs and hash browns made her stomach growl.

Her old manager was there and gave her a big hug and her condolences. She told Kate she'd always have a job there if she ever wanted it back. Kate thanked her and tried to eat, but even bacon didn't taste good.

After breakfast they drove toward the sunrise, and Kate could see as far over the barren corn fields as she could see over the ocean. Despite the general discomfort of the cold, there *was* something beautiful about a fresh blanket of white snow softly covering everything.

Chad turned up the radio. The Beatles were on: "She Loves You." Kate thought of Marco.

When Chad put the car into park in the driveway, Kate squirmed. She didn't want to have a moment with him. She opened the door abruptly, said thank you, and closed the door before he could say anything.

The visitors had left tire tracks and footprints in the spongy snow. As she rushed past, she peeked into the garage and saw Jim's car. And her dad's. She felt a little sick climbing the steps to the back porch.

She tried to be as quiet as she could while she knocked the snow off of her boots, but the screen door creaked when Kate stepped into the kitchen. She thought her mother would be sleeping, but instead she was sitting at the dining room table. A tuft of steam wafted into the air from a freshly poured cup of coffee.

"Where have you been?" Rose asked.

"At the falls, with Chad." The last part didn't appease her mother the way she thought it would. Kate closed the door quietly. The oven door was open, spilling warm air into the kitchen. She began peeling off her hat, gloves, and jacket.

"No daughter of mine will be a spinster and stay out all night with boys she isn't married to. Nothing good happens after ten o'clock."

"Mom," Kate said, surprised. "We just went to the falls. And talked."

"And now you're lying to me." Lying to her? Kate didn't understand. She'd been living her own life for too long.

"I'm not lying." Kate wanted to sit at the table, but she was afraid that her mom would smell the smoke. "I'm tired, I need to go to bed."

"Kathryn Wyse, you will talk to me first. Sit down." Kate reluctantly sat. "Have you been drinking?"

"Yes," Kate said. Her mother sipped her coffee in a familiar sound that said, it's still too hot. Kate draped her jacket over the back of the chair.

"Have you been smoking?" The eyebrow up meant *angry*, but Kate also saw hurt in Rose's face.

"Yes." She had never been able to lie to her mom.

Rose put her head in her hands. "My husband is gone," she said under her breath. "And now my daughter is rebelling."

"Rebelling? I'm not rebelling. I was just out with my friends." She pulled the bottom of her shirt down over her jeans.

"Until daylight. All night. What did you do with him?"

"I didn't do anything, Mom. We went to breakfast. Chad and I are in the past. He, he is different than he was before, and I am too."

"Does that mean you're not going to marry him?"

"*Marry him?* He didn't ask."

"He asked a long time ago."

"And then he left me and *stopped writing*."

"He left for a noble cause."

"His last letter to me did not describe a noble cause. Would you like to read it?" Kate hadn't shared with her mom in words how much her heart had broken when Chad described his travels and all of the beautiful women around. Still, she thought she must have known.

"He was fulfilling his civil duty," Rose said.

Instead of sharing that pain with her, Kate tried to hurt her back. "Will you feel that way if Jim gets drafted?"

Her mother tightened her lips. Kate felt a pang in her heart for being so nasty. For her friend Noah. She wanted to tell her mother about him, but Rose wouldn't approve. She wanted to tell her how he'd stood up for her, twice, to protect her, but she couldn't explain it all. She wanted to tell her mother that she had fallen in love, even though she hadn't meant to. But instead, as her mother's eyes pierced hers, Kate said, "I have to go to bed, Mother. I'm tired. I love you."

Kate stood up and hugged her around the shoulders. Rose's warm fingers lightly brushed Kate's hands and then moved back to her coffee cup. As Kate closed her bedroom door, she heard her mother sniffle as if trying to breathe back tears, but Kate knew Rose wouldn't want her to hear it.

CHAPTER TWENTY-SIX

As the snow melted, Kate tried to get used to her life again. Nights spent sitting around watching The Lawrence Welk Show on television while her mother knitted. Everybody calling her *Kate*, instead of *Library*, or *Katie*, or *Katie Bella*. She helped her mom cook and clean, trying to find small moments of joy in her dad's memory.

Her dad's things were just as he'd left them: lottery tickets on the table, shaving cream on the sink, clothes hanging in the closet. As if he were going to come home any minute.

One morning in early April, she lay in bed, listening to the first robins home from their winter break. Sparrows were building a nest in the apple tree. The phone rang.

Kate got up, put her robe on, and went into the bathroom to wash her face and brush her teeth. Her tan had faded.

Staring into the mirror, she tried to remember who she was in Florida, how in love she once felt. How alive. Even though it was spring now, she still felt gray. The scent of her dad's talcum powder lingered after all of these months. She wanted to hear his voice.

Her mother knocked on the door. "Are you decent?"

"Yes, Mom," she said.

Rose opened the door a crack. "Chad's on the phone for you."

Great. He'd been calling, and she'd been avoiding him. He stopped by at least once a week, and Kate always tried to find a way to shorten their visit.

"Can you tell him I'm busy? In the bath?"

"Well, that would be lying, wouldn't it? You know I'm an honest woman."

"Uggh." Why wouldn't her mom just treat her like an adult? "Okay. Be out in a minute." She wiped her face in the towel and wanted to scream into it.

"Kate," Chad said, "I've been trying to get a hold of you. How are you?"

"I'm as good as can be expected," she said, wiping at her eyes. "How are you?"

"I got tickets for us to go to the race today. Johnny's riding in his new Chevy."

The race? "Oh, well, thanks, Chad. But I can't. I have to help my mom clean today." It was the best thing she could think of, but as she studied the cobble of rotting flowers and cards still on the dining room table, it sounded like it could be true.

"Clean? Well, I'm sure I can get you out of that. Let me talk to your mom."

Kate didn't want to go. She didn't want to tell him and disappoint him. She didn't want to do anything, actually, but lie on the couch and watch television. She reluctantly handed the phone to her mom. She didn't know what else to do.

"Oh, yes, Chad. Sure," Rose said. "Of course, she can come. Yes, of course, I can do the cleaning by myself." Her mother glared at her. Kate glared back. "I'll make sure she is ready." Rose hung up the phone. "He's picking you up at one."

"Mom," Kate said. "I don't want to go. I want to stay home. I want to spend time with you and Jim."

"Well, we'll be here. It's not every day that a handsome, young, successful man is calling to take you somewhere."

"But *Mom*. I don't even like him anymore. I mean," Kate trailed off.

"You mean you don't want to get married and have kids? This is your chance, Kate. You might not ever get any more chances. You just don't know." Her mom sat down at the kitchen table and scratched at a lottery ticket. "Love just doesn't come around all the time."

She froze. Noah had said those same words to her. *Love just doesn't come around all the time.* It made her think of Marco. She wanted to be in his arms, she wanted to swim. She wanted to dance with him, to hear him sing to her.

"You're going, young lady. Get ready."

Kate was out of energy to protest.

Maybe she could turn Chad off, somehow.

The race was loud and dusty, and everybody seemed to be cheering for somebody. Kate knew Johnny from high school, but even though she had a soda and a good seat, her heart wasn't in it. Chad had tried to kiss her when he opened her car door. She turned the other cheek with as much grace as she could.

"Chad!" A girl yelled from down the bleachers and waved. She climbed over a row of fans to get to them. Kate didn't recognize her.

"Karen," he said. "Hi." He rubbed his palms on his jeans.

"I hoped I'd see you here." She flipped her blonde hair and then gazed at him wide-eyed, like she was expecting something.

"Well," he said, "you did."

Was he stammering?

"Hi, I'm Kate." She chuckled. Maybe this was her way out.

"I'm Karen. Nice to meet you." Chad glanced at Kate then back at Karen. "Isn't this a great race? I mean, Johnny is really putting it to 'em?" She ended her statement with a question mark, as if she needed them to agree with her. The cars came around and the noise of the engines halted their conversation for an awkward moment.

"They keep on driving in circles," Kate said.

Karen flipped her hair again, but this time her eyes narrowed.

"It takes a lot of talent and precision to do what Johnny does," Chad said. "He's been leading the pack for almost seven laps now."

"Yeah," Karen said. "He's really in his zone."

Karen sat on the other side of Chad and they both whooped and hollered when the cars drove by. Kate wanted to go back home and go to bed. A woman walked up the steps of the bleachers, and for a minute Kate thought it was Steph.

It was just a girl who looked like her. Steph was in Florida; Kate was in Ohio. A longing took over her heart. She wanted to go back to the beach.

On the way home, Chad tried to apologize for Karen joining them, but Kate tuned him out, the same as the cars driving so fast for so long and going nowhere. In a different time and place, she might have enjoyed this. If Marco and her friends were there, or if she were at the beach.

AT HOME, Kate found a ham sandwich in the fridge, and sat at the table to eat it. Her mom was out in the garden. When she was finished, although it was too early to go to sleep for the night, she lay down anyway.

In a dream, Marco was holding a crown of orchids. Kate woke up to Jim opening her door.

"Kate," he said. "I'm going out. You want to go?"

The clock. Ten p.m.

"Mom says nothing good happens after ten," she said and rolled over. "Where is she?"

"Tomorrow's your birthday, you know. You have to start having some fun."

Her birthday. She had not looked at a calendar in weeks, and sort of hoped everyone might forget. "Come on. You've been moping around here for long enough. I'll take care of Mom. Let's go have some fun."

She wasn't sure if it would cheer her up, but she wasn't sure she could feel any worse. Kate got dressed and put on a little bit of makeup.

"Mom, we're going to meet Chad at The Limbo," he said.

"What are you going to do at The Limbo?" Rose asked.

Jim seemed so calm and cool. "We're going to dance, Mom."

Rose laughed. Kate hadn't seen her mom laugh in a long time.

"Okay," she said, "be careful."

In the car, "Downtown" came on by Petula Clark. Jim turned down the radio and asked, "What's up with you and Chad?"

"What do you mean what's up with me and Chad?"

"I mean," he tightened his grip on the wheel. "What's he saying to you? How do you feel about him?" Kate reached into the console and took out one of his Salem Lights.

"Do you mind?"

"It's fine," he said. "Mom doesn't think it's lady-like to smoke, though."

"I know," Kate said. "I know." She lit the cigarette and tried to blow the smoke into rings. "What's up with Chad and me? Nothing, I mean. How do I feel about him? I feel nothing. I feel like there's a big, empty pit in my stomach, and I feel like my heart is numb. He's, I mean, I don't really feel anything for him, anymore."

"Mom told me he would make a good husband," Jim said.

"She told me that, too, Jim. I'm not looking for a husband."

He lit a cigarette for himself. "You want to work your ass off for the rest of your life? At a diner? You know he'll be a good provider."

"I can't think about that, okay? I don't want to just be taken care of by a man. I want to do my own thing."

"Like what?"

"Like maybe, write. My friends in Florida were going to school and I might take a poetry class."

"Poetry, huh. That'll make you rich."

"I don't want to be rich," Kate said. "I just want to be . . ." what was the right word? Free?

"Happy."

Elvis came on the radio, "I Can't Help Falling in Love with You." Maybe he was right. She kept trying to talk herself into going to the diner, but every day she found something else to do instead. Her boss in Florida had said he would keep a job for her at The Wave, no matter how long it took for her to return. But why did she really want to go back?

"Jim, I met someone, in Florida, someone I like, a lot." Her stomach jumped.

"Oh, yeah? Miss, I-don't-want-to-get-married? Who is he?" Jim asked.

"He's kind. He's funny. He plays music."

"A musician?" Jim butted in. "Smart."

"What do you mean by that?"

"I mean, you know those guys in the band from high school? The Porch Swings? There are girls lined up all the way around their garage while they're practicing. I went to one of their parties. The girls just, fall all over around them. Because they play music?" He shook his head and said, "I should have kept taking those guitar lessons when I was a kid."

Kate didn't want to hear this, from her brother of all people. "I know," Kate said. "But Marco, is somehow, different."

"Marco," Jim said. "Is he Mexican? Mom's not going to approve of that."

"He's from Texas," she said. Kate trailed off thinking of his soft, velvety skin.

"Marco the Mexican musician," he smiled. "And my sister Kate. In rebellion."

"I'm not *in rebellion*, Jim. I'm living my own life. Anyway, what about you?" Kate stubbed out the cigarette in the ash tray. "How's your love life?" Their dad used to ask them that when they were kids. He turned his head over his left shoulder, and back to the front before he answered.

"I've kind of got my eye on this girl named Karen."

"Karen, like the blonde with big—"

"That's her. She's pretty, right?"

"I guess so. I met her today with Chad, at the race."

"I wondered where she was earlier," Jim said. "I called and left a message at her house to see if she wanted to meet up with us tonight."

It wasn't often that she didn't like somebody right away. She usually just liked people, but something about Karen put her off and she didn't know what it was.

"I got her into the back seat last week," he said.

"Jim," Kate said, "I can't," she put her hands over her ears and laughed. "Not everybody needs to know everything about you."

"I think she likes me. Or maybe she's just fast. But anyway, I can't stop thinking about her."

The word 'fast' hit Kate like a knife in the gut.

"Maybe she's not," Kate said, giving Karen the benefit of the doubt. "Maybe she really likes you, and she was just, you know, ready."

Cars were parked bumper to bumper all around The Limbo. Convertibles with their tops down, Fords and Chevys with their doors open. There were people everywhere, laughing and flirting. Guys held beer cans and cigarettes, and girls in short skirts giggled and whispered into each other's ears.

"Let's go in," Jim said. "See if anybody's dancing."

Inside was dark. Kate remembered being at Junior's. A cloud of smoke hovered over the dance floor and burned her eyes.

"Look," Jim said, grabbing her hand. "It's The Porch Swings." It was new to see a band playing on stage here. Usually they just had a disc jockey who alternated records while everybody danced.

"And there's Chad. And Karen." Kate stopped and folded her arms.

"Hey guys," Jim said.

Chad sauntered over to Kate and tried to put his hands on her waist. She removed them quickly and folded her arms back to her chest.

"Karen," Jim said. "He kissed her on the cheek. "I tried to call you earlier."

"Right. I'm sorry I didn't call you back. I thought I might just run into you." She glanced at Chad.

"Yeah, no problem," Jim said. "You wanna dance?"

"Sure," she said.

The band switched into a James Brown cover.

"*I Feel Good*," Jim sang, and started moving, leading Karen by the hand. Chad asked Kate to dance, and though she thought the song was catchy, she didn't want to.

"No thanks," she said. She couldn't remember the last time she felt good.

"Come on, Kate. You haven't had any fun since you've been back."

"Well, I haven't exactly been back on the best terms."

"I know. You want something to drink?"

"Vodka and cranberry," she said. Kate watched Karen and Jim on the dance floor. He twisted and jived, showing off his new moves. He was wearing their dad's wing-tip shoes, the ones he only wore for special occasions.

Karen's face didn't light up when she looked at Jim, but her eyes gravitated toward Chad. Kate didn't care. She didn't want to be with him, anyway. Maybe tonight she would be able to tell him. She hoped at least that Jim wasn't going to get hurt.

When Chad brought back the drink, she drank it down quickly. She watched the band as they played and sang. The lead singer looked her way and raised his eyebrows, which only made her think of Marco.

"What's on your mind, Kate?"

"Nothing," she said.

The lead singer said, "We're going to slow it down for a minute." They started to play a slow version of "My Girl," by the Temptations.

Chad said, "Excuse me," and ran up on the stage.

Karen and Jim joined Kate.

"What's he doing?" Jim asked.

"I don't know," said Kate.

The lead singer stepped back and Chad got in front of the microphone. He reached into his pocket and pulled out a box. The same box he had given to Kate when she was sixteen, with the ring in it. Was that hers? How had he gotten it?

The microphone popped and squealed when he grabbed it. He lowered himself down on one knee and said, "Kate Wyse. You're my sunshine on a cloudy day. Will you marry me?" Karen's mouth dropped.

No! Kate thought. Jim grabbed her by the elbow and ushered her through the crowd, until she stood right in front of Chad. His face twisted in the silence. *This can't be happening.* Everybody stared.

She'd been duped. She closed her eyes. Jim lifted her hand up and held it to Chad, who slipped the ring on her finger, jumped down from the stage, and kissed her quickly. *No.* She pulled away.

All eyes on her. The crowd began to cheer.

The lead singer took back the microphone and said, "Congratulations to Chad Smith and Kate Wyse. Everybody lift up your glasses in cheers!" Everybody cheered louder.

She turned to Jim and spoke softly. "Get me out of here, please."

"What?"

"Get me out of here, now, please. I can't do this."

He shrugged his shoulders at Chad, still on stage, and followed her out the door to the car.

"What are you doing, Kate? That was a beautiful gesture. He wants to be your husband."

"I don't want a husband," she said. "I don't want Chad to be my husband. Take me home, please, now."

Jim tried to talk to her on the drive, but Kate brimmed with anger and didn't say a word. Rose was waiting by the door when they got home.

"Congratulations," she said. "Where's Chad?"

"Mom," Kate almost yelled, but she stopped herself. "Did you give him the ring back?"

"Why, yes. It looks great on you."

Kate wriggled it from her finger. "It does not. I don't want it. I don't want to marry Chad." She began to cry. "He just embarrassed me in front of the whole town."

Jim fiddled with his belt loops. "Umm, Kate. You might have just embarrassed *him* in front of the whole town."

Kate heard her own voice getting louder. "I already told him I don't want to marry him. He knows. I don't know why he won't let it go. I don't love him, Mother," she said.

"Marriage isn't always about love," she replied. "You loved him in high school."

"I'm in love with someone else," Kate sighed. "I fell in love with someone in Florida. He's, well, he's amazing. I've, I've never felt like this for anyone else.

"And he's *Mexican*," Jim said. "A musician."

"Jim!" Kate said.

Other than the sheriff using the term 'brown boy,' Marco's heritage had never come up with anybody in Florida. Nobody there cared about that.

"Kathryn," Rose said. "Whom you've known for six months? Have you forgotten who you are?"

No. She hadn't. She was discovering who she was. She was finally, for the first time, speaking up for herself, asserting her own truth to her family. "I told you, he's from Texas."

This was new territory; she needed to speak carefully. She slowed down. "A man came on to me one night, the first night I wore a short skirt. He, tried to touch me and, Marco *saved* me. I mean, he came out of nowhere and had the guy on the ground so fast before he could hurt me."

Rose said, "Absolutely not. Not my daughter."

"But mom!" Kate was pleading now. "Maybe he doesn't feel the same way about me now, but he wrote me a song—"

Jim cut in, "That's what musicians do, Kate. They write songs for pretty girls to bed them."

"Jesus, Jim, thanks."

"Kathryn! You will not use the Lord's name in vain in my house, young lady." She lowered her tone. "You didn't lose your virginity to some—"

"Stop," Kate said. "Both of you." She squeezed her hands into fists. "I don't tell you how to live your lives, and I don't need you to tell me how to live mine."

She needed her dad. He would be on her side for this one. He would defend her and call her a free spirit and tell her she should be true to herself. He would hug her and tell her that it was going to be all right. He would talk to her mom. Reason with her later.

"If Dad were here, he would say I should follow my heart," she said finally.

"If your dad were here," Rose said sternly, "he would have drunk a bottle of whiskey by now, and he would not be able to form a coherent sentence."

Jim winced.

Kate ran into her room and slammed the door. She couldn't take either one of them right now. She was growing up. She was not their property.

CHAPTER TWENTY-SEVEN

"*H*appy birthday, time to get up." Rose's voice was cheerier than last night.

Kate rustled under her covers. She wasn't ready to get up yet. She wasn't sure she could face them. *They knew.* They'd both known that Chad was going to propose again and neither of them had told her.

Kate said, "I'm still sleepy."

"You've been asleep for twelve hours," Rose said.

"No, I haven't." She had spent half the night seething with anger. "Okay, well, I'll be out in a minute."

She wandered into the bathroom, again confronted with her dad's shaving brush. How long were they going to leave his stuff lying around? It didn't matter. Maybe she preferred it there, so she could remember. There was a white box with a pink bow on the dining room table. She had hoped everybody would forget her birthday this year.

The salty smell of bacon led her into the kitchen. Her mom had made her favorite: sunny-side-up eggs. "Thank you, Mom," Kate said.

Kate poured herself a cup of coffee. Rose stood over the

stove, carefully scooping bacon out of a skillet. She held each piece and let the grease drip, before she moved it onto a plate lined with paper towels.

Kate tore off a piece of toast and broke the egg yolk, watching the yellow seep over into the white.

"I don't think it's wise that you've been drinking and smoking," Rose said. "I don't think it's good for you." A raw piece of bacon sizzled.

"I don't have a problem with it. I only do it when other people are drinking and smoking." Kate dabbed the toast and put a creamy bite onto her tongue.

"What about the night Heather brought over the wine? The night of the funeral?" As Rose added more bacon, the sizzles intensified.

"Gosh, mom. Who told you about that?"

"It doesn't matter. I know you're in a lot of pain right now, and we all are. But I expect more from you. You're my daughter and—"

"I'm your daughter. But I'm an adult. I'm not your property anymore." She thought twice about the tone of her voice.

Her mother turned around and took on her sternest look, lips flat and an eyebrow raised. She pointed the fork at Kate. "I raised my daughter to honor her family. To respect God, her home, and to respect her elders."

"Well, maybe I want to go back to the beach. Which is my home, now. Maybe God and my elders could appreciate that."

Rose shot a brief look at Kate. "And how are you ever going to get there?" She turned back to the stove. The bacon sizzled even louder as she flipped each piece, one by one.

"I don't know yet." Kate had spent all her money on the bus ticket back home. Even the emergency money.

"I've arranged for you to stay here. I found you a respectable job."

"What?" Kate wanted to take another bite of the toast, but suddenly she wasn't hungry. "Where?"

"Chad's dad's shop. You start tomorrow." The bacon grease popped. Rose startled back, and then turned down the burner.

"Mom, I don't want to work for Chad's dad. What will I even be doing there?"

"You'll be a secretary. They already have one, but she needs some help."

"A secretary? Mom, no, please. I don't want to be someone's secretary, especially Chad's dad. Please. Can you call them and apologize, and tell them I won't be able to? Please, Mom?"

"Kate, you need some money. Your dad was not paid up on his insurance, so I'm going to need some help with the house payment, plus, those medical bills. And since you'll live here with me—"

"But Mom, I don't want to live here. I want to go back to my life in Florida."

"I need the help, Kate." Her mother's face hung lower and lower, but her voice stayed stern.

"What about Jim?" Kate said. "He has a good job. Can't he help with the house payment?"

Rose shook her head as she pulled out the last piece of bacon. "Jim needs to start saving for his own family. He shouldn't have the burden of his poor, old mother on his back."

Kate stood up so quickly, the chair scraped against the linoleum. "Do you know how ridiculous that sounds? Jim needs to save for his own family? He doesn't even have a girlfriend."

"Yes, he does. Her name is Karen."

"Karen? The blonde? The two times I've met Karen, she doesn't seem so hot on Jim."

"Watch your tongue, young lady," Rose said. "You will go and work for Chad's dad. You will call Chad today and tell him that you're sorry that you ran out of The Limbo last night, but you were just overwhelmed. You will tell him you will be honored to marry him."

"Mom," Kate pleaded.

"That's it! End of conversation."

Kate left her full plate and slammed the door to her bedroom. She tried to turn the radio on, but all she could get was static. She curled up into her bed. What was happening? Why was this happening? She wished Steph was here to make some sense of it all. Or Noah.

She could call Heather, but she was afraid that Heather would tell her that she should marry Chad. She laid her head on her arm and felt metal pressing into her cheek. The anchor bracelet. *My heart is the place where you can always anchor,* Marco had said.

She went to her drawer and fished out the piece of paper with his phone number on it. She stared at his handwriting, as if it were the only part of him she knew now. Kate waited until the kitchen became quiet. She snuck through the house, to the back door, and saw her mom in the garden. Even though it was long distance, and her mom would be mad at her when the bill came, she dialed the numbers. One at a time. The phone shook in her hands.

Kate's heart tightened with the first ring. She didn't know what she would say. On the second one she let out a deep breath. She just wanted to hear his voice. She checked that her mom was still out back. On the third ring, her heart dropped. She could always hang up.

The phone rang and rang, and he didn't answer.

She hung up the phone and a deep sob came from her soul. She went back to her room and let herself cry. How long had all of this pain been stuffed in her body? She missed her cat. She missed Noah and Steph. She missed feeling independent, like she belonged. She missed feeling free.

She cried until she didn't have any energy left, until all of the pain of doing everything her family always wanted her to do, subsided. Until her mind broke open into thoughts again. Slowly, they began to form sentences. Sentences that asked for solutions.

What could she do? How could she get back to Florida?

She could hitchhike, but that meant she couldn't take all her stuff; the trunk would be too heavy. And she'd only hitched a few times with her brother when they were in high school.

Could she hitch all the way? How would she eat? Maybe she could borrow some money. From whom? One of her uncles? They were always asking her dad for money. Maybe Jim. Probably not Jim. She could try to ask Jim, if she needed to. Maybe she should call Steph.

Kate crawled back into her bed and fell into a fitful sleep. She dreamt of Marco's face, and then Gina. Different places, with different people, and every time a new girl showed up and latched around his arm. Or sat down next to him before Kate could get there. Or stood right in front of him as he was singing.

In one, he kissed a girl right in front of her, from the stage, then went back to playing the guitar. In the last one, he was waving at Kate to come and sit with him on a porch swing, when a giant dog showed up between them, teeth baring and barking at her. The dream ended when she fell backwards, and the dog charged. She woke up cold and sweaty.

By now Marco had surely found some other girl to sing to, and Kate was old news. She hugged the comforter around her. What was she thinking, that she loved him? She didn't really even know him. Not as well as she knew Chad, anyway. At least not for as long.

Maybe her mom was right. Maybe marriage meant things other than love. Maybe a stable guy with a good job was what she should be interested in. Was there something wrong with her heart that she didn't love Chad anymore? Maybe she could try to learn to love him again.

In the mirror, she didn't recognize herself; her eyes were so swollen from crying. She found her mom on the porch snapping beans. Kate sat down next to her and grabbed a handful.

"Okay," she said to her mom. "I'll do it. I'll take the stupid secretary job and I'll agree to marry Chad, but only if you stay out of our business. I'm a grown-up now, Mom, and I can handle my own relationships."

"Oh, Kate!" Her mom stood up and hugged her. "I'm so proud of you and I'm so happy for you. I know he's going to make you happy; you just have to believe it. Then you can make me a grandmother." Kate snapped a bean, peeled back the string, broke off the ends, and tossed what was left into the bowl.

She didn't know what other choice she had.

Rose ran into the house and came back out with the birthday box. Kate wiped her hands on her mom's apron, opened the bow, and lifted out a wedding dress.

"It's only been worn once," Rose said. "When I married your father."

CHAPTER TWENTY-EIGHT

The first day at her job she met her new boss, Karen. Chad had started working at the lumber yard with his dad. He was set to inherit it since he was the only son, and it was one of the most successful businesses in town. She listened to Karen giggle and bumble through instructions, but most of all, Karen treated Kate with a certain contempt.

Kate was back to wearing her long skirts and blouses, and Karen wore skirts above her knee. Kate was to do the memos and typing. She spent her mornings crunching numbers and her afternoons typing letters and statements to customers and potential customers.

It was even more unfulfilling than Kate had imagined.

She'd called Chad and apologized for running off. She told him she was just scared because it was so soon after her dad passed, but she was excited to marry him. She didn't tell him her mom had guilted her into it, or they needed the money to keep their house. She didn't tell him she was in love with someone else.

In fact, she wasn't even sure if she was still in love with

Marco anymore. It had been so long since she'd seen him, her nightmares began to replace the good memories.

Still, she didn't take the bracelet off.

Jim spent more and more time going to The Limbo, without asking Kate to go. They hardly ever saw each other, except for on the weekends, but according to him, he and Karen had begun going steady. Karen tried to talk about it sometimes, but Kate tuned her out.

She couldn't watch the news about Vietnam. She would walk by it in the evenings when her mom had it on, go to the kitchen for some tea, and retreat back to her room. When she got her first paycheck, she went out and bought a new record player. She pulled out the old LP of The Dolphins and she listened to the whole thing from beginning to end.

They played upbeat melodies and sang about life and love. Love and loss. Her heart and body yearned for him. She felt encompassed by Marco's voice, but it had been too long now to call him, so she shrugged it away. She thought of writing to Steph, but she didn't. By now Steph had probably found new friends, and she might not even remember Kate.

Rose put an engagement announcement in the newspaper, enthusiastically lined up the pastor, and enrolled the church ladies to bake a wedding cake. Easter Sunday bloomed into summer, and pretty soon, it was the night before the wedding. Kate invited Heather over for one last girls' night. Heather arranged a baby-sitter, and Harold and Chad went to The Limbo.

Kate and Heather picked up some wine and a pack of cigarettes, drove around in Jim's car, and listened to music. They decided to park by the falls, which they used to do when they were in high school. Kate turned up the radio and opened the windows, and they sat out on the hood and listened to the music mix with the water.

A full moon rose. It started out pink, and then turned yellow, then white. Kate couldn't help but wonder what it looked like rising over the bay. Or the beach. She wondered if Marco could see it.

"What's marriage like?" Kate asked Heather.

"Oh," Heather said. She reached her hand out. "Wine me." Kate handed her the bottle. Heather took a long, long gulp and then wiped her mouth with her sleeve. "It's like a never-ending circle of cooking and cleaning, dishes and laundry. Just when you get one thing clean, another thing is dirty. It's like following everybody around, just picking up their stuff all the time. Baby on hip, washcloth in hand."

She took another sip and handed the bottle back to Kate. "But I love my babies." Heather's eyes brightened. "I wouldn't trade them for anything."

"How are the girls?" Kate asked.

"They're a lot of work, but they're fun," Heather said. "They give my life a different kind of meaning that I didn't have before. Are you and Chad going to have kids?"

Kate took a drink. "He wants to," she said. "I'm not sure. I still want to do things, you know? Like, maybe go to college, or something."

"Right," Heather said. "You've always wanted to do your own thing." Heather must have noticed her distance. "Do you love Chad?" She lit a cigarette and leaned back on her hands.

"Sometimes I think I do. But sometimes . . . ." She wasn't sure she could admit it, even to Heather. Then finally, she said, "I think I was in love with someone. In Florida."

"You were!" Heather said. "You didn't tell me!"

"I know. After my dad passed and you were busy with the kids, my mom, she sort of, talked me into staying."

"What was he like?" Heather asked. "How did you meet him?"

"Well," she thought of Marco's eyes on her.

Kate felt joy for the first time in a long time. Since she'd been home, anyway. Since her dad passed. She told Heather every-thing. She told her about the night they met when he'd played Elvis, and the Beatles, how he stared at her from the stage. And then the night he brought her orchids at her job. How it was like they could talk without talking.

She told her about Linda, and about Chip, and about Captain, Steph, Noah and Jack. She told her about everything but Donny. She didn't want to remember that.

Heather listened intently. They finished the wine and opened another bottle. Heather said, "Really?" and "Oh my gosh, Kate." She squealed in the parts about their first swim, with the algae around them like constellations, and the day at the Love-In when they went to the beach and the restaurant. She gasped at the part with the sheriff. Kate told her about their night-times, making love in the water, on the hammock, and in his bed. She told her about Gina showing up, and how Kate had closed off. Then how he'd written her the song and sang it to her the night they were alone. Going to the jazz club, and danc-ing, and then finding out he had a daughter. About Noah's talk with her before he left for the Army. She told her about how her mom and Jim had reacted when she'd tried to tell them. It felt so good for Kate to be able to tell somebody. She'd been holding it all in since she got home.

"Wow," Heather said. "It certainly sounds like an adventure. Like a dream, almost."

"Yeah," Kate said. "I guess it was. I just, you know." She puffed on her cigarette. "Wonder what would have happened sometimes, if Dad hadn't passed away, you know? If I would have stayed."

"Harold ran around on me," Heather blurted out.

"What?" Kate turned to Heather in confusion. "Right after I had Laney, our second."

Kate thought they had it all, the perfect relationship. But the pain in Heather's face resounded. She reached her arm out and hugged her. "I'm so sorry, Heather. That's awful."

Heather smiled through tears. "His secretary." She gulped back a sob. "She ended up telling me. Not even him. He couldn't even tell me himself." Then she slumped her shoulders, "I guess he felt so guilty."

Kate had no idea what to say. "What did you do?"

"I yelled. He denied it at first and got defensive. And then he admitted to it. Said he was sorry. It was just with the weight that I'd gained and being busy all the time with the kids. I stopped doing it with him altogether." She wiped at her eyes and took the bottle from Kate in a long, drawn-out swig. "But I'm not working, you know? I have two little babies, and I don't have a job, and what am I going to do? The babies, they need to eat."

"What about your mom?" Kate asked, though she knew this was a sore subject. Heather's father had left when she was small, and her mother lived from paycheck to paycheck, always struggling.

"I didn't tell her," Heather said. "My mom thinks that Harold is the greatest thing that ever happened to me." She wiped her nose on her shirt. "I didn't want to jeopardize any chances of having a future with him. You know how she is. I didn't tell my sister, but I want to."

"What are you going to do?" Kate asked.

Heather kept wiping her eyes as the tears kept flowing. "I'm going to be a good mom," she said, "and stay married, I guess." Kate held her close and let her cry harder. "Thank you, Kate. I haven't told anybody. I thought I was over it, but I guess, well, thanks for listening." Kate took the wine bottle from Heather. She lit a cigarette and looked over at the water. Crickets and frogs hummed. The falls crashed into the river below.

"Do you love him?" Kate asked. "I mean, I know you guys met in high school and I remember being around you and stuff, as friends, but do you feel like you love him?"

Heather wiped one more tear from her cheek. "I mean, yeah. Of course, I do. But I guess, well, after hearing your story about Marco, I wonder if maybe I didn't let myself experience enough. Like, if I would have gone out on my own a little bit. Maybe I don't even really know what love is, you know?"

Kate didn't ask, because she knew the answer. She knew Harold was the only guy Heather had ever been with. They stayed silent for a while, listening to the Ohio night sounds. A light fog drifted up and the trees seemed to glow in the moonlight. "I wish we had something to smoke," Kate said, "other than this."

"Like grass?" Heather said. "My sister smokes grass." Her face lit up like the sun. "We could drive by her house and get some." She sat straight up. "Do you want to?"

"Tomorrow I'm signing my life away to a man I don't know if I love. To appease my mom." Kate didn't have to think very long before she said, "Yeah, let's go."

Heather's sister's house wasn't far away. Kate stayed in the car as Heather ran in. The mid-summer corn had begun to sprout a sugary scent into the air. They drove back to the falls, resumed their spot by the water, and rolled a joint.

"I didn't know you smoked," Heather said.

"I mean, I don't," Kate laughed. "You know, I haven't ever even actually smoked. It's just that Marco, he would blow it in my mouth, and I wanted him to kiss me so bad," she said. "Like, his mouth is so, and his tongue touching mine, wow. Then, well, I always felt pretty pleasant afterwards."

Heather snorted out a huge laugh. "Seriously, you're so graphic. And you're the only one I know who would say, *felt pretty pleasant afterwards,* in the same sentence."

"I'm serious," Kate laughed. Linda had said the beach would shake the Midwest out of her.

"Harold smokes," Heather said, "but he doesn't like it when I do. And I know Chad does."

"Really?" Kate didn't know this about either of them. "How do I not know this?"

"The boys will always have lives we won't ever know about. That's just the way it is."

Kate tried to tidy up the ash of the joint around the wine bottle. She could feel herself getting lighter. Brighter. She missed the way she could see a million stars over the ocean.

"After I do all this marriage stuff with Chad, we should go on a vacation to the beach."

Heather snort-laughed again, and Kate couldn't stop laughing. "I mean, like, seriously. I'm making money now, and I'm giving a lot to my mom but—"

"You're giving money to your mom?" Heather straightened her face and stopped laughing.

"She wasn't sure she would be able to keep the house if I didn't."

"Geez," Heather said, taking the joint. "That sounds like a lot of pressure."

Kate hadn't thought about it for a while. "Yeah, I guess. But my mom, you know, she, like raised me." Kate was trying to find more eloquent words, but all she had were these. "She spent her whole life just, so she could give us the best life she could, you know? Dad spent most of his money at the bar, and mom kept on growing things, and canning things." Kate stared off into the distance. "I feel like I owe her something."

"You think you owe her your life?" Heather asked.

The silence widened.

Did she owe her mom her life?

"Hey," Heather said, "Don't you think that tree looks like Harold? Shaking his finger at me?" She pointed out into the distance.

On the other side of the river dark green silhouettes of trees mingled and swayed. A light breeze rippled across Kate's skin.

"No," she said. "It looks like Marco singing to me." They both busted out into hysterical laughter.

After they calmed down Heather said, "We should go and find the boys."

Kate sighed. "I'm feeling so good, I'm not sure if I want Chad to ruin my mood." Then she laughed.

"Ruin your mood? Is he that bad?"

"I mean, he's just not—"

"A hunky musician who lives on the beach and sings to you?" Heather snorted again, and Kate had to hold her belly because she was laughing so hard. Tears ran down her face, and when Heather noticed Kate was crying, Heather laughed harder. They shrieked and slapped their knees. Heather rolled off the hood into the grass and Kate laid back onto the windshield, cackling until her stomach hurt.

When they gathered themselves, Kate said, "I mean, we can go find the boys if you want to. Do you think Chad will be able to tell that we've been smoking?"

"Let me see your eyes." Heather reached out, grabbed the bottom of Kate's cheek with her thumb, and held up her eyelid with her index finger. This made Kate laugh, which made her eye blink, which made it hurt. Heather snorted again. Kate swatted at Heather's hand.

"Probably." They both laughed. Heather from her throat, and Kate from her belly.

"Okay," Kate said. "Let's go then."

Maybe Chad would back out. Maybe he would change his mind about wanting to marry her. As Heather drove Jim's car now, and Kate swigged at the wine bottle she thought, *how can Chad even be in love with me? He doesn't even know me anymore.*

It was almost closing time at The Limbo. The girls were still giggling as they arrived, but they strutted in like they were the prettiest girls in the place. It was dark; The Porch Swings played from the stage. Kate and Heather looked around for the boys and didn't find them.

"Where do you think they are?" Kate asked.

They walked around the entire place. They laughed and danced their way around, but the guys weren't there.

"Excuse me," Kate said to the bartender. "We're looking for two guys, Chad Smith and Harold Turner. Have you seen them here tonight?"

The bartender leaned over and said, "You're Kate, right? Congratulations on your engagement."

"Thanks," Kate said. "I'm getting married tomorrow!" She giggled when she said it; it didn't even feel real. "So anyway, have you seen them?"

"Yeah," he said, putting a cigarette out in an ashtray. "They left about a half an hour ago." He hesitated.

She took a sip of her drink and tried to look innocent, so he might feel for her. She knew he knew something else.

"Well," he said, hesitantly. "I don't usually talk about other customers' business, because I like my job." He smashed the cigarette butt and wiped his hands on his pants. "But you're Jim's sister, right?"

"Yes," Kate said.

"Jim's my friend, man. And he's not here tonight. And you're, well, they left with Karen, and some other girl." Then he put his hands up, palms out, and shrugged his shoulders. "They just left, not too long ago. Please don't tell them I told you."

Kate bit her lip and made straight for the door.

In the car Heather said, "What should we do?"

"I don't know," Kate said. "I could go for a milkshake."

"Me too, but I mean, they left with two other girls?"

She let that sink into her body like some form of twisted acceptance. "Not cool," was the only thing she could think to say.

"Do you want to go look for them?"

"Not really," Kate said.

"Look," Heather said, "this is my life. That is my husband. If he's with some other girl, I want to know. I want to know where. I want to find him and—"

"What will you do?" Kate said. "How will we even find them?"

A guy in cowboy boots and a belt buckle came out of The Limbo. He looked at them, put one hand in the air like he had an imaginary lasso, and said, "Whooooo-weee," as he waved it around.

"Right," Heather said. "I guess we go home, and you get married tomorrow."

Kate sighed. "What a life."

Heather put Jim's car into gear, and Kate turned up the radio. A new song by The Supremes came on, "Stop! In the Name of Love." Despite her sadness, Kate rolled down the window and listened to the lyrics. By the end of the song, they were singing the chorus together.

CHAPTER TWENTY-NINE

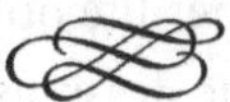

Kate's mother buzzed around the house excitedly. Jim had taken the day off. He sat at the kitchen table staring off into space. Rose interrupted his moments and gave him duties. "Jim, I need you to go and pick up the flowers. Jim, we're going to the beauty shop at noon."

He drove them to the beauty shop, where Heather met them. Kate wanted to be excited. She wanted to feel like she was doing the right thing. But she didn't, and she wouldn't, so she tried to talk herself into small moments of joy.

The hairdresser reminded her of Brenda from the beach. Brenda who said, "Stay away from men for as long as you can." She wound the girls' hair into hair-spray beehives and curled bangs, and when she was done and presented the mirrors to them, they both looked like movie stars.

"Thank you," Kate said. They looked ready for a wedding.

The church smelled like old wood and Pine Sol. Jim was poised to walk Kate down the aisle. He had rented a white tuxedo, and his hair hung over his eyebrows like one of the Beatles. Rose's radiance shined over everybody. She hugged and kissed Kate in the dressing room, pinned on a carnation corsage, and told Kate that she looked like a princess.

Chad's family showed up in full color. His dad and his mom trotted down the aisle like they owned the most lucrative business in town, as they did. Onlookers snapped pictures; the newspapers had sent reporters. Kate found it strange and uncomfortable, but so was her life now. She shrugged it off.

Heather wore a baby blue dress, as beautiful as Kate had ever seen her. Harold had both girls in the second row, struggling with the younger one, who was crying.

Heather said, "Are you ready for this?" She pulled at Kate's bangs. They stood at the back of the church facing the altar.

Kate shook her head 'no' and said, "You're my best friend. Thank you."

"Marriage isn't that bad," Heather said. "At least you'll be taken care of, you know, financially." She turned and walked down the aisle to the organist playing Canon in D, clutching a bouquet of white roses.

Kate's mom had already been seated by an usher, and it was almost time for her to go when Jim said, "Kate. I'm sorry I've been so distant."

"It's okay. You look really handsome." Kate wished her dad was here. She focused on the bouquet in her hand to avoid her mascara running.

"Kate," he used her name again. The big-brother voice. "I feel like I have to tell you. I don't want to tell you, but I don't know who else to tell. I think that Chad's having a thing with Karen." Kate linked her arm with his as they stared down at the preacher.

"You're probably right." She adjusted her veil.

"So, what do we do?" he asked. Kate took a step toward the altar. Jim stayed in step with her. She glimpsed down at her bracelet. The anchor.

"We pray for a miracle," she whispered. "I don't know what else there is."

The organ began. Everybody stood up.

Kate blushed now that she was wearing white in front of all of these people. But she knew she wasn't Chad's only girl. Last night, even, she hadn't known where he was. Everyone in the chapel stood and swooned. She wished Marco were here, or at least Steph.

Heather was crying, and Kate's mom was crying, and Jim, forlorn, did his procedural, give the bride away to the groom. He lifted her veil and kissed her on the cheek. The pastor asked everybody to sit down. Kate handed her bouquet to Heather and then turned to Chad, who looked sheepish. And, in love, almost.

Kate was just going through the motions. She felt empty.

This was the least she could do for her mom. This was the only option she had. She was going to have to kiss him soon, and she wasn't excited about it.

The pastor read some verses. Rose continued sniffling. But Heather looked great. And Kate felt like she looked great, regardless of Chad's family glaring down at her.

She stood poised.

When the preacher began his talk, her mind drifted. How did I get here? What am I doing? If I wouldn't have come home for my dad's funeral, then . . . then her mother would never have forgiven her, and she wouldn't have ever forgiven herself.

Kate thought of the beach. She thought of Marco Del Rio. She looked at Heather's face, clutching the roses and wiping her eyes with a tissue, and the words popped into her head.

Did she owe her mom her life?

The preacher said, "If anybody in the congregation knows of a reason that these two should not be joined to unite in holy matrimony, then please speak now, or forever hold your peace."

CHAPTER THIRTY

November, 2014

Curtis stomped down the steps and found Skylar where he'd left her, on the floor surrounded by letters.

"What did I miss?" he asked.

"Noah got drafted, Mom's high school sweetheart showed back up, and now Grandma is making her marry him."

"Marry him? She can't marry anybody but Dad. And what happened to Marco?"

"He's still out there, I guess. But mom's stuck in Ohio."

"What! I was gone for like, three hours."

"I know, here." Skylar handed him the letters she'd read since he'd left.

"Skylar," Curtis said. He put his phone in his pocket and took her hand. "I just want you to know that I'm sorry about that stuff in college. That fraternity party? I didn't know."

"Yeah," she said. "I know."

"It makes me crazy that I couldn't protect you. That I didn't."

"I know," Skylar said.

She knew.

CHAPTER THIRTY-ONE

August, 1965

Kate wanted somebody to stand up. She wanted somebody to say something. Anybody. Even Jim. Kate's eyes fell on Karen. Maybe she would say something. And then, as Kate's mother wiped her tears of joy, she heard the words come out of her own mouth before she really knew what she was saying. Like the first night at the beach. It was her own voice, but from somewhere primal. "Stop," she said. "I can't."

All at once the congregation gasped.

Chad grimaced.

Maybe this was a bad dream, but if it was, she had to listen to and follow that voice. She took his hands and said, "I'm sorry, Chad, I just can't do this." His face reddened, and anger brimmed on his lips.

"You're fucking that Noah guy, aren't you?"

The congregation gasped again, but louder.

Then the church doors creaked open in the back, and in waltzed Jack.

Everybody turned and stared.

Heather smiled and held the bouquets in a perfect balance.

"Greetings," he said. "Sorry I'm late. Please let me introduce myself." He was wearing a white tuxedo with fluff down the front, and a blue bowtie. "I am Library's friend. Library, whom you all might otherwise know as Kate. My name is Jack Miracle."

He flaunted a flask in one hand, and a ring of white orchids in the other. His dark sunglasses did not hide his Shakespearean impression. He wasn't wearing shoes.

"I travel from a faraway land, called Florida."

She tried to hide her elation and gratitude, but a tear of joy fell down Kate's cheek. *Thank goodness, Jack.* She wiped the tear and didn't look at Chad. Instead, she stole a glance at Heather, who nodded enthusiastically, though she didn't lose her composure.

Jack continued, "We have gathered here for the lovely matrimony of Katie Wyse and Chad," he looked down at a card he had in his hand, "Smith," he said, and smiled. He was a good performer. *Thank God, Jack.* And then, as she adjusted her eyes, Steph's face emerged behind him, standing in the doorway.

Steph had a side bag wrapped around her, and she was wearing a lovely green flowing sundress and round sunglasses. Her hair was almost to her waist. She flashed a low peace sign with two fingers. Kate's heart burst with happiness.

"We're gathered here for a celebration of true love, but—" Jack started down the aisle, swaying, almost dancing. "It has come to my knowledge that Miss Katie is already promised to another. He has sent his wishes with me, via road trip. Miss Katie Wyse, if it is all right with you, I would like to read you a letter from a long, lost friend."

Kate nodded. A wave of relief flooded her chest. He reached into his pocket and pulled out something that looked like a scroll.

Jack was almost at the altar. Steph stayed under the oak

front doors of the church, in the background. The pastor began to move, to say something, but Kate put her hand on his arm. Rose had a look of panic on her face.

Nobody said anything, though. The onlookers were entranced by Jack's performance. He raised his sunglasses and cleared his throat.

"Ladies and gentleman, we are gathered here today for a celebration that need not be celebrated. My brother, a certain Marco Del Rio . . . " Jim stared at Kate. She felt her heart warm up for the first time in a long time, like somebody had lit the pilot light of her soul after a long winter of hibernation. "Has requested my presence at your ceremony, to ask Kate to rescind her invitation for matrimony as he wishes to invite her sacred presence into his court.

"'Mr.—"Jack looked at his card again and then at Chad, " . . . Smith, Mr. Del Rio does send his deepest apologies for being an inconvenience at your ceremony. He only received word very recently that his love was promised to another. His Majesty has requested that I receive Miss Katie Wyse into my care at this most opulent time and in heed, for now." Jack approached Kate and put the crown of flowers over her beehive. "Good people of Ohio, here is his letter." Jack cleared his throat. He made eye contact with Kate's mom. "It is written in Spanish, so please, allow me to translate." He pointed one finger in the air and moved it as he spoke.

"*Katie Bella, por favor, volver a mí.* Please, return to me." Jack read from the paper and moved his eyes around the congregation as he translated. Kate's heart turned from gray to pink again. "*Yo nunca te mostré que eres la chica más hermosa y la más importante en mi mundo, de mis sueños.* I never showed you that you are the most beautiful and most important girl in the world, of my dreams. *Así, Katie Bella, por favor, no casarse a él.* So, Katie Bella, please, do not marry him. *Vamos a nadar.* Let's go swimming. *Estaremos juntos para siempre.* We will be together for all time. *A menos que sea cierto que es un hombre respetable y lo amas.* Unless it is true that he is a respectable man, and you love him. *Eres mi amor, y yo quiero que seas feliz.* You are my love, and I want you to be happy. *Pero si no tienes a amor a él; entonces, por favor, vuelve a mí, porque mi corazón se está rompiéndo.* But if you do not love him, then, please return to me, because my heart is breaking. *Y Henry también te echa de menos.* And Henry misses you also. Amor, Marco."

Jack slowly rolled the scroll back up and put it in the breast pocket of his tux.

Was this a dream? She watched her mom's face fade into horror. She pinched herself, ever so discreetly, blinked, and here she was at the altar leaving Chad.

He stared at her, his expression stunned and silent. She hugged Heather, in the biggest bear hug she'd ever given and whispered in her ear, "Come to visit me," taking the bouquet back from her hands. Then Kate walked down the steps, holding the bottom of her dress in one hand and her roses in the other. She kissed her mom on the cheek, quickly, and said, "I'm sorry, Mom. I love you, but I have to go. I have to live my own life."

"Kathryn, no," Rose said. But Kate turned away from her.

"What are you doing?" Jim asked in the big brother voice.

"Following my heart," she whispered. "Please, take care of Mom. I'll send money when I can." She met Jack and hugged him. He offered his elbow and wrapped her arm in his.

"Las personas simpáticas," Jack said, "Nice people of Ohio, we will see you in another time and another place, and until then, many blessings." He bowed as if he were a court jester addressing an audience. "And the queen and king will address you when necessary."

At this, Chad leapt from the steps and lunged at Jack. Jim caught him just in time, and Kate's uncles helped hold him. "You fucking bastard!" he yelled. As Kate and Jack passed

Karen, Kate handed her the rose bouquet and said, "He's all yours."

Then Kate and Jack ran to Steph and out the back doors of the church.

"Holy shit, Library, you were going to get married! Come on!" Steph grabbed her hand, and they ran down the steps.

"I can't believe you found me," Kate said. "How did you find me?" Steph helped Kate hold up her dress while Kate removed her heels. Jack lit a cigarette.

Steph said, "My mom cuts out articles for me from the newspaper. She sent me your engagement photo. When I showed it to Marco, he didn't speak. For days. He missed two shows in a row, and when Captain went to find him, he said he couldn't play 'because his heart was breaking.'" Steph said the last part with her fingers up like quotation-mark bunny ears, and she rolled her eyes. "Anyway," Steph said. "You said you didn't want to get married yet, right?"

Right. Panic and relief swept over Kate.

"He was not a sight to see," Jack said. "Our lively musician friend turned into a wilted flower without you."

"We told Marco we'd try. We just made it," Steph said. "It was a long drive. Sounds like you were handling it, though. You don't love him, do you? The Chad guy?"

"No," Kate said. "I don't feel anything for him."

"Okay," Steph said, tugging her hand. "Let's get you out of here." Kate followed them around the corner and there was Noah, sitting in the driver's seat of a white convertible and wearing dark sunglasses.

Steph and Jack jumped into the back and Kate climbed over the passenger door.

"Noah!" Kate said. "How are you? You're home! Are you okay?" She wrapped her arms around his neck. Before he could answer, they turned around to see the congregation had followed them out of the back door. Among the sea of shocked faces, Kate only caught a glimpse of her family. Jim nodded and smiled at Kate, while he held Chad back by his shoulders. Rose frowned, and Heather cheered.

Jack said, "Let's go, let's go, let's go!"

Noah screeched the tires, and they took off. He lifted the sunglasses and turned to her. "Hey Katie, yeah. I made it back. Where's your house?"

"My house?" His hair was clipped almost to his scalp.

"We've got to get your stuff, quick, if you want to get it."

"Okay," she said and gave him directions.

Kate packed her things faster than she'd ever done anything, and she remembered her winter jacket this time. Noah threw her trunk into the back, and they all drove south toward the beach. Jack pulled a pizza box from the floorboard and said, "Hey Library, want some pizza?"

Noah jammed out to the radio and Steph and Jack laughed in the back seat. Jack took off his bow tie and tux and settled down into a white tank top.

"That was a stellar performance, Sir Jack," Kate said in her best British accent. "Did Marco really send that letter?"

"I helped him with it. I told him I only want half of the royalties if he turns it into a song."

"How's your mom," Steph asked. "And how are you?"

"I think she's going to be okay," Kate said.

"You know," Steph said, hovering into the front seat to light a cigarette. "Chad is sleeping with that girl from his dad's office, whatever her name is, Karen?"

Kate turned to her in surprise. "How do you know that?"

"She's from my hometown," Steph said. "My sister went to school with her brother. And everybody knows. Even my *mom* knows, which is just weird."

"You know she was seeing my brother, that Karen girl?"

"Yeah," Steph said.

Kate couldn't believe how complicated it all was. How she'd

almost gotten stuck there again, living the wrong life. She was not going to miss Ohio for a while, except for one thing. "I wish we could have brought my friend, Heather."

"Do you want to get her?" Noah asked. He had one hand on the wheel and one hand on the gear shift.

"No, she's got a family . . . "

"Okay," Noah said.

"Your hair is so long," Kate said to Steph. She had pulled it back to keep it from tangling in the wind.

"You've been gone, like, six months, Library." Steph said. "Glad to have you back."

Jack reached over the seat and put his hands on her shoulders. "You're one of us now," he said. "Like it or not."

They drove through the night and decided to ride out to the beach and to take the rest of the trip down the coast. At one point they pulled over and switched out driving. Steph drove the nighttime leg and Noah crawled into the back seat, settling his head onto Jack's shoulder. He had lost weight.

Kate woke up to sunrise colors over the ocean, the comforting smell of salt water, and a light breeze on her skin. Steph parked the car under a sign that said, "Country Breakfast."

"You guys wanna get some food?"

Jack and Noah rustled in the back seat. A man in a white coat with a broom walked by their car.

"Guys," Steph said. "Breakfast time." She put her hand on Jack's knee and shook them awake.

"Where are we?" Jack asked.

"North Carolina," Steph said. "Almost to South Carolina."

"I'm hungry," Noah said.

A bell rang as they entered the diner, and only a few customers sat dispersed around brown tables. The smells of bacon and coffee wafted around. A waitress in an apron said, "I'll be with you in a minute."

They all sat down at the bar counter and began looking at

the menu. Kate noticed the man in the white coat eyeing them. He whispered something to the waitress, who looked at Noah and Jack. She shook her head, but the guy pointed at her.

Reluctantly, then, the waitress put up a sign that said, "This section closed," right in front of Noah and Jack.

"Excuse me," Kate said, "we'd like to order some eggs."

The waitress was young, younger than the rest of them, and her face took on a dour frown. She mouthed the words, "I'm sorry."

"We don't serve your kind here," the man in the white coat said. Kate noticed his southern drawl, something she had always associated with hospitality.

"I'm sorry?" Steph asked. Her cheeks reddened.

"Fairies," the guy said. "We don't serve fairies here."

Jack bent his neck back and put both hands on the counter. Kate saw his knuckles getting white. Noah put his head down.

"Oh," said Steph, standing up. "You must have us confused. You see," she pointed to Kate. "We *do* dress in long flowing skirts, and my friend here has a crown of orchids, but we're not actual, real fairies. In fact," she smiled. "I'm not sure that real fairies would come to a place like this. It's a little, you know, non-magical."

The guy picked up his broom again and said, "I'm going to have to ask you to leave." The few customers set down their silverware, the clinking noise intensifying the silence. Kate wanted to say something, but she wasn't sure what would help.

"Really," Steph said, "We were just talking about leaving because it smells like rat's ass in here, and you probably," she held up her menu which had a dead moth plastered inside the plastic, "haven't cleaned since the fifties." The guy gritted his teeth and scrunched his eyebrows.

"Come on," Steph said. Noah and Jack's chairs squeaked as they rose. "Let's go someplace where it's clean."

The guy started after them with his broom. The group

rushed out. As the bell rang behind them, Noah kicked a hole in the newspaper dispenser, and the glass crashed around his foot. Jack jumped into the driver's seat, and they took off.

The guy followed them out, cussing in indecipherable yells.

"What an asshole," Steph said.

"Karma will come to all," Jack said.

Noah didn't say anything.

Sometime later, the car rolled over some railroad tracks, and Jack pulled up to a place called "The Friendly Diner."

A couple of boys sat outside on a bench, whittling at some sticks.

"Hello," one of them said.

"Hey guys," Jack said. "What are you making?"

"A flute," one of the boys said. The other one just smiled. "He don't talk much."

Jack admired the kid's handiwork. "Ka-pow, man, that's cool. Keep up the good work!" When they entered the diner, the waitress said, "Well, hello y'all. Have a seat wherever you like." Her nametag said, "Sissy."

They took seats at the bar counter and Sissy tipped over their coffee cups. "It's a beautiful day out there, isn't it?"

A cook peeked out from the kitchen.

"Ay, Ma'am, it certainly is," Jack said.

"So, what'll you have?" They all ordered eggs and bacon.

As she refilled their coffee cups Sissy said, "So what brought you all to Randolph County?"

"We just saved our friend Kate here from marrying the wrong guy." Steph said. Noah finally smiled.

"Aw, marriage," she said with her hand on her hip. "It ain't something to go into lightly. Are any of y'all married?"

"No Ma'am," Jack said. "My friend Noah here just got back from Vietnam, and my friend Steph here only believes in free love."

"Jack," Steph said, punching him on the knee. A laugh sounded from the kitchen.

"Whoo—eee," the voice said.

Sissy smiled over her shoulder. "Me and Bobby jumped the broom about five years ago. Smartest thing I ever done," she said.

"Ain't for the faint of heart," Bobby said. He came out with a spatula and kissed Sissy's cheek. "She's my girl, though, my one and only."

They settled quietly into eating when Kate's attention turned to Noah.

"What was Vietnam like?" she asked.

Noah set his fork down on the counter and sipped from his coffee mug. He made eye contact with each one of the friends, separately, then shook his head, 'no,' and picked his fork back up.

CHAPTER THIRTY-TWO

When they arrived in town, they drove straight to the beach where The Dolphins were playing at The Parrot. The band was on a break, and when he saw her, Marco stopped mid-sentence and carved through the crowd.

"Bella," he said. He picked her up by the waist and kissed her. She locked her ankles behind his hips and wrapped her arms around his neck. As he carried her all the way out the back door, away from curious eyes, and set her down on the picnic table, she took in his eyes, his scent, his touch. She felt her heart opening again.

"¿Cómo estás? I have missed you like no other." He peered into her face. "You look like a princess."

She kissed him again. "Steph and Jack showed up just in time." She smiled at the memory of Jack's performance. "And Noah's home!"

"You were going to get married? Why, Katie?"

"My mother. She wanted me to stay there and help her." Kate wiped her palms on the sides of her dress. "But I can't live the life she wants for me. I want to be here, with you."

Marco pulled a piece of hair-sprayed curl from her face. "My beautiful Katie, climbing out of the family box."

"I can still send her money from here. She'll be lonely without my dad, I know."

"I am so *sorry* about your father. Why did you not tell me?"

Kate lowered her eyes. "I don't know. You were busy with work, then your daughter, and I didn't want to worry you, and then, it all happened so fast. I didn't know he was going to, you know."

Marco held her close. His musky, sweet scent enveloped her.

"My mom always says, 'not everybody needs to know everything about you.'" She let her head rest on his shoulder.

"Ah," Marco said. "So, this is why Katie does not always tell me what she is feeling." Then he pulled her back and studied her face again. He kissed her softly, quickly and said, "Do you love him? This man you were to marry?"

She shook her head and hoped her gaze told him how she felt. She still couldn't put it into words.

"Okay, my princess," he said. "Where are you staying?"

"I don't know," Kate said.

The door opened, "Hola, Miss Katie," Timbale said. Marco took a step back so Kate could stand up and hug him. "We missed you, señorita."

"I missed you guys, too!" She squeezed his arms. "How's Melaney?"

"Ah," he said, "she is very fine, thank you." He placed a cigarette behind his ear and said, "Marco, it's time."

Timbale went back through the door and Marco pulled Kate close again.

"Stay the night with me? Come in and listen?" He picked her up, kissed her long and hard, and carried her into the bar.

"Shawn," he said. "Give mi amor whatever she would like on our tab, okay?"

"Aye aye, Marco," he said. "Welcome home, Katie." Marco set her down onto a bar stool.

Home, she thought. *I am home.* Kate waved at the old sailor.

The friends settled their drinks at the round table against the wall, but Steph and Jack got up to mingle. Kate and Noah sat in silence for a while, until Kate mustered up the courage to say, "How did you get out early?"

Noah's shoulders tightened up and he swirled the ice cubes around in his bourbon.

"I kept my mouth shut, my eyes up, and my head down."

His voice trailed off and his eyes stared over her shoulder toward the wall. Although he hadn't really answered her question, she decided not to ask any more.

After Marco's set, Kate hugged her friends one more time before she got into Marco's van, and they rode out to his trailer. She couldn't wait to get out of her wedding dress.

When Marco opened the door, Henry jumped up at her, wagged his tail, and then sat down, nuzzling his muzzle in her hand.

"All right, boy. Sí." Marco said, "Yes, I am happy to see her, too."

Queen Kitty came around the corner from the kitchen and meowed at her, as if she were yelling against her absence. Kate scooped her up and held her until she purred.

"Steph brought her to me before they came to get you," Marco said. "I am so glad they got there in time. I think she missed you, too."

Marco unloaded his equipment and carried in Kate's blue trunk. Then he led her to the couch and said, "My body and my soul have missed you." Kate felt alive again. "Would you not please stay with me for a long time?"

Kate was sweaty and she was pretty sure she didn't smell like roses. "Can I take a shower?" she asked. It was a long trip.

He led her to the bathroom and pulled back the shower curtain to the porcelain claw-foot tub. "It is not huge, but—"

"It's perfect. Thank you." She stood awkwardly, then.

"Can I help you out of your dress?" he asked and kissed her neck.

She felt shy. It had been months since they had been together. She had lost most of her tan and had gained some weight. Would he still find her attractive?

He turned on the water, squeezed a bottle into the stream, and a million tiny bubbles formed, some of which rose into the air.

"Ah, I know what we are missing." He disappeared into his bedroom. A jazz trumpet whispered from the record player. She took her dress off and slid into the tub, cleaning herself as fast as she could before he returned. She dunked her hair under water and tried to rinse out the hairspray.

Marco returned with a bottle of champagne, two glasses, and a candle. He turned off the light, lit the candle, and popped the top off the champagne, filling each glass and setting them on the small table by the tub. One of the glasses bubbled over.

"Can I join you?" he asked.

Kate bit her lip and nodded.

She pulled the bubbles over her legs with her hands in the yellow glow of the candlelight, and took a sip of champagne, savoring the sweet on her tongue. He climbed into the tub from behind, placing his legs on either side of hers. She rested her arms on his knees and let her hands rest around his ankles.

Marco kissed her neck on either side, scooped up bubbles from the water, and drew patterns in them against her body with his fingertips.

He breathed gently into her ear, "you are sweet as honey."

Oh my gosh.

Sweet as honey.

A sudden wave of fear.

Donny's body pinning hers.

His awful smell.

Pain.

Water crashed over the rim of the tub. She grabbed a towel and wrapped it around her. Frozen on the rug, wet and dripping. Trembling.

"¿Qué pasa?" Marco said. "What is happening? What is wrong?"

"I'm sorry. I'm . . ." Kate snapped out. "I'm—" *oh my gosh.* She began to cry. "I'm sorry." She went to the bedroom and sat on the bed. "Oh my . . ."

Noah's anger.

Disgusting Donny.

Standing over the bed.

"Oh my gosh," Kate repeated.

Steph yelling the f-word.

Marco rushed in with a towel wrapped around his waist. "What is wrong? What did I say?"

He lit a cigarette and brought the ashtray onto the bed. "What did I do? I am sorry. Por favor, talk to me."

"It's. I just, had. An. A memory." She couldn't get the words out.

"What is it?" He leaned in closer, pushed her hair off her shoulder and kissed her neck. Her body curled away from him.

He tilted his head and studied her face. "I cannot read your mind," he said. "I cannot understand what you need if you do not talk to me."

Kate didn't want to talk. She didn't want to remember. She was embarrassed still; she had drunk so much that night. If she wouldn't have put herself in that situation then . . . maybe it would have never happened.

She struggled to speak. Had to tell him.

"Will you get the champagne?" she asked.

He went to the bathroom and retrieved it. He handed her a

glass, took a drink of his own, and sat it on the nightstand. He tried to cuddle up close to her, their naked bodies only covered by towels. "You can talk to me," he pleaded.

She scooted away. She almost spilled the champagne. Her brain was still flashing in broken memories, like a television picture going in and out. *Images. Fear. Pain.*

"I didn't want to tell you this, but I guess . . . that night . . . ." She heard her voice shaking as if it weren't hers.

She told him the story. She told him how she had been trying to drink to forget. To ignore her heart. About Noah and Steph coming in. She sobbed, but she finished the story. And then she lay back on the bed, looking at the ceiling, afraid of what he might be thinking.

"I understand," she said, "if this changes the way you see me."

"Why would this change the way I see you?" He took her hand. "You are *everything* to me."

"The memory," she said. "It just came out of nowhere. And I, I guess it scared me." She guzzled the rest of the champagne. "I guess I feel, like, maybe you'll think I'm some kind of fast girl or something. But that's what he said when I woke up, that you said I was *sweet as honey.*" She cringed.

"Oh," Marco stood up, towel around his waist. "I will kill him." He paced back and forth and said some words in Spanish that Kate didn't understand. He gritted his teeth.

"No, please." Kate said. "Noah put him in the hospital. We think that's why he got called to service. Please, just please. Don't tell anybody?"

He shook out his wet hair, flicked it back and forth against his face and stared at her as if he were making an important decision.

"If you wish, I will not say anything. But I am very angry. How dare he? How dare he touch my princess? This is why you wanted me to lock the door here that night? When our friends were over?"

"Yes," Kate said.

"And this is why our friends would not talk to me? I thought you had told them to stay away from me."

"I figured word would get around to you. It does with everything else." She couldn't believe he hadn't heard.

He shook his head. "Katie. You must learn to talk to me, okay? I overheard Donny bragging about something with you, but I thought you must have wanted to be with him. My heart was breaking, which is why I had someone cover for me at The Wave. I wanted you to be true to you."

"I did not want that to happen," Kate said.

"I understand now," Marco said. "And I want to beat his face in, but I will respect your wishes." He touched her hand. "Please, you can trust me to tell me things. I want to know you. I want to know who you are and what you dream about, what you want to be and do. I want to know everything. And I pray to have you all to myself, but I also want you to feel free."

It was late. It had been a long day. "Can we just go to sleep?"

He nodded and put the ashtray and her champagne glass on the nightstand and pulled down the covers. Kate kept her body wrapped in the towel, and she laid down on his pillows.

"Can I put my arms around you?" he asked. "Is that okay?"

"Yes," she said. She didn't know why she was still crying.

CHAPTER THIRTY-THREE

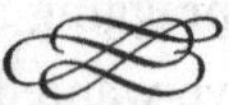

Henry lifted his head as Kate woke. She went into the bathroom and remembered the lovely bubble bath, and then how it ended so abruptly. She felt horrible about it all, like it was still somehow all her fault. In the mirror her scraggly hair was going everywhere. She ran some more conditioner in it, washed it out again, and brushed her teeth.

As she pulled a comb through her softer tangles, she wandered into the kitchen where Marco was packing a basket with sandwiches and champagne. Henry followed her.

"Good morning," he said. He wiped his hands on a towel thrown over his shoulder and approached her. "Can I kiss you?"

"Yes." Her body, after rest, had tuned back into his.

He pointed at Henry. "It looks like you may have a new dog." Henry wagged his tail and sat down. "What do you have to do today?"

"I guess I need to go and talk to Butch about my apartment. See if it is still for rent. If I can get my job back." She pulled the last tangle out of her hair, finally.

Queen Kitty sat down and meowed at them.

"Can it wait two more days?"

"Why?"

"I want to take you somewhere." Marco's tongue touched his top lip. "Just you and me. Make a new memory."

"Where?"

"Ah," he said, putting his hands on her waist. "It is a surprise." He kissed her again. "Pack a change of clothes. I will feed Kitty, then I am almost ready."

"But where are we going?" Kate wasn't good at surprises. She was worried about money and felt like she needed to get back to work. But, then again, what were two more days if she got to spend them alone with him?

"Es una sorpresa, Bella. If I tell you, it will not be a surprise anymore."

"What should I wear?" Kate finally asked.

"Whatever you want, mi amor. Bring sunglasses and a bathing suit. We will take Henry with us, but you," he reached down and scratched the cat's ears, "will have to stay here and watch the house." Queen Kitty moved her head around and sniffed at his fingertips.

Kate decided to put on her swimsuit and cover it with her red sundress. She hadn't worn it all the time she was in Ohio. She steadied her sunglasses on her head, so they held her hair out of her face, and packed a small bag.

She had seen the boat pulled up against the trailer, but she hadn't thought much of it. Marco locked up the house and led her outside where he uncovered a simple rowboat with a small motor. "Do you like being on the water?"

She nodded.

"You do not get seasick?"

"I don't think so."

It took both of them to pull the boat out from the sand. It was heavier than it looked, but they managed. He loaded in a tent, a picnic basket, a cooler, and when he had everything settled, he called for Henry, who splashed in the water before he leapt into the boat.

"It looks like he's done this before," Kate said.

"Henry loves the water." It was still morning, and the sun shone through a few clouds and sparkled on the ocean. "It is a calm day," Marco said. "We should make it in only a few hours. Are you ready, my love?" He covered his eyes with a pair of sunglasses.

"Yes," Kate said. She tucked her bag under her feet and sat down on the front bench next to Henry.

Marco took off his shirt, and Kate's body prickled with yearning. She watched the muscles in his arms tense as he lowered the motor into the water and pulled the line to start it. With one hand on the motor to steer, he pointed the boat south, and they crossed over a few small breaking waves and then puttered down the beach.

When the boat seemed steady, Marco opened the picnic basket with his free hand and poured them both a cup of champagne. He pulled out an orange and offered her half. The motor hummed, and the boat splashed over small waves.

She decided to take off her sundress and let the sun wash over her shoulders. Marco lifted his sunglasses, and his eyes drilled into hers. He said, "You are the prettiest girl I have ever seen." He reached into the basket and pulled out some beef jerky. "Will you give this to Henry?" He lowered the glasses back over his face.

Henry scarfed up the jerky. Marco pulled out a bowl and poured some water in it from a glass bottle. "He might also need this." Kate sat the bowl at his paws, and he slurped it up.

"We are leaving Sunrise Beach, now," Marco said. "Then next, see the big, pink hotel? He pointed to a giant pink and orange building that resembled a castle. "That is Prince's beach. Many famous people stay there. Baseball players and such. I used to work there. My friend works at the pool, still. We should go sometime."

A few sunbathers and folks out for early morning walks waved at them as they passed. Kate and Marco waved back. As the sun rose, they passed the end of the strip of land, and all Kate could see in the distance was water. She felt a little uneasy. Maybe she should have at least called and told Steph where they were going.

"There are life jackets here." He pointed to them. "The weather is clear, and you have me. I am certified in deep-sea diving, and I have my captain's license."

Kate fidgeted with her suit strap. "Why do I feel like sometimes you can read my mind?"

He smiled. "I like watching you."

They continued floating out into an expanse of open blue. Kate adjusted her sunglasses over her own eyes, trying to be more mysterious.

"Okay, Mr. Del Rio, if I'm going to tell you everything, then also, I get to ask about you."

"I am an open book for you. What do you want to know?"

"How old are you?" she asked.

"How old do you want me to be?"

"Marco," she threw an orange peel at him, and he laughed, showing off his straight teeth and his dimples. "That's a fair question. How old is the infamous Marco Del Rio?"

"How old are you?" he asked. She had to think for a minute about her last birthday. Time seemed to be going so fast.

"I'm twenty. Annnnd you?" She put her arm in the water and drizzled the water over her legs.

"I am twenty-five," he said.

"Really?" Kate couldn't believe this. "But you seem, I mean, you look, so much younger." He laughed again.

"My grandmother, Abuela Maya, says that you are only as old as you think you are. So, I am thinking, I am about twenty."

He looked up at the sky now and put his finger to his forehead. "Okay, maybe twenty-three." It was as if the sun turned him even bronzer each second, his eyes greener. She wanted to put her hands on his glistening body. "But Abuela Maya is ninety-five. And she is walking around like she is fifty. Gardening, canning, singing, dancing. So, I believe what she says."

Kate couldn't help but smile. Twenty-five sounded old. Why would she care, though? She couldn't remember the last time she felt this happy.

"My turn, Katie Bella." His face turned a little more serious, and he lifted his glasses, so she could see his eyes again. "Do you have kids?"

"Marco," she said. "Do you think if I had kids, I would have left them somewhere else and come chasing you around the beach?"

She laughed at herself. She was feeling the champagne loosen her body.

He laughed. "Are you chasing me around the beach? It seems as if I had to chase you all the way to Ohio."

"You had your friends chase me," she said.

"*Our* friends," he corrected.

No," she smiled. "I don't have kids."

He softened. "Do you want to have kids?"

She leaned her arms back on the bench and crossed her ankles on the seat. "Sometimes. I sort of want to be able to take care of myself, first, though, you know? Have a career? Do something good for the world. What about you?"

A drip of sweat trickled down her stomach. He put his free hand on her ankle and ran it toward her knee. "I would like to, with your permission, climb on top of you and kiss your entire body from top to bottom," he said. "And take your bathing suit off with my teeth."

"Marco," Kate blushed. "We'll rock the boat over. Is Lily your only daughter?"

"You can rock my boat over any time, Katie." He laughed again, this time the sound of a little-kid laugh. She'd never seen him so unrestrained. "Sí," he said. "One is enough for me right now. I love her. But her mother hurt me very badly."

"What happened?" Kate asked.

He lowered the glasses back over his eyes and took a swig of champagne.

"I mean, you don't have to tell me if you don't want to."

"No, it is okay. I proposed to her when we found out about Lily. I was not sure she was the one, but it was the right thing to do. My family is very *Católica*." He set the cup down and wiped his forehead. "I was working during the day at the hotel, then playing at night. She said that I would never make enough money to make her happy."

Kate wished she could see his eyes, but his face turned off toward the horizon. "She left me for some guy who came to my shows. A businessman." He cocked his head to the side and looked at the sky. "It was hard, but it was for the best, because now, I am here with you." He lifted his sunglasses and moved his eyes back to hers. "People think playing music is so easy, but it is a lot of work. A busy schedule. I know I am good," he said. "But I think if I work hard enough, that I could be . . . great."

Kate loved his passion for music. She wished she knew exactly what she was passionate about.

"What is it you want to do, Katie? Save the world one smile at a time?" She took a second to process his story before she sat up straight and answered.

"I think I want to go to college, maybe. Take a writing class or something." She reached out her glass and Marco poured her more champagne. "My mom wanted me to get married and be a secretary, but I never liked working in an office. I want to eventually work for myself."

"Katie Bella, my young free spirit."

Stuck for words, she gasped. A moment of deja vu, just as a

pelican crashed into the water beside their boat and started to glide. "My dad used to call me that."

"You have this way about you. Independent, self-assured, free. I mean it as a compliment."

Though Kate saw herself as everything but self-assured, she said, "Thank you. I'll take it that way."

The couple quieted for a time. Kate studied the layers of blue in the water, heard the hum of the motor, dangled her fingers into the water. If she hadn't spoken up for herself at the wedding, and if it hadn't been for her friends, she would not be here in this moment.

Land revealed itself in the distance.

"We are almost there," Marco said. "¿Tienes hambre?"

"I love it when you speak Spanish to me," she said, "even though I don't understand it."

"I will teach you," he said. "Are you hungry, Bella? We are almost there." Henry stood up and panted, wagging his tail. On the side of the boat, a dolphin appeared, and then another.

"Oh my gosh," Kate said. "I've never seen a dolphin this close before!"

"They have come to receive us. They are very curious animals. They want to know who we are and what we are doing in their water."

Kate put her hand in the water and one of them rose to the surface, close enough that she touched its smooth skin. "Oh my gosh!" Kate said. "I touched it!"

Marco smiled. "Their brains are bigger than human brains. Dolphins are very smart animals. Henry likes the dolphins, as well."

Henry let out a bark, and then a growl-talk. "He wants to play with them," Marco said. He turned down the motor to a purr. "This, up here, is Turtle Island. It is still protected land, but it is my favorite place to camp. We will get the tent set up, and then we can have our lunch."

Kate took another sip of champagne. Marco was surprising her. She put her dress back on as he guided the boat onto the island shore. When Kate and Henry got out into the sand, she helped Marco pull the ropes to beach the boat. "We are here," he said.

Henry ran across the sand, jumped in the water, then jumped out, and ran and ran. "Henry likes Turtle Island."

They carried their things up onto the beach where a small sand dune hid a clearing under a mangrove tree. "We should set up the tent here," he said.

Marco worked quickly and diligently, and Kate helped him when he asked. She had only camped a few times when she was young, but Marco was like a boy scout. He effortlessly erected the tent and then laid a soft blanket in front of it. He opened the picnic basket to turkey sandwiches and an array of snacks. "Do you like pineapple?" He pulled one out of the cooler. Kate sat on the blanket in the shade.

"Where did you get this blanket?" she asked. "I do like pineapple."

He pulled out a knife and a cutting board and trimmed it, quickly, cutting it into cubes. "My mother gave it to me."

"What's your mother like?" She leaned back onto her elbows and crossed her legs.

He ate another piece of pineapple and handed her one. "She is like feisty, fiery. She is an excellent cook, and she does not take any flak from anybody. Sometimes she has to, porque my dad's family is even feistier. My aunts really gave her the runaround at first. You know, he is from México and she is American. They tease her and test her, and she is very small, like five-foot-nothing, but she handles them with the strongest poise. The white girl in the Mexicana family. My dad, he tells stories about her, how she will never take any crap from anybody, even his sisters."

"And your dad?" The pineapple stung her tongue and puckered her lips.

Marco smiled, almost distantly. "My dad is more complicado. But sturdy, and stable. He had problems coming to the states. Some white people, even in Texas, are not nice to Mexicans. But he found a job at a cattle farm, and he worked hard to support us. He plays the Spanish guitar better than anybody in Texas. I think if he would have stayed in México, then he could have made it big there, but when he met my mother, he says he heard angels sing. She says that when they met, his guitar put a spell on her and she has been cursed ever since. He grins when he tells the story. He left Mexico to be near her, and he had to put his music at the background."

Marco's eyes were off into the water. "They own a ranch now, and my siblings are all grown. I think he may be able to retire someday and play guitar again. Also, they are very religious, and they often tell me that I am not living up to God's will for me." He wiped his hands on the blanket. "I just think, if there is a God, that He wants me to be happy." He shrugged his shoulders.

This sounded familiar. "What can I do to help?" Kate asked looking at the spread of snacks and feeling like she hadn't done much.

"You can sit in the sun or the shade, and just look beautiful, as you do."

"But I want to do something."

"Okay," he said, "I brought some cheese, in the cooler. Do you like cheese?"

"Yes," she said.

"Here is the knife if you want to cut them into pieces. Kate was surprised. There was Swiss, cheddar, and a white cheese in the shape of a wheel that she had never seen before.

"What is this?" she asked.

"This is brie, the sweetest of white cheeses. There are blueberries and almonds, and we can go to the spring and fish later, and that is why I brought the salsa. Do you like to fish?"

Kate had been fishing with her dad when she was small.

"Sí," she said.

"You are working on your Spanish," he said. "Muy bien." He leaned over and kissed her, put a piece of pineapple in his mouth, and offered her another. She took it from his fingers and put it in her mouth, tasting the sweet and sour.

"Katie Bella," he said, "I would like to take you out of that red dress."

"And what might you do to get me out of it?" she teased. He got close to her.

"I might approach you like this," he said, "and kiss you once like this."

He put his lips against hers, sweetly, then he opened her mouth with his and she could taste the pineapple on his tongue. He ran his hands up her arms, then down them again, and pulled her dress up and over her shoulders.

"It's the daylight." She felt suddenly shy.

"There is nobody here but us, and Henry, but he is busy chasing dolphins in the water."

"Do you want to go swimming?"

"Sí, Bella, but first I would like to have you here, on this blanket, if you will allow me to. "Te quiero a todos para siempre."

He laid her body down on the blanket, so she was on her back, and he took her over, all of him encompassing her again. She whimpered so slightly as he hovered over her, curving and curling his body into an intimate tangle of delight.

Kate caught a glimpse of the blue, blue sky before she burned so intensely from the inside out, that she thought she might erupt. She found his eyes and then his lips, and then he cradled her head with his hands, moving slowly, then slower, then falling onto her, his head in her neck. She opened her eyes, and she laughed.

Marco blinked through his heavy breath. "What is funny?"

"Henry's here." He strutted up slowly.

"Tiempo privado, nosy."

"What does that mean?" Kate asked.

"Private time," Marco said, nibbling at her bottom lip. "He knows what it means. ¿Sí, señor?"

Henry put his tail down behind his legs and walked back toward the beach side of the sand dune.

"Oh, no." Kate said. "He's sad."

"He will survive. I would like to stay with you always, Katie."

A thought welled up from her heart that Kate couldn't shake. She didn't want to talk about it, but Marco had said that she needed to tell him how she felt. "I'm sorry about that day with Gina."

"That day was not your fault."

"No," Kate said. "I want to. I mean, people on the beach kept warning me that you were bad news, that you weren't faithful. And so I guess, that day, I didn't believe you, and I started to believe them." Kate cleared her throat. "I mean, I just wanted to say I'm sorry for doubting you. I was just, scared I guess, that they were right." He rolled off her body, balancing his weight with his elbows, and onto his back. He reached for the cigarettes and tapped one out of the pack.

"I am sorry she came into our lives like that." He took a puff and then handed it to her. "I was not always a good guy, in the past," he said. "But after my daughter was born, I wanted to be the kind of guy that she would want to love someday. You know, kind. And respectable. But, with my lifestyle . . . ." he rubbed his face, " . . . it was hard to find a good girl. A girl who can handle my playing every night, you know? But now I know, I was on my way to finding you."

They lay there for a while in the shade, and then Marco got up and resumed his position by the picnic basket. Kate slid her sundress back on and sat cross-legged. Marco fed Kate a piece of brie, taking time for his finger to touch her tongue and then he said, "How is it?"

"It's delicious." They ate until they had their fill, and then he said, "Okay, how about that swimming?"

The water was warm. They took turns jumping in and out of the waves. Henry re-joined them, and then Marco said, "Look, Bella." Only five feet from them, a sea turtle surfaced. He poked his head out of the water and paused at their faces.

"Hola tortuga," Marco said. Kate was in awe. "You know they live for a hundred years or more." The turtle looked back and forth between them. Its eyes were kind and curious. She wasn't sure how she had landed in this life, in paradise, swimming with sea turtles and Marco and Henry. She could do this forever.

The turtle took one more look at them. Kate reached out to try to touch his head or his shell, and he ducked under the water, and swam on. When it was out of eyesight, Marco said, "Let's go fishing."

They got out of the water and found the fishing poles. He grabbed a tackle box and led her over white sandy paths, through trees and jungle plants. Henry trotted behind them. Marco knew the names of all the different palm trees. "This is a queen palm." He touched its trunk. "And this is a king." They came to a clearing with a waterfall, and a small, clear pool of water.

"Our destination," he said.

The scenery took Kate's breath away. The water was so clear they could see the fish swimming in the pool. It smelled like the freshest air, the cleanest. Pink, white and orange flowers the size of Kate's hand spread out around the pool.

"Oh my gosh," Kate cradled one with her hand, careful not to bruise its petals. "What are these?"

"These are hibiscus flowers. Florida means "flowering Easter." A dragonfly flitted between them, paused, and then flew on. "Ponce de León came to Florida first on Palm Sunday."

"You are like a walking encyclopedia." Kate was mesmerized. "What do we do?"

"We put our hooks in the water, and we catch our dinner." He rigged up the poles with hooks out of the tackle box. "Pero," he said, "we need bait. We catch some small fish, with these small hooks, and then we catch bigger ones." He rigged up the hooks with tiny meal worms he had brought.

He put them on the hooks, and they dropped them in the water. They watched the fish eye the bait, and then a rather large, pink fish bit on Kate's hook, and she pulled. Marco said, "Maybe we do not need small bait."

Kate pulled it onto the shore. "A sunfish, a delicacy of the sea." Kate bristled with excitement. "It is enough for dinner, and maybe for lunch." Marco guided her hand to put it into their net. "Henry, no," he said. Henry sat and wagged his tail. He looked like he wanted to play with the fish. "*No tuyos*. Not yours." Henry laid down and put his head on his paws.

"Can we swim here?" Kate asked.

"We can do whatever you want."

Kate removed her bathing suit and jumped into the water. Marco followed her quickly. When he emerged, she wrapped his body with her legs and kissed him. She put her hands over his slick, black hair, and touched his supple lips with hers. "How did I get so lucky?"

Marco breathed heavily into her ear. "I am the lucky one." Kate had been careful not to profess anything to Marco, after all — she wasn't looking for a husband. But now she said, "I know we haven't known each other for a long time, but I feel like I've known you forever, somehow."

He carried her under the waterfall. The cool water poured over their bodies and massaged Kate's shoulders. He pulled her up onto the rock underneath, and kissed her lips, then her neck, then he climbed up next to her and sat.

"There is something I have to tell you," he said.

Oh, no, Kate thought. "Are you going steady with someone else?" Kate had never asked him that. It came out of her mouth before she even thought about it.

He turned and put his hand on her face. "*You* are my dream girl. My future." They sat there bare skinned on the rocks with the water falling all around them.

"Then what is it?"

"I am going on tour. My agent called me last week and finally booked a national tour for me."

CHAPTER THIRTY-FOUR

Kate's insides folded in fear. "The band," he said, "has a pretty good following. I have done some studio work for them. They do not have a big name, yet. But my agent thinks that this could be my big break." He waved his arms as he said the word, 'break.'

Oh, no, Kate thought. She splashed water over her face. "What will happen with us?"

"Would you come with me?"

Oh, no. Kate felt okay about picking up and leaving Ohio, but could she just pick up her life and leave Florida?

"What will I do on tour with you?"

"Whatever you want," he said. "You could write, you can read, you can do whatever you like. We can see the country, maybe the world . . . ."

Kate couldn't wrap her mind around this. She wanted to be with him, but she didn't know if she wanted to follow around a guy, even Marco.

"Oh," she let out a loud sigh. "I need to think about this. I don't know if I'm ready."

He pleaded with her then. "I will do whatever you want me

to do. In our life. I will not go if you do not want me to. I could get a job, with better pay. Or I could go back to the hotel, and we could start our own family."

"Marco," Kate said. She didn't know if she could handle this. She certainly couldn't ask him to stop living his dream. "Let me think about it, okay? For now, would you just make love to me? Please?"

Marco said, "You never have to say 'please' after you ask me to make love to you."

He let himself off the rock, took her body into his, and pulled her close. "I love you, Katie. I will have you any way I can, forever and for always."

BACK AT THE CAMPSITE, Marco showed Kate how to carve the fish. He heated some garlic and oil in a cast-iron skillet and fried it up for them. He pulled out the salsa.

"This is Abuela Maya's recipe. Black beans and corn." He spread it all over some steamed rice, and as the sun set, they ate fresh fish and stared out over the water in silence. Kate didn't realize how hungry she was. She gulped down one helping of fish, and then another. Henry sat patiently next to them until they had their fill. Then Marco fed him their leftover meat, placing the rest in the cooler for the morning.

Marco carried the blanket out onto the beach, and they laid silently next to one another, looking at the stars in the clear night, listening to the waves push and roll against the sand.

"Now it is me, who cannot resist you," Kate said, "and it is unlike me."

He propped himself onto his elbows, took a deep breath, and said, "I asked God for this."

"What?" Kate asked.

He reached over and clutched her hand. "I prayed for this

very moment, and now it is here. *Gracias a Dios.*" Then he laid back down and stared at the sky.

He had his arms around her when she woke, and his head between her shoulder and her neck. She spent a few minutes just holding him. Henry laid next to her, raised his head from his paws, and panted. Kate had never had a dog before. Her heart welled up in gratitude.

The first thought that crept in, she tried to push away. But it came back. Could she go on tour with him? What would that even look like? And what if she didn't go? If there were a million girls on the beach in love with him, how many would fall in love with him while he was touring the country? Would he be faithful? Even if she were there? Would he keep his promises? Would she be able to tour with him? What should she do?

She untangled from Marco's arms and waded into the water. Henry rose, stretched, and followed her. Sunrise spread over the water, and Kate had no idea what time it was, which felt like its own kind of freedom. A small boat bounced up and down on the horizon.

Part of Kate wanted to travel, and have new adventures, but the other part of her was afraid. Sure, she could do her own thing. Sure, she could write and read. But how would she make money? She didn't want to depend on Marco, and she didn't see herself being able to support herself on the road.

She kept coming back to the other girls. It was one thing to be in the midst of sultry eyes focused on him at The Wave and The Parrot, but it was quite another to think about traveling the country and seeing girls from all other walks of life eyeing him all of the time.

But maybe she was overthinking it. Her dad had told her to follow her heart, and so far, it had worked out. She had at least experienced love. But was she willing to let it go? Could she hang on to it? There were so many unknowns. She wasn't sure what to do. She said a silent prayer to the sunrise and then Henry barked.

Kate looked ahead. In an approaching boat she made out the profiles of Steph, Captain, Jack, and Noah. Heading their way. She ran back up to the towel, and quickly put her bathing suit back on. She leaned down and kissed Marco awake.

"Marco," Kate said. "Our friends are here."

"What? Who?" He opened his eyes and rubbed at them.

Kate handed him his shorts. "You might want to put these on."

"Dios mío," he said as he put one leg on at a time. "We cannot be alone for even one day?"

"How did they find us?" Kate wondered out loud. "Did you tell anybody we were coming?"

"Only Timbale," he said.

As the boat approached, Jack stood up, beer can in hand.

"Ahoy!" He yelled.

"Jack," Steph yelled. "You're going to rock the—" and then the boat rolled over, spilling their friends into the ocean. Kate and Marco laughed uncontrollably, but Marco stood up and walked toward the shore.

"You amigos okay?"

Each one surfaced, and they all struggled to retrieve the life jackets and miscellaneous that were floating out in all directions over the waves.

"Jack," Captain said, "you rascal." They were all laughing now.

"Look, friends, I saved my beer!" Jack treaded water with it raised above the surface.

"Of course you did," Steph said, swimming now toward the sand. "You guys, get the boat."

The guys managed to roll the boat back over, and put the items they'd saved back in. They swam it in, pulling it by the rope.

"What are you guys doing here?" Marco asked. "Katie and I are having a wonderful private time." He was smiling. "By ourselves."

"I see that," Steph said, wading out of the water. She was wearing jean shorts and a bathing suit top.

"There's a storm coming," Captain said. "Tropical. We came to let you know."

"Yesterday the weather report said clear all week." Marco ran a hand over his hair.

"Yeah," Captain said. "It was just a storm hovering over the Bahamas, but apparently it's gained strength and is coming this way. It's supposed to hit this afternoon. They're talking one-hundred mile-an-hour winds, eight to ten-foot waves. We weren't sure when you guys were coming back, but we were afraid of you getting stuck in the middle of it."

"Timbale told us you were here," Steph said, "we decided to take a boat trip to let you know."

"You know how we like trips," Noah said and smiled. Kate hugged him.

Marco stood facing the horizon. He put his hands on his hips. Noah and Jack pulled the boat up onto the sand next to Marco's. Henry put a stick in front of Noah's feet, and Noah smiled and threw it into the waves.

Marco said, "We should probably go then."

"It's about eight o'clock now," Jack said. "If we leave in the next hour, we should be able to beat the storm."

"We can help you guys pack up," Steph said.

They all gathered up the camp site and helped load Marco and Kate's gear into the boat. Marco grabbed Kate by the waist, in front of everyone, and kissed her. "I guess we will have to have our dinner at home. Is that okay?"

She was disappointed that their trip was ending already, but she had not yet been through a Florida storm. "I mean, I don't want to get stuck out here in bad weather."

Jack passed out beers from the cooler. "For the going away party," he said.

When the boats were loaded up, Kate climbed in with Henry and Marco, and Steph and the guys piled into the other one. They started up the motors and headed back north.

The morning sun rose higher and higher. Kate draped her fingers through the water and propped her feet up on the edge. The boats stayed close enough that they could hear the others' conversations now and then. When Jack stood up to get something, Steph said, "Jack, I swear, if you tip us over again, we're leaving you out here." Everybody laughed. After about an hour, Kate could see an outline of the storm looming. There was a cluster of gray and yellow clouds moving toward them.

"Do not worry," Marco said. "We will be okay."

She reached into the cooler, retrieved the open bottle of champagne, and poured them both cups. "No thank you," Marco said. "I want to be completely alert, just in case."

She drank hers, then his.

CHAPTER THIRTY-FIVE

$\mathcal{H}$enry whined, and the hair on his back stood up. As the wind picked up, Kate felt a chill on her shoulders. The storm built as if in slow motion, picked up air and clouds from the land, and dragged them out over the water. Yellow, gray, and reddish clouds formed in a threatening rotation.

Kate could see land, but they were still quite far away. Marco's face became stern and serious as he steered their little boat. Everybody stayed quiet.

A puttering sound broke the silence. Their friends' boat slowed, then stopped. The waves had grown taller, and when the engine cut off, the boat bounced and kicked around. Kate and Marco began drifting away.

"What happened?" Marco yelled. He steered toward them, until both boats were side by side, but pointing opposite directions. He cut their motor. Kate smelled something burning.

Jack pulled at the motor string. It sputtered and stopped.

"Do we have gas?" Steph asked.

"I think so," Jack said.

"What do you mean, you think so?" She clutched the side of the boat as it rolled. "Did you fill the tank before we left?"

"No," Jack said. "I mean, I just borrowed it from my friend this morning. I figured it already had gas."

"Did you check?" Steph asked.

"How do you check?"

Steph's face turned red.

"We have gas," Marco said. "Here."

Kate, Captain and Noah held the boats together and Marco handed Jack a gas can. Jack pulled off the cap and dumped it in. He pulled the throttle. The motor sputtered again, but it didn't turn over.

"Shit," Jack said. "I don't know what it is." He pulled at it again.

"Let me see," Marco said. He climbed into their boat and lifted the top off the motor. The sky rumbled.

"I can't tell, man. I cannot tell what's wrong."

Noah reached into the electrical lines, and moved them around with his hands, then pulled one out that appeared broken. "It's burnt," he said. "Old wires, maybe."

"What do we do?" said Captain.

Steph said, "Can you guys go and get help, and then come back for us?"

"We are not leaving you out here, Steph," Kate said.

Marco said, "I do not think we have time."

"We could tie the boats together," Noah said. "And row."

The guys looked around, then at each other.

"Okay," Marco said. "Let's get going."

"Girls, get in the back boat with Henry." Noah said. "Guys up front." Kate led Henry into the other boat, and the guys climbed into the front boat one by one. It started to rain. After the lines were secure, Marco sat down and steered.

The guys rowed as the rain grew steadier and steadier. The

first bolt of lightning cracked, drawing a line from the sky to the water. Kate and Steph huddled together.

"So, Library," Steph said. "Your first ocean adventure?" Kate closed her eyes and took a deep breath. "We're in good hands," Steph said. Kate believed her, but she said a prayer anyway. The sky grew darker. They were still too far to swim.

"We can roll onto Prince's beach," Marco said over the sound of thunder. "And then find shelter there." They kept paddling. The waves splashed over the sides of the boat. Henry whined again. Another bolt of lightning struck the beach in a long and bright yellow zigzag.

Kate pet Henry's head. His fur was starting to mat under the rain. "It's going to be all right, boy," she said. She wished she believed it.

A large wave came over the front boat and knocked Captain and Noah from their seats. They got back up and kept paddling. Another one came and splashed over the back of the boat. The motor made a sputter noise, and then cut out.

"Shit," Marco said. He used some words in Spanish that Kate didn't understand.

"What's up?" Noah asked.

Marco pulled the throttle, and it didn't even make a sound. They started to float away from land. "Keep paddling." They did, but all their strength combined only seemed to keep the boats static.

"Girls," Marco said. "Put your jackets on." Kate and Steph both wrapped themselves in orange life jackets. Kate shivered. Marco pulled at the throttle again.

Nothing happened.

"It's washed out," he said. "Guys, life jackets. One at a time. Jack, you first." One by one the guys took turns paddling and putting their life jackets on. They were getting pulled out farther into the ocean. It was still morning, but the sky looked like dusk. Layers of gray, blue and purple hovered over them. The rain came down harder.

"It's a whiteout," Captain said.

"What do we do?" Steph asked.

"Pray," Marco said. Kate said another prayer. Even Jack was quiet now, paddling, to no avail. A wave hit the back boat and suddenly Kate was alone in the vessel.

Henry and Steph were in the water.

Kate gasped. Steph's head bobbed up a few feet from the boat. Henry paddled frantically. He was moving farther out into the ocean. A bolt of lightning flashed, and thunder rang at the same time. A wave covered them.

Kate heard a voice in her own mind, *trust yourself.* It sounded like her father's voice. She saw Marco's eyes say, *no,* but she grabbed the white and black safety ring and jumped into the water toward Steph.

Salt water stung her eyes. Choked her nose. Cold. She found the surface and took a deep breath. A flash. Marco on the bow. "Raft, to your right!" A splash of orange, felt something, grabbed Steph by the life jacket.

"Steph," Kate sputtered.

"I'm okay," she coughed.

The lifesaver pulled them under.

"Kate, raft to your right!" On the other side of a wave, the other lifesaver floated. She dropped the first one. Hooked her arm around the other, holding Steph.

"Henry," Kate said.

She started toward him, but the lifesaver pulled them against the current.

They bobbed against metal. A biting sensation at her left arm, and in the next flash of light, hands on the sleeves of Steph's life jacket. Her outline rose from the water.

"Kate," Steph said. Kate released the side of the boat.

"Jack, Flare!" Noah yelled.

"Henry!" Kate screamed.

"Your left!" A red streak in the water. Another wave over the head. A hint of white. A whimper.

Orange.

"Almost!"

A paw. She grabbed it. The line reached its limit and tugged her backwards. His leg cracked as they jerked. He yelped. She didn't let go. Marco's face. Water. Henry's collar. Noah. Henry's snout bobbed under. Noah's voice. "You got this, Kate. Swim!" Henry's eyes, glazed.

Another wave crashed over their heads.

"Hold tight," Marco said. Kate swallowed water; held her breath. Arms around her.

An orange light flashed. She moved her feet. Kept hold of Henry.

The metal side of the boat. "Henry," Marco's voice. Henry's body in the air, water hanging from his limp body. Captain standing over them. "Kate," Marco said. His body against hers. Her life jacket tightened around her.

Then she was in the boat, too.

"You're crazy, Library. Are you okay?" Captain.

She coughed. Nodded. Water everywhere. Wind blocked her ears.

Noah lifted Marco by the jacket and into the boat. Jack paddled, still with the oars. The rain encompassed them, now, falling all over them in sheets. She couldn't see anything in front or behind. Only water. All of them in one boat. Knee deep. Rolling violently back and forth.

"We're too heavy," Captain said. The back boat was sinking.

"It'll pull us under . . . untie the lines!" Marco and Noah scrambled to the sides. Jack shot another flare into the dark. Steph held on, and Kate hovered over Henry, keeping his head above water.

A green light shot out of the corner of her eye.

"Jack, flare!" Noah said.

"Last one," he yelled, as a wave crashed into them again.

Marco leaned into Kate, panting. "I love you, Katie Bella."

"I love *you*." Lightning and thunder hit at the same time, and everybody ducked.

The last flare lit up the sky like a firework, highlighting a million droplets of rain in an ominous twist of giant gray clouds. A glowing outline turned toward them. Kate's nose burned. She clutched the seat of the boat.

"Thank you, Jesus," Steph said.

The second boat was gone. Sunk. They took turns holding onto one another and trying to scoop out the ocean from their remaining sinking rowboat. As the ship approached, Kate could hardly see anything through the sheets of rain, but one shadowy mass.

"Ahoy!" a guy said. The boat banged against their starboard side. A life raft appeared, then a ladder. Kate's teeth chattered over the pattering of the rain. Everything sounded like she was in a tunnel. She wiped blood from her arm.

"Kate and Steph, go!" Noah said.

Steph climbed into the bouncing life raft and up the ladder.

"Katie," Marco yelled, "Henry!" Jack held Henry in the lifeboat, struggling to get him up the ladder. The sailor said, "I've got it," and moved Kate to the side. In a stilled moment of panic, like a slow-motion photograph, Kate thought he had the sweetest, kindest eyes. Like a child.

Another bolt of lightning. Crack of thunder.

"I think his leg is broken," she said.

"I've got him, get into the cabin," he pointed, "hold on to the lifelines."

She and Steph stumbled through the wind and rain, following the bars, their hands slipping on the cool, wet metal. Wind howled in their ears. They turned the corner to find another man at the helm. He had dark hair and sunglasses on his head, tied to his neck with a string.

"I'm Ed. I'd shake your hand, but I can't take them off the wheel."

"Steph," she said, "And Kate."

"You're bleeding."

"Yes, I," Kate touched the wound for the first time. A small layer of skin had peeled from her arm. "It's just a scratch."

"Go downstairs and dry off." Ed said. "First aid kit in the salon. My buddy's got the guys."

"Are you sure?" Kate asked.

"We're squids," he said.

"Squids?"

"United States Navy, miss. We've got you." Henry, soaking wet and panting, found them. He was limping. Kate hugged his neck.

"Oh, my gosh, boy, are you okay?" Henry sniffed at Ed's back, water spraying out of his nose. He shook the water from his fur before Kate and Steph carried him down below.

Steph helped Kate wrap her arm in gauze, then they wrapped Henry's as best as they could. The guys came down, one at a time. Marco, Jack, Captain, and Noah. They were all soaked, cold, and tired, but they were alive. The guy from the deck of the boat shook each one of their hands and introduced himself.

"I'm Jay," he said. Blonde hair peeked out of a floppy hat. He indeed looked like a very grown-up child.

"Thank you, Jay," Marco said.

"Not a problem. I'm going to help Ed get us to land. What the hell you guys doing out here in that little boat, by the way?"

Marco said, "Two boats. We had two, but one of the motors burned out and the other one flooded just as we could see shore. We were camping." Guilt washed over his face. "Our friends came to find us, to warn us about the storm."

Jay nodded. "Me and Ed just got called to duty. Wanted to take one last fishing trip before we go. Had the radio off so the fish wouldn't scare but got caught in it as we were coming into shore. Good timing, though, I guess. We just happened to see your flare."

"Thank you so much, Jay," Kate said. "You were an answer to our prayers."

"Thank you," Noah said, shaking his hand again.

"Welcome aboard the Dixie, named after my mom who passed."

"Jay," Ed called from the helm, "still in a storm up here!"

Jay touched the bill of his hat. "Duty calls. Make yourselves at home. Booze in the fridge, smoke in the galley cabinet. But don't tell anybody about the smoke, if you don't mind. We're gonna get her in and get you guys home safe."

"Can we help?" Noah asked.

"We'll probably be okay, now. Me and Ed have ridden the rough seas together many times before. It's kind of our thing."

Noah saluted, and Jay saluted back. Then he climbed up the stairs.

The boat rocked and pulled from the inside now. Kate dried off and took a few deep breaths to let her panic subside.

Jack said, "Just another day in paradise." He reached into the fridge and pulled out a bottle of vodka. "Drinks?"

Marco's eyes drilled into Kate's. "I am so sorry for putting you in danger."

"You didn't know," Kate said.

"Yeah, man," said Captain. "Even Jay said he hadn't heard about the storm." Marco crouched next to Henry. He panted and turned his head for a pet. Jack handed Kate a drink, and she took a sip.

"Who knows what would have happened to us if you guys had not showed," Marco said. "Thank you for finding us."

"Cheers," said Jack.

"To living the dream," said Captain.

Everyone was drenched. The storm continued to pound and blow, but Jay and Ed found a slip on the edge of Prince's beach. They all climbed into Jay's truck, girls in the cab, guys and Henry in the bed, and Jay drove them back up to Marco's place.

"Are you sure you'll be okay here?" Jay asked as they all loaded out. The tide had risen halfway up to the trailer. Rain fell all around them.

Marco said, "We have vehicles here if we need to get farther inland." Lightning crashed and thunder roared. The wind howled. Kate held onto the side of the truck as they said their goodbyes. Everybody was soaking wet again.

Steph stood up on the lip of the truck and kissed Jay on the cheek. "Thanks, man," she said. "You saved our lives."

"Oh," he said, a slight of pink twinged above his little-boy cheeks. "Don't mention it." He glanced over at Ed, who had climbed into the cab. "It's what we do. Only a small adventure in the days of sailing the high seas." He flashed Steph a peace sign. "You guys take care."

Then Jay and Ed pulled away, and Kate never saw them again.

CHAPTER THIRTY-SEVEN

The friends ran inside. Marco passed out towels and warm clothes, and they changed, one by one in the bedroom and the bathroom, the girls first.

As they warmed up Steph said, "Kate, tell me about your night, please." Noah and Jack sat on the couch, the girls stood in the kitchen, and Marco and Captain were changing.

"Tell you later," Kate said.

"Oh, my, gosh, Library," Jack said. "You're such a prude."

Kate picked up a dishtowel from the counter and threw it at him. "I don't kiss and tell, Jack. That's all."

He ducked under the towel. "So, you kissed him," Jack said. "Well, this is a start." They all laughed.

When Marco and Captain joined them Kate said, "Should we still be worried? About the storm?"

Marco looked out of the kitchen window and studied the wind and the water. "I don't know, guys, what do you think?"

"This is the best hurricane party I've ever been to," Jack said. "Anybody wanna go surfing?"

"Jesus, Jack," Kate said. "Can we take a minute to acknowledge that we almost just died out there?"

Marco grabbed Kate by the belt loops of his jeans she had put on. "I am so sorry, Katie."

"It's okay," she said. "We're okay." She brushed her wet hair behind her ears. "That was just, scary." For a moment Kate forgot that the others were in the room. She searched his eyes.

"Yes, it was," he said. "I will never put you in that much danger, ever again."

"It wasn't your fault. I'm sorry about your boat."

He licked his lips. "I can get another boat. I cannot get another Katie." He kissed her then, softly.

"Get a room," Captain said.

Marco smiled. "We have a house," he said. "On the beach. And you are in it."

"A *free love beach house*," Jack said. Steph laughed.

Marco released Kate's belt loops. "What do you guys think?"

Noah peered out the window. He scratched his head. "I think we saw the worst of it in the water, but the tide is still rising."

"What do you guys want to do?" Marco said.

"Can we stay here?" Steph asked. "And we'll leave if the tide gets too high?

"Sure," Marco said. "However long you need."

"Play us some songs, Rio," Steph said. She cuddled up next to Captain on the couch. Marco took one of his guitars from the wall, sat down and started to play. Kate sat next to him and curled her toes against his waist. She was so glad to be out of the water. To be warm. To be with Marco and her friends. It wasn't long before she fell asleep.

Kate woke up in Marco's bed and looked out the window. The sun was shining brilliantly, the tide had gone back down, and though there were trees and rubble scattered along the beach, she could barely tell there had been a storm. Henry laid on his blankets, head on his paws, looking at her. Marco was asleep by her side.

As she crawled out of bed, Henry stood up and stretched and

followed her to the bathroom. Kate giggled. "I'll only be a minute." She shut the door in his face. Her toothbrush was lost at sea, so she spread some toothpaste over her teeth with her finger and washed her face.

She almost didn't recognize her reflection in the mirror. Her eyes were wild and alive, her heart open. She said a prayer of gratitude again. She truly believed that Jay and Ed showing up, even their friends showing up at Turtle Island, had been divine intervention. She looked at herself again and she smiled.

She liked who she was.

Henry jumped when she opened the door, and then led her to the back. He still limped slightly but seemed to be putting more weight on his injured paw. "Oh, I see," she whispered, "you want to go outside." She opened the sliding glass door. He ran out to the beach, sniffing and galloping.

Steph and Captain were cuddled on the couch, and Jack and Noah on the floor. Kate realized she was starving. In the kitchen she found eggs, bacon, and some red potatoes. She had to open a few different cabinets, but she located a skillet, a loaf of bread, and made some coffee.

Kate's friends woke up one by one to the smells of breakfast after the storm. Marco wandered in wearing only a pair of shorts. Kate eyed his stomach muscles and had a memory of them bristling on top of her.

"Katie Bella," he said, hugging her and then kissing her. "Cooking in my kitchen." He smiled and pulled a coffee cup from the cabinet. "I could get used to this."

Jack awoke and said, "Throw me a brew."

"Jack," Marco said, reaching into the refrigerator and pulling out a beer. "You are a lush, my friend. We also have coffee." He tossed the can to Jack.

"I'll have coffee," Steph said. Kate realized she hadn't even asked Steph if she and Captain had made it official. Or about Peggy. She needed to ask Captain about getting her job back. Or did she? She didn't even know when Marco was supposed to leave.

Noah stretched and yawned as he came into the kitchen. "Kate, you were really brave yesterday."

"Yeah," Steph said. "I owe you one."

"We were all brave. I wouldn't want to be stuck in a storm with anyone else." Her mind was already drifting to the future. "When does your tour start, Marco?" She thought she whispered it.

"Two weeks," he said.

"Tour?" Steph asked.

Marco pulled plates out of the cabinet. "My agent booked a tour for me. It could be big."

"Are these the same music people from New York?" Steph asked.

"Different," he said. Kate stepped back and gestured that the eggs and bacon were finished. "Come and get it, my friends. Breakfast made by the lovely Miss Katie."

Captain stood up first and made a plate.

Marco backed Kate up by her belt loops and held her against him on the far counter.

"I let Henry out," she said.

"You let your dog out, and now you must watch to let him back in." He laughed. She looked over her shoulder and kissed him. "We should probably get his leg checked out."

"Where you going, man?" Captain asked.

"It is a North American tour," he said. "Major cities." Kate sipped her coffee, glad to be awake and alive.

Noah made himself a plate. "Thanks for breakfast, Kate," he said, and kissed her on the cheek.

"You're welcome." It felt like the least she could do for her friends.

"Yeah," Captain said. "Thanks for cooking. It's nice when I don't have to," he smiled.

Steph said, "You should see this guy. At your place he makes these elaborate seafood specials, and at home he eats pizza rolls and frozen fish sticks."

"But I'm a master at pizza rolls and fish sticks." He gave Steph a swift kiss on the lips.

"Ho," Jack said. "And we have another couple, courting."

"What about you, Kate." Captain said. "What are you going to do next?"

"I don't know," she said.

After their friends left, Marco cleaned up the kitchen and Kate fell asleep on the couch. She dreamt of the storm and woke up in a cold sweat.

"I am here, Bella," Marco said.

Kate, still half in dream world, saw him tinkering with his guitar on the chair. Henry lay next to her, on the floor between the couch and the coffee table.

"How long have I been asleep?"

"It is seven-thirty."

"Oh my gosh," Kate said. "For hours?"

"You must have needed it. The vet says that Henry has a sprained leg, and that we should continue to wrap it."

Kate reached down and patted Henry's head. Marco tucked his guitar under his arm, stood up, and kissed her. Smoke flickered from a stick of incense.

"Have you thought any more about going with me?"

"No," Kate sat up. "I mean, yes. I mean, I don't know, Marco." He got down on his knees.

"What do you want to do? I do not want you to give up your dreams for me, but I want you to stay with me, as long as you will." She held his chin, then guided him up to face her.

"Lay on the couch with me?"

He propped the guitar against the chair and laid down in front of her. Kate wanted to just lie here and hold him.

"I have a show tonight. I have to load up in a half an hour."

"I don't know what to do. I honestly," she stopped. "I want to be with you, but I don't know if I can just, like, leave everything."

"I know you like your life here. I like my life here. But I am afraid that if you do not go with me that we will lose this thing that we have going." He sighed. "I do not want it to end. What if you decide to not go, and then you fall in love with somebody else while I am away? I don't know if my heart can take losing you again. I almost lost you."

Kate wished she knew what to do. She kissed his neck, and then he turned around to face her.

"Come with me, Katie Bella, *eres la chica de mis sueños*."

She lifted his shirt over his head and held his chest to hers.

"Henry," Marco said. "Cama, bed." Henry stood up and limped out of the room. Marco stared at her. "You have the most beautiful body."

Kate ran her hands up and down his back.

"I want you to be my girl, para siempre."

She looked into his eyes, where she felt most at home. "Come with me," he said. "Por favor. I am begging." She pulled him closer.

Her body tingled and warmed, and then his eyes sparkled in pulses of pleasure. His face fell onto her chest. He leaned down onto her, letting the weight off his hands, and onto her shoulder, in her neck, then, he lay, slowly panting and whispered, "We are meant to be together."

HENRY HAD RESUMED his position on the floor next to Kate. Marco had covered her with a blanket.

She got up and went to the bathroom and saw her eyes again, in Marco's mirror, happy and alive. He had left her another note, in the kitchen. She found it as she poured herself a glass of water. *"I hate to leave you every time. Please come with me, Amor, Marco."*

Kate found a tee shirt in one of his drawers and put on a pair of his shorts. Maybe she could go with him. Maybe she should. What else would she do here at the beach? Hang with her friends? Take a poetry class? She wanted to do those things, but she wanted to be with him.

Follow your heart, my little free spirit, her dad had always said.

She settled onto the couch and lit a candle. She studied his bookshelf and found a book that called out to her. It had a blue cover, with what looked to be like an Indian princess on the cover. The title read, *The Journey of Self Discovery.* She opened it. Then she stopped and walked back into the kitchen. On the note he had left, just in case she fell asleep before he got home, she scribbled, *"I will go with you."*

Kate thought of her mom, sitting alone at the kitchen table in front of a coffee cup. She couldn't change the way her mom's life had worked out, but she could trust herself to make her own decisions for her life, to follow her own heart.

She found another piece of paper and thought deeply before she penned the letter. *"Dear Mother,"* she wrote. *"I hope you and Jim are well. I am going on a trip with my new friends. I will write when I can."*

CHAPTER THIRTY-EIGHT

November, 2014

*A*s Skylar tucked the last letter back into the envelope, the siblings sat in silence for a while. Then Curtis, who had never been much for quiet, said, "Did you ever hear mom call herself Katie?"

She hadn't. It was 'Kate' to all her church friends, her colleagues, to everybody. "And she used the word *love* at the end of every one of these letters to Marco."

"Mom *loved* everybody," Curtis said. He gestured quotation marks. "Like Jesus."

"I can't believe she had all these interesting friends she never told us about. And this, like, epic love." Skylar said, "Do you think Dad knew about this?"

The last letter had been postmarked years later. It had not been memories, but a declaration that no matter what, Kate was coming to see him.

"He never mentioned if it he did. Mom was kind of wild, though."

"She was so brave," Skylar said. "But I need to know . . . I'm going to find Marco."

"Skye, even if he's still alive, with their lifestyle, he's probably —he might not even remember her."

"I've got to see," Skylar said. "If he's still living, I've got to bring him these letters."

CHAPTER THIRTY-NINE

February, 2015

The Pink Flamingo Retirement home had more than two-hundred residents, according to its website. Ice-cream socials and bingo every Sunday.

The old man sat in a rose-colored chair, staring out the window. He moved his eyes away from the pond, blinked twice, and quietly grunted.

"Katie, is that you?"

Skylar froze in the doorway, hands clutching the letters inside her bag. She hated these places, she thought, then felt ashamed. He had to live here, in this tiny little room that smelled of stale potpourri.

As she stepped inside, she saw a glimpse of what her mother was talking about in the letters. Marco's almond-shaped eyes were both gentle and penetrating, deep and green. She imagined his pale skin once glowing bronze.

In her mother's words, luminous.

"Hi, umm. No, I'm not Katie." The man frowned. A bit of light came through the room, but otherwise it was dark, too dark, for a Florida afternoon. "I'm Skylar. Katie's daughter. Are you Marco?"

"On a good day. Today I am, since you are here." He grinned.

"It's a beautiful day." She didn't like small talk, but she was good at it, like her mother had been.

"It is too hot. Unless you are going for a swim or a whiskey, I would wait until dusk to go out." He ran his fingers over the top of his head, nearly missing his thin white strands, as if he were stroking a mane that wasn't there anymore.

"They do not let me do either here, and so I stay inside." His smile, faint with dimples, completely disarmed her. He was frailer than she'd pictured, but she was learning that age could change your body in unimaginable ways, and fast.

"Skylar." He patted the yellow bedspread. "Please, sit down." An oxygen tank sat next to him. "How is your mom? I have not seen her in a long time, I don't think, but my memories have not been clear for many years now."

She sat down on the very edge of the bed and began to cry. How should she tell him? She patted at her bag. The letters were still there. She dabbed a tear with the strap of her sundress.

"Mom passed in November." She had trouble looking Marco in the eyes when she said it. "Kate. We called her Kate. She wasn't sick for very long."

He cocked his head and sighed.

"My dad had already passed, so . . . " Skylar wiped her hands on the bottom of her dress and stopped talking so she didn't fall apart in front of this man she'd only just met.

He turned his head toward the pond out the window. "I am sorry to hear this." Two mallards floated together, leaving a ripple behind them. A flag waved in the breeze. She thought she heard him whisper, *Katie,* under his breath, but she couldn't be sure.

He smiled gently. "You look just like her. Except, you are a redhead."

Skylar blushed. "It's fake. I really have brown hair. Mom was a brunette."

"Yes, she was. Muy bella."

A nurse came in, and his tone turned upbeat.

"How are you feeling today, Mr. Del Rio?"

"Skylar, meet Nancy the Nurse. Nancy, meet Skylar, lovely daughter of a dear friend of mine who recently crossed to the other side of the pond."

"It's nice to meet you, Skylar," Nancy said. "I'm sorry for your loss."

"Thank you." Skylar never knew what else to say to this.

Nancy's brown skin made her white nurse's outfit seem brighter. "Time for your blood pressure medicine, Marco."

"Did you bring me some whiskey to wash it down?" He raised his eyebrows.

"Not today," Nancy said, handing him a paper cup of pills. "You can have water or a soda."

"Water, please. Soda will rot your teeth." Skylar sat still and waited. She thought of her own father and the Hospice nurse's care when he was dying. It took a special person to do these jobs. Skylar wasn't built to be a nurse.

"How about some whiskey for my friend here?" he said. "She promised she would not let me have any, but she thinks it smells weird in here and a drink would take the edge off."

Skylar and Nancy both laughed, Skylar despite how nervous she felt. He was right about the smell.

"Have you had any luck on getting any of those Camel non-filters?"

Nancy wasn't fazed at all. "You know you can't smoke in here, Marco. You quit smoking, anyway. Remember?"

"Yo recuerdo," he said. "I just thought I would give it a shot. Maybe speed up this ending process a little." He turned to Skylar. "I am just kidding with her. You have to have a little fun around here if you don't play bingo. Right Nancy?" He took the paper cup of pills, put them in his mouth and swallowed them.

"Whatever you say, Marco. You've got the longest line of girls coming to see you in the whole place, so you must be doing something right."

Marco blushed and turned to Skylar. "I have a daughter. And she has daughters." He was impossibly charming. She saw what her mother saw in him way back then, even though age spots covered his forehead and neck.

Skylar wanted to give him these letters. But first, she had a couple of questions to ask him. She stood up and reached into her bag.

"Can I get you anything to drink, honey?" Nancy asked.

"No, thank you." Skylar didn't think she'd be here very long.

"Okay, I'll leave you two alone. Marco, behave." Nancy marked on a clipboard and left the room.

He reached for a cup on the table and drank from it. "How are you liking the beach?"

"It's gorgeous." She thought of the colors she would use to paint the bay scene from earlier, outside of the bar.

"The ocean is a place of magic and mystery," he said. Skylar gazed outside at the flag blowing in the breeze. The ducks floating together. "If Katie has gone on to the other side, how did you find me?"

She wondered how much time he spent looking out this one window. "I went to The Buoy. You're quite a legend around there."

"Oh, it is a small town," Marco smiled. "Once you get a reputation, people begin to tell their own stories."

"There was this artist who passed along the name of this place."

"Diane," he said. "I am glad to hear she is still on this side of the pond."

She finally pulled out the letters. "We found these letters to you in my mom's keepsake trunk." She reluctantly handed the rubber-band bundle to him, with his name scrawled across the front in her mom's handwriting.

His hands shook as he took them from her. "Katie Bella," he whispered. This time a tear rolled down his face and he didn't try to wipe it.

Skylar didn't really know how to breach the subject. She felt guilty now.

"My brother and I . . . she never told us about you, so we, um. We opened them. I'm sorry."

A tear rolled down his other cheek.

"We thought they might be . . . we weren't sure." She suddenly felt as though she had violated his privacy. "They're basically memories from the year you met. Almost like journal entries. And in the last letter she says she's going to come looking for you, but I think it was after she met my father."

Marco looked at Skylar with eyes that seemed to have a lived a thousand lifetimes. He studied her, then paused.

"Your mother. She lived by this phrase, 'Not everybody needs to know, everything about you.'"

Skylar and Curtis had heard Kate say it a million times.

His eyes twinkled. "But she wanted to write everything down, all of her experiences, as if she didn't want to lose them. She loved poetry, and music. When I met her she was very shy, but she grew to be tough when she needed to be, and to talk about her feelings." He sighed. "She did come to see me."

Skylar sat back toward the headboard.

"She showed up like a ghost." Marco stared out the window again. "It was like when movies turned from black and white to color, when Katie walked into a room the colors got brighter. She carried a magic about her that lit up a room."

They shared a moment then. An understanding.

"When she was there, I always felt as if I were dreaming."

Skylar folded her hands in her lap and listened.

"It was raining. One of those Florida downpours that comes out of nowhere. One minute the sun was shining, and the next it was a monsoon. I was playing a show at The Buoy and there she was." Marco's eyes changed as if he were seeing her right in front of him. "She stood on the steps outside, water falling all around her, dripping from her hair, her cheeks. I was stunned. I could barely sing. I was so happy she had finally come back for me."

Skylar's face dropped. She didn't know what she was about to hear. He paused, cleared his throat again, then went on.

"I had not felt like the world was magical in a very long time. I tuned up to the first song I wrote for her. And I began to play it."

"The swimming in stars song?" Skylar asked.

He nodded. "It is the best song I ever wrote. As I played it, I realized that it was not just rain all over her face. First, I thought they were happy tears."

Marco's lips drooped and the faraway look in his eyes grew more distant. "At night I always pray I will see her again."

He lifted a pair of glasses from his bedside table, put them on, and gave her a look she couldn't interpret. "How long are you visiting?"

She wasn't sure if he meant today, or this week. "I can stay however long. I'm in town for three more days."

He handed the bundle of letters back to her. "My eyes are not what they used to be. How about this? If you have time, maybe you could read the letters to me? And when you are finished I will try and pick up where they leave off, if I can, and tell you the rest of the story."

Skylar didn't have anything planned. This is what she had come for. "Sure, I would like that."

She began to unwrap the bundle, and pulled out the first of the delicate, yellowed paper.

"It may take me some time," he said. "Some of my memories now are unclear, and some of my memories are like dreams."

"I have time," Skylar said. She slipped her shoes off, tucked her feet under her legs on the bed, and focused on her mother's cursive script.

"Dear Marco," Skylar read. They could hear Katie's sweet and tender voice in their minds, as if she were there in the room. "I remember . . . "

CHAPTER FORTY

EPILOGUE

August, 1965

"You've got issues, Library." Jack and Kate sat on the beach behind Marco's house, the cooler between them. Kate breathed in the smell of salt and seaweed. It was still early. She didn't feel like talking, but curiosity got the better of her.

"What do you mean?"

Jack played with the top of the beer can, running his finger over the condensation on the outside. She put her arms around her knees and studied the line separating the blues on the horizon.

"I mean, you can't go on tour with Marco." Jack meant well, so she listened. A seagull squeaked in the morning air.

"Why not?" Jack directed his eyes at her. They were blood-shot and serious.

"*Because*, he's Marco Del Rio."

Kate pushed her toes into the sand. "So."

She had already decided. She'd written her mom to tell her.

She'd begun to pack her things, though she didn't own much anymore. It all fit in the blue trunk.

"So, he's the beach's biggest womanizer." Jack guzzled at the beer and sighed as he lowered it. "Musical genius. Better than the best of them. Better than Dylan. Better than the Beatles. They're more popular than Jesus, you heard?" He set the beer can down in the sand and put his own arms around his hairy legs. "He's the real deal, Library."

Did Jack think she didn't know how much talent Marco had? "I know," Kate said. "He's amazing." She wanted to tell Jack the other ways she thought Marco was amazing, but she thought better of it.

Steph approached them. An imbedded pattern covered her cheek from sleeping on the hammock.

"Good morning," Kate said.

"Morning." Steph plopped down next to Kate on the blanket and handed her a mug of coffee.

"Thanks," she said.

Jack continued, "Look. You've seen the Beatles on TV, right?" Kate remembered seeing them on the Ed Sullivan Show. "The girls screaming?" He scratched his nose. "Or, okay, Elvis. You ever seen the way the girls react to Elvis?" Kate nodded. "That's what I mean, Library. That's the way the girls will react to him. You just going to hang out backstage and watch them all fall over like dominoes?"

Kate had been through a lot with Jack. She respected what he thought. She hadn't pictured the details of the tour yet. She was in love with Marco, she knew, but now Jack had her getting anxious.

"Plus," Jack said. "We all know, Marco doesn't exactly have the best history with women. I mean, neither do I, but he's—"

"¿Qué pasa?" Marco came up behind Kate and kissed her on the neck. "Mi amor," he said quietly. Kate smiled and rubbed goose pimples from her legs. "What are we talking about?"

Kate smelled his cologne on her. It opened a memory of their nighttime, and she had to push it away to stay composed.

"Good morning, Rio," Steph said. "Jack was just telling Kate about how many girls there are going to be screaming for you when you go on tour." She scooted over and patted at the blanket, so he could sit next to Kate. "Like the Beatles. And Elvis."

Marco sat down and glanced at Jack, who hunched his shoulders and picked up his beer. "I hope there are many screaming girls in the crowd who will then buy records and tell their friends to buy records, so Katie Bella and I can buy a big house with a swimming pool and have lots of niños running around. Then, Katie Bella will not have to work, and she can do whatever she wants."

Jack didn't answer. Kate felt a weight lifting from her chest. Steph slurped at her coffee.

"What are we doing today, guys?" Jack said. "Where's Captain?"

"Still asleep on the hammock," Marco said.

"We could take a boat to Turtle Island," Jack said.

Kate said, "No more boats for a while, please."

"Plus," Steph said, "ours are sunk."

Everybody laughed, but Kate still felt uneasy at the thought of the storm. They had almost drowned. If it weren't for the two Navy sailors, they might have.

"When do you guys leave?" Jack asked.

"This weekend," Marco said. "Saturday."

"What day is it?"

Steph giggled. "It's Sunday."

"Okay," Jack said. "Let's take a road trip." He stood up and rubbed sand from his knees. "To the Keys. A celebration before we send our friends off on their grand musical tour adventure."

Despite her closeness to Marco, the way she'd never felt so comfortable, enthralled, and *herself*, sitting next to him, she couldn't get the image of the screaming girls out of her head.

"We have to get ready for classes," Steph said to Jack.

"Which classes?"

"I don't know, all of them: Philosophy, English, Religion."

Jack stood up. "I, Madam Stephanie," he raised his arms and twirled around, "will teach you philosophy, English, and religion. On the road." Marco laughed. Kate loved watching him laugh. "In the van," Jack said. "On the way there." A flock of seagulls landed in front of them, screaming and scattering at the edge of the tide.

Marco pulled his shirt over his shoulders and kissed Kate. "Do you want to go to the Keys, my love?" She felt a twinge of excitement in her stomach.

"I don't have any money left since my trip to Ohio."

"I have money," he said. "From my shows this weekend."

"We won't need much money," Jack said. "Food and gas. We can sleep in his majesty's van, right Marco?"

"If you don't mind cuddling up with Henry," Marco said.

Kate turned to Steph who was pulling a piece of blonde hair from the corner of her mouth. "Are you going to go?"

"I'll go if you go."

"Then it's settled!" said Jack. "Road trip to the Keys, right Library?"

"Okay," Kate said.

Marco held out his hand to Kate. "Before we start packing, let's go swimming."

"Cheers," Jack said. He tipped the can up to his mouth, squeezed it, and put it back into the cooler.

They all ran out to the water. Kate stopped at the edge and felt the ocean lapping on her toes. As her friends went deeper past the waves, she thought about her year. How she'd left home to go out on her own despite her mother's wishes and her brother's advice. How everybody had told her to stay away from Marco. How she had followed her heart, anyway.

If she would had listened to them, she would have missed

out on all of this. She trusted her friends. And Marco. She couldn't explain the way she felt about him. Sure, he was older. Sure, he had a different lifestyle than she was used to.

Despite Jack's negativity, she was going to go on tour with him. And what a better way to say goodbye to her friends than to take another road trip with them.

"Katie Bella," Marco called from deeper water, "the water is warm."

Jack hollered from behind a wave. "We're going to the Keys!"

"Who are?" Noah was smiling. Captain kissed Steph on the forehead and said, "Who's going to the Keys? When?"

"We all are, Captain Franky-poo." Jack said. "Pack your things and meet back here at three."

"Can we go to breakfast first?" Noah asked.

"You" Jack said, "are always hungry." He dove under a wave and walked back up to the shore. With their friends gone, Kate and Marco retreated to the bedroom.

"I bought you something." Out of his dresser he pulled a beautiful nightie of black and baby blue silk and handed it to Kate. She turned over the soft fabric and thanked him as he put his lips on hers. "Would you put it on for me, so I can take it off of you?"

She emerged from the bathroom to incense burning and laid down on the bed. She felt silly for only a moment, before he exposed his tanned stomach and began tugging at the silk. He teased her and ran his hands up and down her arms before sliding off each strap, kissing her neck and kissing her stomach as he pulled it off and dropped it on the floor.

THEY OPENED the bedroom door just as Captain and Steph arrived. It was four o'clock when Jack and Noah returned with their backpacks. Kate had decided to wear the red sundress.

Steph wore a beautiful flowing skirt of orange and red patch-work colors.

Steph said, "I brought you something. I made it." She handed it to Kate. It was a small blue wooden sign with a rope tied around the top. On it were painted the words, *Free Love Beach*, with a peace sign and flowers painted inside the 'o.' "Thought you could use a housewarming present."

"Oh my gosh, Steph." Kate laughed. "Free Love Beach . . . I love it!" She embraced Steph. Marco smiled.

"And I made you this." Steph held up a white and blue dress, with squares of green and sea colors. "Thought these were your colors."

It was the most beautiful dress Kate had ever seen. "Steph, I don't know what to say." The fabric was soft in her hands.

"Well, don't get all sentimental on me. I'm just tired of that red sundress." She smiled. "Buy me a drink later. I had fun making it."

"We can put the sign above the back door," Marco said. "But Katie Bella's love is mine. Not free for all." He wrapped his arms around her and kissed her neck.

"Well, that goes without saying," Captain said.

Jack stood up from the couch and opened a beer from the cooler at his feet. "Shall we go, free love beach spirits? Who needs a road soda?" Foam from the beer erupted over the top and he wiped his hands on his pants. "We can call it our Free Love Tour."

ACKNOWLEDGMENTS

I have been blessed to have strong women in my life who have shared with me their journeys, wisdom, obstacles, and over-comings, and this story is for you, as well as for the women who will come after us. Thank you for living bravely and authentically.

Thank you to Jimmy and Linda for reading early versions of the manuscript, and believing in it enough for me to follow through to the end. Your encouragement and input helped mold Kate's journey into the adventure it became.

Judy, Ron, and Onita, thank you for helping me with the historical details, the accuracy points, and those pesky, never-ending typos. Thank you to Cathleen for the help with the Spanish translations, and to Ryland for the information about saltwater fishing. I happen to be a chronic perfectionist/tinkerer, so all of the typos, historical inaccuracies, and mistakes in translation after their readings are mine.

My friend Vicki was the reader I needed when I wanted to give up. Thank you for your support and your honesty—for everything.

Thank you to AU Creative Writing Program: Rebecca, Denny, Katrina, Dr. Martin; Antioch Writers' Workshop, and MV Writers Network. April, Tim, Jennifer, Judy, all of you. You all keep me informed and inspired. Thank you, Andrea, for your eagle-eye insights.

Finally, thank you to my guy and our dogs, my best friend, my family, my beach friends, my live music friends, my poetry friends, my college friends, my restaurant people, my students, and my writing-creative friends. You all keep me company, keep me smiling, and help me to live and write more authentically: with courage, spirit, soul, and a sense of adventure.

All of your love and encouragement has mattered on my journey, and means the world to me.

Before he passed on to whatever comes next, my dad said, "We had fun, didn't we?"

I intend to keep writing books because it is fun, and it makes me feel free. Thank you again for your support and for reading.

ABOUT THE AUTHOR

Sarasota Green is a writer, editor, and poet. She loves beach towns, live music, indie bookstores, boat trips, reading, and painting. She currently lives in the Midwest.

If you liked Free Love Beach, it would mean a lot to me if you would leave it a review on Amazon, Goodreads, or Barnes and Noble. Write me a message, sign up for my postcard list and newsletter, and stay tuned for updates and new releases at sara sotagreenauthor.com.